SNOWFLAKES OVER PRIMROSE WOODS

JILL STEEPLES

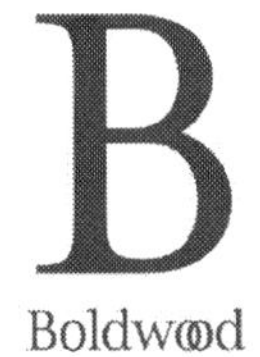

Boldwood

First published in Great Britain in 2022 by Boldwood Books Ltd.

Cover Design by Debbie Clement Design

Cover Photography: Shutterstock

A CIP catalogue record for this book is available from the British Library.

Paperback ISBN 978-1-80280-702-8

Large Print ISBN 978-1-80280-703-5

Hardback ISBN 978-1-80280-701-1

Ebook ISBN 978-1-80280-705-9

Kindle ISBN 978-1-80280-704-2

Audio CD ISBN 978-1-80280-696-0

MP3 CD ISBN 978-1-80280-697-7

Digital audio download ISBN 978-1-80280-700-4

Boldwood Books Ltd
23 Bowerdean Street
London SW6 3TN
www.boldwoodbooks.com

For Nick, Tom and Ellie. Thank you for everything

1

Lizzie Baker was an early riser, but even so, the insistent knocking on her front door at half past seven on a Saturday morning took her by surprise. She couldn't think who it might be, she wasn't expecting any deliveries and anyone who knew her would surely have texted first to warn of their impromptu, impending arrival. She took a sneaky peek through the thick velvet curtains in her bedroom window, but it offered no clues, apart from the sight of a dark saloon car pulling away and disappearing around the corner at the bottom of her road. Perhaps someone had popped something through the letterbox, probably another one of those charity Christmas brochures, she had quite the collection accumulating on her kitchen table.

Rat-a-tat-tat. There it was again. Whoever it was, they were persistent and obviously not going to take no for an answer. With a sense of curiosity bubbling in her chest, she padded down the stairs and gingerly pulled open the door.

A blast of cold air rushed past Lizzie as she took in the scene before her, her mind trying to make sense of it all. Good job she was hanging onto the door, or else she might have fainted on the spot.

'Hello, Mum!'

'Katy, what on earth are you doing here?'

'Nanna, Nanna!' Rosie, Lizzie's little granddaughter, who she'd wished a happy third birthday to only a week ago, via the wonders of modern technology, twirled around on the spot on the doorstep, waving a fairy wand in her hand. Was it a dream? Had her family really been magicked all the way here? Lizzie blinked her eyes open and shut a couple of times to make sure. They were actually here in the sleepy little village of Appleberry, not on the other side of the world in an apartment in Sydney. *But why?*

'Come in, come in.' Lizzie ushered them inside, away from the perishing cold of the late November morning. She peered into Katy's arms to see little Pip fast asleep, blissfully unaware of the enormity of the occasion. Lizzie had so many emotions fighting for attention in her head, happiness, excitement and apprehension, along with a dozen questions waiting to trip off her lips, but really she didn't know where to start. Besides, Katy was looking weary and in desperate need of a cuppa.

'Let me put the kettle on and find a drink for you, Rosie. Oh, come here!' She whisked Rosie up in her arms, hugging the little girl close to her body, laughing as Rosie's cold nose touched her own. 'I really can't believe it!' she gasped, pulling her daughter into her embrace too. 'But where's Brad?' she asked, the thought only just occurring to her.

'We've left him behind,' said Katy matter-of-factly.

'What?'

'Oh, only until he's worked out his notice,' she quickly added, seeing her mum's stricken expression. 'He's got another two months out there, so I thought we might stay with you while I try and find us somewhere to live.'

'Well, of course you can. You know that. This is your home, but I had no idea any of this was in the offing.'

'I wanted to surprise you, Mum.'

'Well, you've certainly done that,' said Lizzie, laughing, still shaking her head, as she went to pop the kettle on. Katy saw to the children, placing the sleeping Pip on the sofa, while Rosie slipped off her rucksack and, eyes wide, wandered around the living room, her little hands reaching out to touch all of her nanna's trinkets, eliciting a kindly but firm warning from her mum. A few minutes later, after having eaten a very welcome ham sandwich, Rosie made herself at home and snuggled up on the sofa beside her baby brother, her eyes soon fluttering closed, and she was fast asleep in next to no time.

'Bless her, it's no wonder she's completely exhausted,' said Lizzie, peering over at her from the other sofa, 'travelling all that way!'

'I know it might seem a bit mad, but once I got the idea in my head, that was it, I had to do it. I can't tell you what a relief it is to be home, though.' Katy hugged her mum so tightly Lizzie wondered if she might ever let her go. When they'd finished their tea, Katy lifted her feet up on to the sofa and allowed her head to nestle onto her mum's lap.

'You know I haven't been happy for months now. I never really settled in Aus even though I tried hard to. With Brad out at work all day and me with a new baby at home, I found it hard to adjust. I missed everybody here so much, but especially you. I sometimes wonder if I didn't try hard enough, but I just found it so difficult. Overwhelming, really.' Katy gave a heartfelt sigh. 'It's all your fault, Mum.'

'What?' Lizzie stopped with her mug halfway up towards her

mouth, and ran her other hand through Katy's hair. She'd known Katy had found it difficult settling into their new way of life overseas, but Lizzie had hoped that given time, she would have grown to love and embrace the new opportunity.

Now, Katy looked up at her mum and smiled.

'I missed you too much. Besides, I want you to be a part of the children's lives on an everyday basis so that they can really get to know you, and not just have you as a face at the end of an internet connection. Someone who they might only get to see every few years. It's not the same.'

'It isn't,' Lizzie agreed, 'but it was the next best thing in the circumstances.' The family had made regular weekly video calls and Lizzie had read stories and sung songs to little Rosie from across the ether. They'd formed a lovely relationship of sorts, but Katy was right, it could never replace the familiarity and closeness that came from sharing at first hand the daily ups and downs of family life.

'When you came to stay in the summer, Mum, it made me realise just how much we were missing out on. Rosie loved having you around and everything seemed so much easier with you being there. I just want to be close to my mum, that's not too much to ask, is it?'

'Not at all. But what about Brad, how does he feel about all this?'

'You know Brad. He's pretty easy-going. He knew it wasn't working out for us as a family, so he's been looking around for a while now. The good thing is that this new lectureship position he's found means he can carry on with the research work he's been doing in Aus. It's a brilliant opportunity, and the uni is only a twenty-minute drive from here.' She clapped her hands together excitedly. 'His mum and dad are thrilled that we'll be back home again.'

At least someone was in on what was going on, mused Lizzie. Her expression must have given away her own bemusement.

'Oh, I'm sorry, Mum, that I didn't say anything earlier, but once Brad's new job came through, I thought what a great idea it would be to surprise you. I swore his parents to secrecy.'

Lizzie laughed.

'Don't apologise, I'm over the moon that you're here. What a Christmas this one will turn out to be! It's just a bit of a shock, that's all.'

'It's a shame Brad can't be here too, but we'll celebrate again when he finally comes home in the new year.'

'Well, it sounds as though you have it all worked out.' Lizzie, whose head was still buzzing from the early morning's strange turn of events, gave a thought to Brad, left behind in Australia, and hoped he was as happy with the arrangements as Katy insisted he was, but perhaps he was relishing the idea of some peace and quiet for a few weeks.

Katy took a sip of her tea, her gaze drifting around the room. 'You haven't got your Christmas tree up yet?' she said, sounding disappointed.

'Oh, I know!' Usually, by this point in the season, Lizzie would have all her decorations up, but she'd had a change of plan. 'I'm having a real one this year.' The silver tinsel artificial tree had served her well for several years, but it was a little threadbare these days and looked rather sorry for itself. She'd felt a pang of guilt at the thought of not indulging in the annual ritual of scrabbling around in the loft, pulling out her old faithful friend, but it was about time she made some changes about the place, even if she had no intention of ever throwing out her little old tree. That was definitely a step too far. 'Bill and I are going over to Primrose Woods in the week to pick out a tree together. Sam said he'd sort out a decent one for us.'

'How lovely. I can't wait to meet Bill in person, even though I feel as though I know him already. We'll come with you, if you like. Rosie will love to do that. She's been so excited for Christmas this year. She's convinced it's going to snow, bless her. I've tried to tell her that it's very unlikely, but she's not having it. Hopefully, with all the decorations and the lights and her presents, she'll quickly forget about the white stuff. That reminds me. I've had some of our belongings shipped over, and they should be arriving on Monday. I'm sure we'll find somewhere to store them, won't we?' she said, her gaze wandering off again.

Lizzie nodded, puzzling over where exactly she might find some space in her little house for Katy's gear, but she wouldn't worry about that now. There was always the garage. Besides, she suspected Katy wasn't waiting for an answer, it was more a statement of fact. Katy stood up and checked on the children, tucking their blankets around them tighter. She stretched her arms over her head and settled down beside them, resting her head on a cushion.

'It's so lovely to be home. I really hope I haven't upset your plans for Christmas.' She smiled, stretching and yawning extravagantly.

'How could you ever!'

For the first time in years, Lizzie was actually looking forward to Christmas instead of dreading it. It was her first Christmas with Bill and they'd made all sorts of plans. A trip to the theatre was on the cards, along with a visit to the Christmas market in town, a tea-dance at the Grand Hotel, a meal at a French restaurant on Christmas Eve, and then Bill's daughter Abbey and her partner Sam were coming for lunch on Christmas Day. On Boxing Day, they were intending to collapse in a heap on the sofa with a plate of cold meats and bubble and squeak, accompanied by a glass or two of red wine. A very grown-up kind of Christmas.

Only it looked now as though some of those plans might have to be changed in the wake of Katy's arrival. Still, the more people around her Christmas table, especially her family, the merrier. It would be a lovely Christmas, just not the one she'd originally planned.

'You haven't upset my plans at all,' she said, noticing as she looked up and across at Katy that she wasn't listening at all. She was snuggled up with the children, fast asleep on the sofa, and Lizzie's entire being warmed at the sight, realising that all her Christmas dreams really had come early.

2

Abbey drew up outside her cottage after a hectic day at the care home. Most days at Rushgrove Lodge for the Elderly were demanding in their own way, but at this time of year, with so many activities organised for the residents, it was extra busy, and extra fun too.

She turned off the ignition and glanced at her watch. As much as she loved the excitement in the run up to Christmas, what she didn't enjoy so much was the dark and cold winter nights. She shivered as she climbed out of the car, opened the gate and hurried along the footpath, turning her key in the lock. In the summer months, she'd be heading off for a walk at Primrose Woods at this time of day, but there was no possibility of that now and she had to leave her fix of the great outdoors until the weekends or her days off.

Indoors, she turned on the table lamps, the red and white candle arches on the windowsills and the twinkly fairy lights across the mantlepiece. Although it was still only the first of December, she'd already received a handful of Christmas cards, which looked pretty dotted around the small living room. She bent down to light the wood-burning stove, bringing a blast of warmth into the room, and she lit the cluster of pillar candles in the surround, along with the Advent candle for the first time. She stood in the centre of the room, looking all around her. Those little touches made the house seem so welcoming and cosy.

Upstairs, she changed out of her trouser suit and put on some jeans and a fluffy jumper. She was just untying her bun, allowing her auburn hair to fall onto her shoulders, when she heard the front door open and the familiar sound of paws scrabbling excitedly over the wooden floor. A cold blast of air whooshed up the stairs with Sam and his springer spaniel Lady's arrival. Abbey hurried down to greet them, seeing Sam wrestling with a Christmas tree to get it through the front door.

'Oh, look at that. It's absolutely perfect. Just put it up against the window for now and we can decorate it after dinner. Aw, thanks, Sam. Don't you just love Christmas?'

'I love you more,' he said, wiping his hands down on his work trousers before holding out his arms to Abbey, who walked into his embrace. She took a deep breath, inhaling his lovely scent; wholesome, outdoorsy and with a hint of pine needles right now. Sam worked at Primrose Woods as a senior ranger, which was where Abbey had first set eyes on him. His tall and broad physique was easy to pick out in his distinctive uniform of green cargo trousers and sweatshirt bearing the name of Primrose Woods, and there was no denying his obvious good looks. Ordinarily his role encompassed conservation and preservation of the woodlands and heaths, giving guided walks and talks to visitors, and undertaking practical work in managing the hundreds of acres of the country park. In December, though, it was all about the Christmas trees, his days spent overseeing the smooth running of the yard, selling a variety of trees in all different shapes and sizes.

Abbey grinned, looking up into Sam's eyes, his deep brown gaze always having the power to enthral her. He pulled her closer, his lips finding hers, his touch sending ripples of delight to the top of her head and down to the end of her toes.

'I love you too, Sam,' she said, coming up for air.

So what if Sam didn't share her slightly over-the-top enthusiasm for the festive season, looking on with bemusement when she squealed with delight at having found yet another sparkly decoration that she simply had to add to her collection, or when hearing one of her favourite Christmas tunes on the radio she felt compelled to sing along with. It was only because Sam hadn't experienced the joy of a truly magical Christmas, that's what Abbey told herself, and why she was determined to make this year, their first Christmas together, as special as possible.

'Let me go and change and then I'll start on the dinner.' Sam shrugged off his green Primrose Woods hoodie, throwing it over the newel post at the bottom of the stairs. 'I'll fix us a drink as well. Go on,' he said, grinning, 'I know you're desperate to get started on that tree.'

While Sam disappeared upstairs and the sound of the shower whirred into action, Abbey heaved the tree into the waiting stand and started pulling out the branches, tweaking them this way and that, restoring the tree to its natural shape, while the scent of the pine needles assaulted her senses. She stood back to admire her handiwork. Even in its unadorned state, it looked utterly beautiful and Christmassy. She went across to the cupboard beneath the stairs and pulled out the boxes of decorations, itching to look inside. She loved revisiting the shiny baubles, in different shades of red, green, silver, gold and white, and handling the hanging ornaments like the toy soldier, and the winged angel, her fingers running over their intricate design. Most of all, she loved the decorations that had belonged to her mum. They were kept in a pretty red hexagonal decoupage box and when Abbey peeked inside, she felt a pang of nostalgia at the sight of the trinkets that had held special significance to her mum and reminded her of past Christmases. It was a bittersweet moment. She popped the lid back on the box, for fear of damaging the treasures inside, and put them to one side. She'd keep them safe until she was ready to decorate the tree.

When Sam reappeared a little while later, showered and changed into jeans and a navy V-neck jumper, she couldn't resist throwing her arms around his neck, and kissing the tempting curve of his collar bone. That freshly smelled scent straight from the shower was just as enticing as his natural, earthy aroma that came from a day working outside in the elements.

'Mmm, you smell good enough to eat.'

'While that is a very tempting idea, I should probably make a start on the dinner.' Sam grinned. 'Let me sort us a drink first.' Reluctantly, and with a kiss to her forehead, Sam peeled himself away from Abbey and wandered into the kitchen, opening a cupboard to pull out two wine glasses.

'Here we go.' Moments later, he was back and handed Abbey her wine, his gaze alighting on the doormat. 'Look, there's some cards over there to add to your ever-growing collection.'

'Ooh, yes.' Abbey turned and scooped up the letters from the floor, peering at the postmarks to see where they might have come from. 'Ah, this one must be from Auntie Helen and Uncle Rick in Dorset.' She pulled out the card showing a jolly Santa sitting abreast a chimney stack and popped it up on the mantlepiece with the others. 'And this one...' she ripped off the envelope, '... is from... aw, that's lovely. It's from Connor and his girlfriend Ruby. Oh, look, and there's another card in here.'

Sam placed a hand on her arm as he peered over her shoulder at the card in her hand.

'Connor?'

'Yes, you know Pia, my best friend from school? Well, he's her older brother. We were a right pain to him back in the day, but he did look out for us. He's a really great guy. Oh look, there's a wedding invitation in here too. That's lovely news. *Abbey plus guest.*' She looked up at Sam, grinning. 'That must mean you, I'm guessing. If you want to go, of course?'

Abbey ran her fingers around the edges of the white embossed invitation, a pang of regret twisting in her stomach. Earlier this year, she'd been planning her own wedding, sending out her own invitations, excitedly making plans for a future that she had no idea was about to crumble around her when she discovered Jason, her ex, had been cheating. It was an awful time, having to give up on all her hopes and dreams, the hurt and humiliation she felt absolutely crippling. When she looked back, all she remembered was the black clouds of disbelief, pain and anger. Thank goodness for Primrose Woods. The country park on her doorstep turned out to be a life-saver at the time, a happy place to escape to, somewhere it was impossible to stay sad for too long. That, along with a certain somebody coming into her life when she was at her lowest ebb, was the only thing to have got her through that terrible time.

She looked up at Sam now, a familiar sense of relief washing over her. To think that if she hadn't found out about Jason's deceit then she would never have got together with Sam in the first place, and she might have so easily missed out on meeting her soulmate. What a scary thought that was.

'Sounds good to me,' said Sam, heading back into the kitchen and putting the frying pan on the stove, pouring in some olive oil.

'Are you sure?' Abbey said, moving into the centre of the room so that she could see Sam in the kitchen. 'I can remember you telling me, the first time that we met actually, that you thought weddings were over-rated.'

'Did I?' He paused, spatula in hand, turning to look at her, his brow creasing as he tried to remember the occasion. 'Ah, but I'd just found out that you were meant to be getting married that day. I was only trying to make you feel better.'

She chuckled. He'd certainly managed that. The lunch at Lizzie's, who she'd only recently met at the Treetops Café in Primrose Woods, was such a happy and joyous occasion for her and her dad. There wasn't any other way she would have wanted to spend her non-wedding day.

'You did make me feel better. Although I think the bottle of home-made damson gin you brought along played a big part in that too! Okay, so you're not totally averse to weddings, then?' she said, a hint of playfulness in her tone.

'Definitely not. Well, I've no objection to going along to one, if that's what you mean.' Sam returned his attentions to the frying pan, the aroma of shallots and garlic now reaching her nostrils in the other room.

It wasn't what she meant at all. She knew Sam wasn't the marrying kind, but did it really matter? Her abandoned marriage to Jason had taught her an important lesson: that the biggest, most extravagant wedding in the world didn't mean a thing if you didn't have the love of that special person. Now, she'd found that true and real love with Sam, and that was much more important than the big wedding she'd dreamed of ever since she was a small girl. Wasn't it?

3

Rhi drove into the car park at Primrose Woods and parked in front of the row of towering redwood trees. She took a moment to steady her breathing, soaking in the scenery. Her hands had grown clammy on the steering wheel on the way over and she could feel a heat pinging at her cheeks. *Get a grip*, she told herself. Her gaze searched out the silver hatchback she was looking for and her heart gave a little leap of triumph when she spotted it. Decisively, before she could give in to the nerves bubbling inside, she jumped out of the car and wandered over, attempting to look casually cool but feeling horribly self-conscious.

She'd imagined this moment for weeks, seeing Luke again, after almost three months apart. She'd imagined what she might say, something meaningful to convey just how much she'd missed him, and what he would say in return, the significance of the occasion resonating with them both. Instead, seeing him again in the flesh now, all she managed was a pathetic 'hello' and a gormless expression.

'Hey, Rhi!' His face lit up in a wide smile, and she felt a surge of relief and happiness.

Any awkwardness evaporated in the cold winter air as she reacquainted herself with his bright blue eyes and the sound of his voice, her insides warming to the sight of him, his ability to make her heart stop for the briefest moment undiminished in the months since she'd last seen him.

'It's great to see you again!' she said.

Rhi had been home from her backpacking adventure in Australia for almost a month now and she'd been anxiously counting down the days until she would see Luke again. Part of her, a small part of her, had held the faintest hope that he might have been there waiting for her at the airport on her return, a big smile on his face, telling her how much he'd missed her and how he would never let her out of his sight again, but despite telling herself she shouldn't get her hopes up, she'd still been wholly disappointed when that scenario had never materialised. Trouble was, she'd clearly thought about Luke much more in the intervening months than he'd thought about her. They'd kept in touch while she was away. She'd sent him an endless supply of photos, videos and funny memes, and he'd always responded enthusiastically, or at least she thought he had. Now she wondered if he'd only been being polite.

'And you too, Rhi! Come here.' He wrapped her in a big hug before holding her at arm's length to look at her properly. 'You look great. The trip obviously did you the power of good.'

'It really did,' she enthused. 'I'm so glad I took the plunge and did it or else I might have missed out on the opportunity forever. It was wonderful. I miss the sunshine and the friends I met, but, you know, it's good to be home too.'

She could hardly tell him that he'd been with her every step of the way around Australia, in her thoughts, her mind frequently straying to what he might be doing at any given time, if he might be thinking about her too. She'd wondered if her time away might have lessened her feelings for Luke, but if anything, they'd only grown stronger in the meantime.

'Come on.' He held out his arm with an air of confidence and she happily linked arms, secretly thrilled to be so close to him again. 'Let's walk,' he said. 'It's far too cold to be standing around for too long.'

She took a deep breath, feeling her cheeks tingle with the cold. It was great to be back at Primrose Woods, the sharp nip in the air heightening her excitement and anticipation. It was the natural place for them to meet, as it was the setting for many other walks they'd shared together before she'd headed off abroad. There was something about being amongst the trees, walking side by side, at one with nature, that made it easier for her to talk, to feel a connection with Luke that wasn't always possible in the hubbub of a bar or restaurant. She took a sideways glance at his profile. He was more handsome than she remembered him to be, if that was even possible.

'So how are things going with you? Sounds as though you've been incredibly busy.'

'I have. Sorry it's taken me such a while to find a day to do this, but it's been hectic. Not sure if I mentioned it, but I'm leaving Jansens on Friday.'

'Are you?' She feigned nonchalance. He hadn't mentioned it. She would have remembered if he had. The fact that he hadn't told her made her feel inconsequential, as though he didn't even consider her in any of his plans.

'Yeah, I can't wait to get out of that place.'

'It was the best thing I ever did,' admitted Rhi.

'Yeah, it definitely went downhill the day you walked out. I don't think the company ever properly recovered.'

'Stop it!' she laughed, relieved that they could immediately fall back into the easy teasing and joking that had always been a feature of their conversations.

The job Luke was leaving was where they'd met, working in the same department for a multi-national telecoms company. Rhi cringed when she thought of how she'd treated Luke back then. She'd barely given him the time of day, ignoring his friendly overtures and treating him with haughty disdain. She'd been far too enamoured with Jason, a senior manager, at the time. Brash and confident, Rhi had been taken in by his charms, something that had puzzled her ever since. What on earth had she seen in him? He'd promised her a future together but when she found out he'd been feeding her a pack of lies and was actually engaged to be married, she didn't think twice. She stormed out of the relationship and her job on the same day, putting as much space between herself and Jason as she possibly could.

Luke was the only person from the office to reach out to her in the following days, to make sure she was doing okay. Out of the hurt and humiliation of that period, she'd been truly grateful to Luke for his support and kindness. A friendship had grown from that connection but what had surprised Rhi most of all was just how lovely and kind Luke really was beneath his smart and funny exterior. She'd hoped their friendship might develop into something more, but despite her best intentions, it hadn't happened, and they were still very much in the friend zone, even if her heart was telling her something else entirely.

'So tell me about the new job? When do you start?'

'The second week in January. I've found a flat not too far from the new office and I move in just after the new year. I'll have a couple of days to get myself sorted and then it'll be straight to work.'

'You're moving too? Crikey, there's lots of big changes for you in the pipeline then. Where will you be based?'

'Dashford-upon-Avon.' Rhi could hear the excitement in his voice, but something crumpled inside her. She kept her focus on the path ahead of them, attempting not to show her disappointment. She listened attentively as Luke went on. 'It's a similar role to the one I was doing at Jansens but with more responsibility. I'll have my own sales team to manage. It will be a challenge, but one I'm ready for now.'

'It sounds amazing. Congratulations,' she said brightly, masking the sadness she felt inside. 'I always knew you were destined for great things.'

'Ha! Of course you did,' he said with a wide grin.

Luke was moving over a hundred miles away. How could their relationship ever develop into anything further now with them living in different areas of the country? She had to accept that she'd missed her opportunity as far as Luke was concerned, although it wasn't for lack of trying on her part. Maybe she needed to accept that he wasn't into her in the same way that she was into him?

They walked along the marked woodpecker trail on the path lined with tall, towering trees. There was a definite nip to the air, the ground crunchy beneath their feet, the tips of the branches spun with frost creating a magical winter wonderland scene. Rhi was wrapped up in her fur-lined parka with boots and a woolly hat, with only her face exposed to the air, the sensation of the cold on her skin invigorating and energising. This area, the beauty around her, couldn't have been more different from what she'd recently seen in Australia. There, she'd spent most of her trip in shorts and a T-shirt, the sun blazing down on her bare limbs as she explored the vast and spectacular landscape, marvelling at the blue of the ocean and the endless sky. It had been an eye-opening and wonderful adventure, but being here in Primrose Woods was every bit as awe-inducing. Walking along the familiar trail transformed by the advent of winter, she definitely felt as though she'd come home, and being with Luke only heightened that sensation. At the bottom of the path, they took the small rickety bridge that crossed the stream, Luke lending her a hand as he led the way. He had no way of knowing how much pleasure that small gesture brought her.

'Are you looking forward to it?' she asked.

'Can't wait,' he said with such passion that she knew already his heart was somewhere else. 'Anyway, enough about me, what about you?' he asked, as she jumped off the end of the bridge onto the ground, still hanging on tight to his steadying hand. 'Sounds as though you're going to be just as busy.'

'I hope so. I'm really excited to be setting up the business and working for myself. It's what I've always wanted to do. The website is ready to go live and I've already found one customer, I'll be looking after the social media accounts for the Three Feathers. I'm talking to a couple of other companies too and it's looking promising.' She crossed her fingers in the air. 'I'll still be doing a few shifts at the pub, though, just until I have enough clients to pay the bills each month.'

'You'll make a success of it, Rhi. I know you will.' This get-up-and-go spirit was something he'd always admired about Rhi. She was enthusiastic, resourceful and capable. Okay, so maybe she was spontaneous and hot-headed at times too, but he knew she would take that passion into this new venture and make it work.

'Where will you be working from?'

'Well, that's the good thing about being a virtual assistant, I can do it from anywhere. Initially I'll be working in the spare bedroom at home, but I want to move out as soon as I can. Find a little flat somewhere. Mum has got a new boyfriend, you know?'

'Really?' Luke's eyes widened, dropping his head to one side for her to expand. 'That's great.'

'I know. I'm made up for her. She's said for years that she would never get involved with another man, after Dad, but Robb came along and...' She held her hands up to the air as though she couldn't quite believe it herself. 'It happened, they fell in love, just like that.' It wasn't lost on Rhi that her mum's love life was so much more successful than her own. 'Robb seems like a genuinely nice guy and makes her happy. Trouble is, I feel like a third wheel when he's around. They're at that lovey-dovey stage!' She gave a mock groan. 'Besides, it's about time I found a place of my own.'

'Shall we head for the café?' Luke asked, a little while later as they walked past the lake.

The Treetops Café was abuzz with visitors that morning, the hubbub of conversation and the aromas of warm bread, coffee and cakes mingling in the air welcoming them indoors. Lizzie waved and came out from behind the counter, greeting them warmly.

'Well, it's lovely to see you two together again.' She wrapped them both in a big hug. 'Look, there's a table over there by the window. Go and grab a seat and I'll be over in a minute to take your order.'

Rhi took off her hat and gloves, tidying them away on the seat beside her as her gaze was distracted by the chalkboard with its array of tempting delights. Today's special menu included a sweet potato and Bramley apple soup, turkey sandwiches with cranberry sauce and pigs in blankets, and a Stilton and ham quiche. The smells emanating from the kitchen were totally enticing. Rhi would definitely come back for lunch one day, but for now she would be happy with a cake from one of the glass-domed serving dishes at the front. Trouble was, she was spoilt for choice, changing her mind several times before finally plumping for a cranberry spiced muffin while Luke chose a slice of gingerbread, with them both opting for a cream-topped hot chocolate to drink.

'There you go, my lovelies.' A little later, Lizzie delivered the cakes and drinks, placing them on the table, a big smile on my face. 'I'm going to take five minutes,' she said, pulling out a chair and sitting down with her friends. 'Isn't it lovely to have our girl back?' She turned to Luke, and took hold of Rhi's arm. 'She told me all about her adventures the other week, it sounded amazing. It seems like a lifetime ago that we flew out to Australia together, when in reality it was only a matter of a few months. You know I would never have got out there in the first place without you two urging me on, so I have a lot to be grateful for to the pair of you. I got to see Katy and her family for the first time in years, which made me very happy, and you got to have the holiday of a lifetime. Anyway, it's so lovely to have you both back here in the café together.'

'It's great to be back,' Rhi said. 'Although, have you heard the news, Luke's moving away after Christmas?'

'No, you're not, are you? Where are you going?' Lizzie leaned forward, resting her forearms on the table.

'I've got a new job. It's in Dashford-upon-Avon so I've found a place to live up there.'

'That's a lovely part of the country and good news for you, but we'll miss you round here, won't we, Rhi? Especially on quiz night.'

'Well, it's not a million miles away. And I'll be coming back pretty regularly to see my folks, so you won't be getting rid of me completely.'

Lizzie exchanged a sympathetic look with Rhi as if she realised what disappointing news this must be for her.

'Anyway,' said Luke, with a smile. 'How's life with you, Lizzie?'

'Great. Although it's been hectic.' She wiped her arm across her brow. 'Did you hear that Katy is home? She turned up unexpectedly at the weekend with my grandchildren in tow. What a shock that was. I thought something terrible must have happened, but no, she thought she'd surprise me.' She gave a rueful smile. 'She certainly did that. They're coming home permanently, which is obviously wonderful news for me – no more trips to Australia – and Katy's come ahead to find somewhere to live. They'll be staying with me until she does. It's a bit of a shock to the system to have a full house again but it's great timing. Spending my first Christmas with the grandchildren will be such a treat. The little ones, ooh, they are such a joy, but I'd forgotten how exhausting children can be. It's almost a relief to be able to come to work to get a little respite from it all.'

Despite her good-natured grumbling, Lizzie's eye shone as she spoke, and it was clear to see her pride and delight in having her family underneath her roof again.

'We've got Abbey and Sam coming for Christmas too. I'm not sure how we'll all fit around the table, but we'll make it work somehow.' Lizzie glanced up and across to the door, where a group of customers had arrived together. 'I could sit here and chat all day long, but I shall have to go and do some work.' She stood up, tucking her chair beneath the table. 'You know it's quiz night next week, the last one before Christmas? Are we all going?'

'Try and stop me,' Rhi said, keenly. 'I missed it while I was away, and I'm just pleased you've kept my place in the team open for me. I was worried you might find someone else to fill the spot. You know, someone who actually knew a few answers.' Rhi giggled, but really it was a huge relief to know that some pretty girl hadn't taken her place on the quiz team and in Luke's affections too. Trouble was, there would be another space on the team after Christmas, but who could ever fill Luke's shoes?

'No, never!' said Lizzie, her eyes wide with outrage. 'You're a great asset to the team.'

'And if it's any consolation, we didn't do any better without you being there,' said Luke.

'Thanks for that!' Rhi laughed, unsure of whether it was a compliment or an insult.

'We'll see you there then.' Rhi and Luke held up a hand each to Lizzie as she darted off to see to her new customers.

'She's so lovely, isn't she?' Rhi said.

'A proper sweetheart.'

Rhi tucked into her muffin, picking up every last crumb on her plate with a fingertip, savouring each delicious mouthful. They drank their hot chocolates, laughing as they tried to negotiate the mountain of whipped cream on top, inevitably ending up with cream on their noses and around their mouths, and not caring in the slightest. When she'd finished, Rhi sat back in her chair, her hands resting on the table in front of her. Her fingers played with the turquoise thread bracelet on her wrist.

'It survived the trip, then?' said Luke his gaze dropping to her fingers.

'I've not taken it off since you gave it to me. It was my lucky talisman.' The unexpected gift from Luke just before she left for Australia had taken her completely by surprise and she'd been touched by his kind gesture. For her, it was so much more than a sweet going-away present. It was a token of their growing friendship, and she'd felt certain it had been Luke's way of letting her know just how much she meant to him. Every time she'd looked at the pretty bracelet thousands of miles away from home, she felt a connection to Luke, as though his support and encouragement were radiating across the ocean. Now, in the busy café, she wondered if she'd read far too much into his gesture. Could it have simply been just one friend looking out for another? Now it looked as though her hopes for anything other than a friendship with Luke were dashed again.

'Everything okay?'

Luke's question broke into her daydreaming.

'Yes,' she said, looking up into his bright blue eyes, forcing a smile. 'Everything's great.' Although, if she was being honest with herself, she wasn't sure that it was.

4

'Wish me luck!' Abbey grabbed her laptop bag and her coat from the hall stand, before checking her reflection in the full-length mirror for the umpteenth time that morning. Most days she didn't give a second thought to her appearance, usually some black trousers and a blouse or jumper would do, along with a quick coating of mascara and a dab of bronzer. Today, though, she wanted to make a good impression. After much deliberation, she had plumped for a bottle-green knitted dress with her brown knee-length boots, easy to wear but stylish too. She'd tied her auburn hair back in a smooth bun, allowing a few loose tendrils to fall around her face, and she'd taken an extra few minutes applying her make-up.

'Good luck, although you won't need it.' Sam took hold of Abbey's wrists and looked intently into her eyes. 'You're brilliant at your job and don't let anyone tell you otherwise. Especially that new hotshot general manager. He only has to ask anyone at the home, residents or staff, to quickly realise what a great job you do.'

Abbey let out an involuntarily sigh, grateful for Sam's support, but not sharing his confidence.

'The trouble is, from what I've heard, he has a completely different style of management to the old company, to what I've been used to all these years. He's all spreadsheets, budgets and targets. I just hope he's not going to implement too many changes.'

'There's no reason why he should. Your latest care inspection was excellent. If they can find no reason for concern, then why should he?'

'You're right,' said Abbey, feeling marginally appeased by Sam's positive words. 'Well.' She glanced at her watch. 'I suppose I ought to get going. I can't put this off any longer.'

'Come here.' He pulled Abbey into his arms and she allowed her head to fall onto his chest, exhaling a deep breath as she snuggled into the safety of his embrace. 'You'll be fine. And...' He held her at arm's length now, as his gaze ran the length of her body. 'You look absolutely amazing, really, go and knock them dead.' Lady, the springer spaniel, ran in circles around Abbey's feet as though she was in complete agreement with Sam.

He would say that, Abbey thought, smiling, his encouraging words ringing in her ears. She enjoyed the short drive through the country lanes that wended their way through the neighbouring villages and led to Rushgrove Lodge for the Elderly, situated in a beautiful spot. It gave her thinking time. She was still nervous, but it made all the difference knowing she had Sam's full support and encouragement.

Arriving at work, she didn't have time to dwell on the impending visit from the big boss because she had several emergencies awaiting her as soon as she stepped through her office door. One of the care workers had called in sick, so Abbey was straight on the phone, finding a replacement to cover the day shift. Reg Catling, who would be one of her favourite residents, if she were allowed to have favourites, had had a fitful night with a troubling cough, and despite his protests that it was only a niggle, Abbey wasn't happy with the way he was presenting and she quickly put a call into the local GP surgery to request a visit from the doctor. Then she had to face the issue of the heating in the ground-floor annexe which had clanked to a halt in the early hours and Abbey's pressing concern was making sure her residents were kept warm. She organised Peter, the Lodge's maintenance man, to put an electric heater from the stores into each of the rooms as a stop-gap measure until the heating was back up and running.

'You probably need this,' said Lydia, her assistant, placing a welcome mug of coffee next to Abbey's computer when she finally got back to sit behind her desk in her office.

'Thanks. And that's before I've even started on my to-do list yet,' she said with a rueful smile.

'Well, I'm not sure you'll have much of a chance now, as Matt Walsh just called to say his previous appointment's been cancelled. He should be here any minute.'

'Really?' Abbey let out a sigh, thinking she could have done with a quiet hour or two to finalise the arrangements for next week's carol concert. The local primary school would be visiting and putting a show on for the residents. It was an annual event and one which was a highlight on the Lodge's social calendar, with both the young and the old enjoying it in equal measure.

Never mind, she would have to find an hour later in the day to catch up on her admin as she also needed to plan the rotas for next month, and put in an order for some cleaning supplies.

'He's here,' said Lydia, putting down the phone.

'Great,' said Abbey with a smile that she didn't quite feel. 'Let's do this.'

Abbey wasn't sure what she'd been expecting, but she was pleasantly surprised when Matt came bounding into her office with a friendly smile on his face. He wasn't booted and suited, but was wearing chocolate-brown corduroys with a brown and red jumper that was extremely eye-catching. So much so that she had to force herself to drag her eyes away from his body. If she'd thought that Matt might be intimidating and businesslike, Rudolph's friendly face with his red fluffy nose wobbling on the front of Matt's sweater put paid to any such notions.

Lydia glanced across at Abbey, a glint in her eyes, as she bit on her lip, suppressing a smile, but not before Matt had noticed their amusement.

'Ah, yes, please excuse the jumper. It wouldn't be my usual choice of clothes, but I'm off to the first of many Christmas parties this afternoon so I thought I'd try and get into the festive spirit.' He grimaced as though he might already be regretting his decision.

'It's great,' said Lydia. 'Certainly brings a smile to the face.'

That was never more true than when Abbey gave Matt a guided tour of the Lodge and introduced him to some of the residents, who were always delighted to see a new face about the place. The novelty jumper was a hit with them all and definitely an icebreaker.

'Can I tweak your nose?' said Margie Robotham, giggling like a star-struck teenager.

'Please go ahead,' said Matt. 'It's the best offer I've had today.'

Margie reached forward and gave Rudolph's nose a squeeze, delighting herself and the rest of the residents in the lounge when it lit up and gave a tinny rendition of 'Rudolph the Red-Nosed Reindeer'. Laughter rang out all around. Matt was a natural with the guests, chatting easily with them, his interest and concern for them seeming entirely genuine. From across the other side of the room, Stella Darling peered over the top of her glasses.

'Is that your young man, Abbey?'

'No, this is Matt Walsh, he's the new General Manager of the Lodges. He's just come to have a look around.' There were six care homes under the umbrella of White Dove Care Homes and the group had only recently been taken over by the new company. Apart from some email and telephone contact, this was the first time Matt had visited Rushgrove Lodge in person.

'Ah, I thought he was your new man. The one with the dog?'

She supposed Matt did resemble Sam from a distance. They were of a similar build and height, although Matt's colouring was fairer than Sam's. They were both good-looking men, and Stella definitely had a knack for picking out a handsome young man from across a room.

Abbey shook her head, smiling, as she attempted to direct Matt away from the lounge, and into the newest accommodation wing, but Matt had other ideas. He wandered across to Stella, and Abbey had no choice but to follow.

'He was here the other day, wasn't he?' Stella scrunched up her face as she peered through her glasses to get a better look at Matt. 'Brought the tree along. He's a lovely young man.'

'That's right,' said Abbey. She loved Stella, even if she did show an almost obsessive interest in Abbey's personal life. It was her own fault. She'd always been honest and open with the ladies and gents at the Lodge, so they knew almost everything about her life away from the home, and their interest had only heightened ever since the summer, but they only had her best interests at heart. Still, she really didn't want her love life to be a topic of conversation in front of her new boss.

'You're the new bigwig around here then?' said Stella, addressing Matt, the accusation evident in her tone.

'Matt,' he said, holding out a hand to Stella with a megawatt smile. 'In name only. Abbey here is very much in charge, as I'm sure you know. She's clearly doing a great job and I have no plans to make any changes.'

'That's very good to hear,' said Stella, her manner immediately thawing. Abbey thought so too, with a sigh of relief, just hoping that Matt would be true to his word. 'We all love it here, so we don't need any new-fangled ideas.'

Matt laughed.

'I'll bear that in mind, Stella.'

'Are you married?' she asked with her customary directness.

'Divorced,' Matt replied, just as directly.

'Oh, dear. That's a shame. Abbey was due to get married in the summer, but it all fell apart. She's got another man in tow now.' Stella shook her head indulgently. 'It all seems so much more complicated these days. I can't remember it being quite so difficult when I was a girl.'

'That's probably true,' said Matt, with a wry smile as he glanced at Abbey, who took the opportunity to steer him out of the room, deciding to ignore Stella's comment completely, as they went onto the next part of the tour. Later, when they returned to the office, Lydia made coffee for them all, before sitting at her desk, and Matt took the seat opposite Abbey. For the first time, Abbey was able to get a proper look at her new boss. He was tall, his long limbs seemingly overflowing from the chair. He was much younger than she might have expected too, probably about thirty-five, with short fair hair and brown eyes. Definitely good-looking, if she were being objective about these things. It was his warm and open personality that was most appealing, though. He seemed honest and straightforward, and she liked that. She only hoped he wasn't lulling her into a false sense of security.

'Thanks for showing me around the Lodge this morning. It's

clearly a happy and safe environment, and the residents, those who I spoke to, seem very happy living here which, of course, I knew already. I've read the glowing reports, but it's good to see it for myself. I wanted to reassure you both that I'm not about to make any sweeping changes if you might have had any concerns in that direction.' A smile hovered at the corner of his mouth, his eyes locking onto Abbey's, and she breathed an internal sigh of relief. 'Why fix it if it ain't broke?'

'That's good to hear,' she said with a smile.

'We will be having a rebrand, so that will mean new brochures, new stationery and signage, but nothing that will directly impact on the work you're doing here. I hope that sounds okay?'

Abbey and Lydia looked at each other and nodded.

'One thing, there will inevitably be some extra administration duties. I'm trying to bring all the homes into line and am streamlining the reporting process. Everything will be submittable online, but it will probably require some additional hours initially and I'm not sure if you have the capacity to fulfil that at the moment. It might mean hiring another person if you need to.'

Abbey looked across at Lydia. They'd worked together so long they could almost read each other's minds.

'Shall we see how it goes?' asked Lydia. 'And then make a decision when we have a better idea of the time commitment involved?' Abbey nodded her agreement.

'Perfect,' said Matt, easing himself up out of his seat. 'In that case, I won't take up any more of your time. Thanks once again. Oh…' He turned, just as he reached for the handle of the office door. 'There is just one more thing.'

Abbey knew it. He was leaving the killer blow right until the last moment. Delivering it with casual abandon as he waltzed out the door. She steeled herself.

'Can I take you both out to dinner sometime? My way of saying thank you for the brilliant work you've been doing here and to mark the beginning of our new working relationship.'

'That sounds... lovely,' said Abbey, taken aback by the unexpected offer.

'Great. Email me over a couple of dates that work for you both and we'll get something in the diary before Christmas. Any suggestions of any nice restaurants in the area too and I'll get it organised.'

He breezed out with the same positive energy that he'd imbued the Lodge with during his visit.

'Well, that went much better than we could have expected,' said Abbey when she knew Matt had left the building.

'I know,' said Lydia, sliding down her office chair and fanning herself exaggeratedly with a piece of paper. 'Be still, my beating heart!'

5

'Again, again!'

'Give poor Bill a rest,' Lizzie laughed, as she stood with her hands on her hips, surveying the complete chaos around her feet. There were toys littered across the carpet, baby paraphernalia everywhere and the boxes of Christmas decorations that had been brought down from the loft were still piled up in the bay window, awaiting the arrival of the tree. That job had been put on hold when Katy and the children turned up as Lizzie concentrated on sorting out their sleeping arrangements and finding space for all their belongings. Although she wouldn't say she'd actually succeeded on that front yet.

Little Rosie, and Pip too, had settled into their new surroundings remarkably well, which was the most important thing, and Bill was very much Rosie's new best friend. He showed never-ending patience with her demands, happily brushing the hair and changing the clothes on Rosie's ever-growing collection of dolls. He'd read the *Spot the Dog* book on numerous occasions now, complete with funny voices which made Rosie giggle uncontrollably, and now Bill was on all fours on the living room carpet as Rosie clambered on and off his back as she chanted, 'Go, donkey, go!'

'Aargh!' Bill grimaced, reaching for his knee and rubbing it with his hand. 'I shall have to get up, that's if I can. Give me a hand, Lizzie.' With a lot of huffing, puffing and sighing, Bill managed to struggle to his feet, a pained smile on his face. He flexed his leg, his joints creaking. 'That's better,' he said, chuckling. 'I'm not as flexible as I once was.'

'In the garden, Bill-Bill.'

'Come on, then,' he said. 'It will probably do me good to stretch my legs.' Bill helped Rosie to put on her wellies and they wandered outside, hand in hand, stopping to look at the shrubs and the trees, Bill giving the little girl his full attention as she no doubt bombarded him with a hundred and one questions.

'Bill is just so lovely,' said Katy, watching them through the window.

'Isn't he? I'm so pleased you like him.' She squeezed her daughter's hand. 'He is a proper gent. I always said I would never want another man in my life after your dad. I mean, there's not a person on this planet to take his place, but Bill came along unexpectedly and we hit it off from the outset. He's so easy to be with and it's just nice to have someone to share a meal or to go shopping with. He's very kind, you know?'

'Honestly, Mum, I'm really pleased for you. I can see how happy he makes you.'

'He's certainly given me a new lease of life. I've got a busy social calendar these days, what with our regular afternoon tea dances and the monthly quiz nights at the pub. We've formed a lovely little friendship group there. There's Abbey, Bill's daughter, you'll get to meet her soon, you'll really like her. She's with Sam now from Primrose Woods and they seem really good together. I'm just pleased he's finally found someone special. I was beginning to despair of that man and his love life. He's such a lovely guy and you know what a great support he's been to me, so for him to have finally found someone who makes him happy is a big relief all round. Then there's Rhi and Luke, you'll have heard me talk about them. They're the ones to thank for getting me over to Australia in the summer. Luke put me in touch with the hypnotherapist who helped with my fear of flying and Rhi held my hand on the outward flight. I would never have done it without them. They're such a lovely young couple, and I was hoping for them to get together properly, but they popped into the café the other day and told me Luke has a new job and is moving away, so I'm not sure what's happening there now.'

Katy nodded, listening interestedly. She never grew tired of hearing her mum chattering away happily about her new friends. She already felt as though she knew them all, her mum spoke about them that often, and just seeing her brimming with positivity and enthusiasm made Katy smile. It's what she'd missed the most living in Australia. Keeping up with the daily ins-and-outs of each other's lives. She gave a thought to Brad all those miles away on the other side of the world, wondering what he might be doing right now. She glanced at her watch. Probably working in his study or getting ready for bed. She'd messaged him earlier, but she'd not heard his voice in a couple of days. She missed him, the sound of him, his soft warm gaze when he looked at her, and she had to sniff away the tears gathering in her eyes as she thought about his patience and kindness.

Pip stirred in his makeshift cot in the armchair, his gentle chuntering making his presence felt.

'Hello, sweet little boy,' cooed Lizzie, standing over him. 'Shall I pick him up?' she asked eagerly, not wanting to overstep her position, but her arms were aching to hold him.

Katy nodded.

'I'll just go and put his milk on.'

With Katy in the kitchen, Lizzie collected her grandson up in her arms, inhaling his delicious scent, feeling his lovely chunky legs through the cute orange and white hooped romper suit he was wearing. She could never get enough baby cuddles. Pip was such a happy, easy-going boy, sleeping at the right times and taking his milk greedily, and Lizzie frequently joked that he had clearly read the *Good Baby Guidebook* from front to back.

'Here we go then,' said Katy when she returned to the room with the warmed bottle in her hand.

Lizzie looked up, noticing the subtle shift in her daughter's demeanour, the cloud of sadness wafting around her as she re-entered the room.

'Is everything all right, love?'

'Oh, Mum, what have I done?' She passed the bottle to Lizzie, who positioned herself on the end of the sofa and started feeding an expectant Pip. Katy flopped down beside her. 'I've left Brad behind in Australia and dragged the children to the other side of the world, just before Christmas as well. I was absolutely certain that I was doing the right thing, but now I'm here, I wonder if I've just been really selfish. I should have put my husband and the kids before my own needs. Brad would have been happy to stay in Aus, I know he would, but I was adamant that we should return to the UK. And turning up here without any warning is so unfair on you. Look at the mess.' She held up her hands in a gesture of defeat. 'You don't want all of this, you've got your own life to lead now.'

'Nonsense! You're my daughter, Katy, and you'll always be welcome here. Admittedly it was a big shock finding you on my doorstep, but it was the loveliest surprise ever. How could I be unhappy about this?' she asked, running a finger along Pip's milk-tinged cheek.

'I just feel like the worst wife and mother in the world. I should be happy. I've got everything I always wanted, but...' Her words trailed away. 'I don't know why I'm feeling like this.'

'Katy, darling.' She adjusted Pip in her hold, reaching out an arm to pull Katy into her embrace. 'The children are happy and thriving. Brad has a new and exciting job which you've told me he's looking forward to starting. Everything will work out fine, you'll see. It's just that everything's up in the air at the moment. You're bound to feel unsettled.'

Her mum's reassuring words did little to make Katy feel any better and the tears she'd been suppressing bubbled to the surface, falling in big gulping sobs down her face.

'Oh, sweetheart. I hate to see you like this.' Lizzie stroked Katy's hair, soothing her tears. 'It's understandable that you're feeling so out of sorts. You've got a new baby, on top of everything else you're dealing with, and a lack of sleep always makes everything seem so much harder to cope with.'

'I'm shattered,' Katy admitted, blowing her nose with the tissue her mum had offered. 'I feel so tired all the time but then when it comes to bedtime, I can't get to sleep.'

'Well, you're probably still suffering from jetlag, and on top of that, you've moved, not just homes, but countries too, and you're living apart from your husband. You're hitting all the stress buttons. But you're here now so just try and relax for a few weeks until after Christmas. I can help with the children, and before you know it, Brad will be here too and you'll be back together as a family.'

'Thanks, Mum, I really don't know what the matter is with me. There's so much I should be doing, but I can't settle to anything.' There was a note of panic in Katy's voice. 'I should be helping you, getting things ready for Christmas, but I just feel so useless. I really don't want to be a burden.'

'Never,' said Lizzie, troubled by her daughter's choice of words. 'You never could be. It's lovely to have you home again and we can get ready for Christmas together. Like we used to.' Lizzie cupped Katy's face in her hands, looking into her moistened eyes. How she wished she could make everything better for her daughter with a hug and some carefully chosen words like she had when she was little, but she knew it wasn't as simple as that. 'Let's see how things work out in the next few days and if you still feel as though you're struggling, then it might be worth checking in with the GP. It might help to talk to someone outside of the family.'

Katy sighed heavily, nodding, feeling better already to have offloaded her feelings onto her mum, relieved that she hadn't berated her for her impulsiveness and her selfishness, knowing deep down that she would never be so openly critical. It was good to be home, but it would be much better for everyone concerned when they were in their own place and Brad was back at her side. Lizzie sat Pip up on her knee, gently stroking his back.

'We should get a move on, I suppose. I need to go and choose the tree today or else Christmas will have been and gone. Do you want to come, or would you prefer to stay here and have a quiet hour or two? Bill and I would be more than happy to take the kids, Rosie will love going round the park.'

'Are you sure, Mum?' Lizzie heard the relief in Katy's voice. 'I'm so tired, I might even go back to bed.'

'Make the most of it, while you can. I'll bring you back some cake from the café. What do you fancy?'

Leaving Katy behind at the house, the rest of them wrapped up in their winter coats and hats, and drove the short distance to Primrose Woods Country Park where they parked in the main car park and Bill wrestled the buggy from the boot and manhandled it into position. Lizzie lifted Pip from the car seat, his little legs swinging in the air, and strapped him into the buggy, not before plonking a kiss on his forehead. How could she not when his little face was always so bright and expectant? She took the handle of the buggy and headed for the path that led along the sculpture trail. Rosie, in her brand-new shiny yellow wellingtons, held onto Bill's hand, her excitement plain to see as she skipped along, eager to experience everything she could.

'Look at the deer,' said Bill, directing her over to the family of carved wooden deer, hidden in the shadows of a towering redwood tree. Normally unadorned, now they were decorated with evergreen garlands.

'Rudolph!' said Rosie, running across to the statues, her hands reaching out gleefully to touch the baby deer's nose.

Rosie loved exploring, scrabbling around between the trees and squealing when she found the fairy grotto, trying out the little seats for size. Lizzie stood back watching, her heart warming at the reminder of Katy at a similar age. The sculpture trail was a new addition to Primrose Woods since Katy was small, but they'd spent many happy days in the park as a family and to be able to recreate those special memories with her grandchildren was more than Lizzie could have hoped for. She felt a pang of sadness that Katy wasn't with them today, but it was best that she rested while she could. It hurt Lizzie to see her daughter struggling and she would need to keep a close eye on her. Hopefully her low mood was just a reaction to all the pressures she'd been under recently and nothing more serious.

'Should we go and find our Christmas tree? You can help me to decorate it when we get home.'

With a little bit of coaxing, they managed to guide Rosie away from the animal sculptures, past the play park with a promise they could go there later, and to the large scrubland area behind the café where they were selling the Christmas trees. There was a lively festive atmosphere in the busy arena, helped along by Michael Bublé's smooth tones crooning through a loudspeaker, and the aroma of freshly brewed coffee mixed with pine needles wafting in the air. People were chatting and laughing as they viewed the vast array of trees. Lizzie had no idea where to look first, but she needn't have worried because Rosie led the way. There were big trees, small ones and every size in between. Non-drop and drop. Nordmann Firs, Norway Spruces and Fraser Firs, the sweet smell of fragrant pine all around them.

'This one, this one!' Rosie called, patting the first tree she came across before moving onto the next one, shouting the same.

'Lizzie!' she heard a familiar voice call out from behind her and turned to see Sam's distinctive figure striding across to meet them. He greeted them enthusiastically, shaking Bill's hand and hugging Lizzie, and making a point of introducing himself, and Lady, to Rosie, who looked up at him, wide-eyed. She giggled as Lady wagged her tail furiously.

'Have you chosen your tree yet?' he asked her, bending down on his haunches to meet her at eye-level and holding onto Lady's collar so that Rosie could say hello to the dog in a relatively calm manner, without being subjected to her over-excitable attention.

Shyly, Rosie shook her head.

'Well, we've got lots to choose from. Do you want a big one or a smaller one?'

'A big one!' Rosie cried, predictably.

Lizzie and Bill laughed.

'I'm not sure where to start,' said Lizzie, overwhelmed by the amount of choice. She realised she should probably concentrate on the job in hand rather than allowing her concentration to drift to everything going on around her. Trouble was, she knew everyone working at the Christmas tree yard. They were all regulars in the café, and she liked to stop to have a chat with them all, and of course they all wanted to make a big fuss of Rosie and Pip too.

'Sam, I need a tree to go in my front window. Not too tall, and something that will last until after Christmas.'

'Over here, Lizzie.' Sam led the way over to a particular row of trees. 'One of these will be ideal. It's a Nordmann Fir and will stay looking good over the holidays.'

'Well, if you say so, Sam. What do you think to this one, Rosie?' asked Lizzie.

'I like it!' She nodded eagerly, jumping up and down on the spot.

'Great, I'll get this wrapped up and drop it off later for you,' said Sam.

'Are you sure?'

'Definitely. It's no problem. I'll be driving past your place anyway.'

'Well, that will be super and then we can get busy decorating it, can't we, Rosie? It will really feel like Christmas once the tree is up. We're looking forward to you and Abbey coming for Christmas, Sam. It will be lovely to have a crowd of us around the table.'

'Yep, should be fun,' said Sam, preoccupied with dragging the tree over to the till area and putting it through the netting machine.

'Thanks, Sam,' Lizzie said, after handing over the cash. She stood on tiptoe to kiss him on the cheek. 'We'll leave you to it. Looks as though you've got quite a rush on,' she said, gesturing to the queue that had built behind them.

Afterwards they visited the café and had warming drinks and cakes. Rosie chose a chocolate krispy bar with a babycino and Lizzie and Bill plumped for toasted tea cakes with lashings of butter, alongside frothy coffees. Little Pip, oblivious to everything going on around him, slept the whole way through in his buggy.

'Lizzie, I hope you're not thinking what I think you're thinking,' said Bill, over the top of his glasses, when he noticed her attention drifting behind the serving counter. 'They can manage perfectly well without you, you know? It's your day off, if you haven't remembered.'

'Force of habit,' she laughed, knowing she'd been caught out and making an effort to drag her gaze away and relax into her chair. She loved working at the Treetops Café. Who wouldn't like to spend their days working in such a lovely environment? The fully glazed panels of the café gave a panoramic view of the surrounding landscape with its towering redwoods disappearing into the distance and the grassed picnic area with the fallen tree trunks used as seats. Inside the café, the constant comings and goings of the customers made for an energetic and vibrant atmosphere and Lizzie thrived on being at the helm, serving the wide selection of delicious lunches and snacks from the chalkboards. It was hard to switch off when she was here as a customer, and she had to stop herself from jumping up and lending a hand.

'Are you enjoying that, Rosie?' she said, focusing her attention on her little granddaughter instead.

The little girl nodded, although she'd been very quiet for the last few minutes as she munched on her cake, gazing out of the window.

'Nanna?'

'Yes, sweetheart?'

'How will Santa Claus be able to find me? Will he leave my presents at my old house, with Daddy?'

'Don't worry about that, Rosie.' Lizzie took hold of her granddaughter's hand and peered into her face. 'Santa Claus knows exactly where all the children are and he'll bring your presents to my house this year.'

'Will he?' Rosie's little face was full of hope and expectation.

'Yes, but if you're worried, you could write to him and tell him you're staying at Nanna's house.'

'Yay! Letter to Santa.' She swung her legs in her seat. 'Nanna, help me!'

'I will, we can make a start once we've decorated the tree. And you can help to write Pip's letter too. We're going to be very busy, Rosie.'

'Santa will make it snow too,' Rosie said, with absolute certainty.

Bill and Lizzie exchanged a look and a hesitant smile.

'Well, you never know, Rosie,' said Bill. 'Hopefully it will, but it doesn't always snow at Christmas time. We'll just have to keep our fingers crossed and wait and see.'

Rosie folded her arms crossly.

'The elves make the toys and Santa makes it snow and then he brings the toys in his... car.' Rosie held her arms out to her side, pretending to fly. 'With Rudolph.'

'You're right. That happens in the story.' Bill realised Rosie was talking about one of the picture books that he'd read to her several times already, and no doubt would read many more times before Christmas too. 'Santa will bring some presents and we'll put out a special wish for some snow too.'

'It will snow,' Rosie said with all the authority of a three-year-old girl who had Santa on her side.

Lizzie could only nod in agreement. She couldn't do anything about the weather, however much she might like to, but she could make sure that their first Christmas together as a family would be as perfect and magical as she could make it, with or without the snow.

6

Abbey heard Sam's Jeep pull up outside the cottage and she peered out through the front window into the darkness. Across on the other side of the village green and down her quiet lane, she saw the twinkling lights of her neighbours' decorations. Christmas trees, fairy lights and sparkly reindeers were all aglow, bringing a touch of festive magic to the quiet country village of Wishwell. Abbey watched Sam jump out of the Jeep followed by Lady, her white flashes of fur visible against the dark night sky, her tail wagging furiously, which was its default mode. The pair of them came as a team and it made Abbey's heart swell to see them together. She pulled the curtains closed and hurried to open the door, ushering them inside away from the chilly night air. Sam lifted her off her feet and spun her around in his arms, planting a kiss on her lips.

'Honestly, do you know I still haven't got used to coming home to you each evening? It still feels like such a novelty, one I can never imagine growing tired of. Mmmm, something smells delicious.'

'Probably my perfume,' Abbey quipped. 'Oh, you mean the

coq au vin. Yes, just call me a domestic goddess. I came home at lunchtime and popped it in the slow cooker.'

'You see, what did I do to deserve this?' he said, grinning. 'Let me fix us a drink.'

Sam saw to Lady first, pouring some dry meal into her empty bowl and refreshing her water before washing his hands and grabbing some glasses from the cupboard and pouring the wine. Abbey took the glass of wine offered by Sam as his arm slipped around her waist, and her entire body relaxed into his arms. She rested her head on his shoulder, closed her eyes and savoured the moment. He always smelled so good when he came home from work, bringing the woody aromas of the great outdoors with him. A concoction of the forest floor and the sweet smell of pine rubbed off his sweatshirt.

'Let me go and shower and get changed.'

'Aw, do you have to?' Abbey teased, rather wishing she could stay in his embrace for longer.

'Five minutes,' he said, grinning, 'and I'll be back.'

Abbey pulled out some bowls from the cupboard and dished up the chicken with the creamy mashed potatoes. They took it in turns to cook, whoever was home first would make a start on the supper, and Abbey loved the daily ritual, having a glass of wine together and sharing the details of their day. She wasn't sure how something so everyday and normal could feel so special.

'I saw your dad and Lizzie today at the park,' Sam said when he reappeared, fresh out of the shower, changed into some jeans and a plum T-shirt. 'They brought the children with them to choose their tree. Little Rosie is such a cute little thing. I think she wanted to take all the trees home with her. Lizzie's in her element, having her family home for Christmas. I know how much she's missed them these last few years. I was thinking actually, they're going to have a houseful on Christmas Day. It seems like an awful lot of work for Lizzie. Should we leave them to it, do you think? It might be nice, just the two of us at home. It is our first Christmas together, after all.'

It did sound lovely, romantic and intimate, but they'd already agreed to spend it with Lizzie and Bill, and Abbey would hate to let them down. Besides, she'd spent every Christmas with her dad since her mum had died and couldn't bear the thought of not being with him on the big day, even for just one year.

'Well, you know what Lizzie's like. It will be a case of the more the merrier as far as she is concerned. And I'd really like to spend some time with Dad on Christmas Day too.' She looked across at Sam to judge his reaction. She knew Christmas wasn't his favourite time of year – it was more a case of enduring rather than enjoying it for Sam – but Abbey was hoping that she'd be able to show him just how lovely Christmas could be, sharing it with the right person. 'Do you really not fancy it?' She didn't want to force him if he was really opposed to the idea.

'No, it's not that. I just thought we could...' Whatever he was about to say, he obviously thought better of it. He shrugged off the words before pulling out a chair and sitting at the table, tucking into his dinner. 'I'm fine with whatever you think. I'll have a word with Lizzie. See if there's anything we can take along to contribute.'

Abbey observed Sam from across the table. Her thoughts drifted to last Christmas when she'd still been with Jason. With hindsight, she should have realised that their relationship wasn't working then, but she'd pushed any doubts to one side, determined to make it a happy Christmas for them. Despite trying her best to please him, organising get-togethers with his family and their friends, all Jason had wanted to do was stay at home and drink himself silly. She'd spent far too much time pandering to his moods, tiptoeing around him for fear of upsetting him, she realised now.

Sam was much more easy-going and accommodating and had shown her that a happy, healthy relationship needn't be like that. It was still early days in their relationship, though, and she didn't want to impose her wishes for the festive season onto him, if he really wasn't keen on the arrangements.

'You know, you must say if I'm overstepping the mark, making too many plans. Sometimes I get carried away,' she admitted.

Sam laughed.

'It's what I love about you, though, your enthusiasm! Honestly, it's fine.'

He sounded happy enough. She just hoped he wasn't appeasing her.

'Everything okay?' he asked a few minutes later, when she'd been lost in her thoughts.

'Sorry, I was miles away thinking what an eventful year it's been. I'm just happy I've made it here with you and that we'll be together this Christmas. It could have been very different. Just think if we'd never got together.'

'It was always meant to be, I reckon,' Sam said, a lopsided smile lighting up his face. His hand reached across the table, squeezing Abbey's fingers. It was such a lovely sentiment, but she wondered if it could really be true? One thing she knew for certain was that her ex and Sam were such hugely different characters, she shouldn't really compare them.

'What did you do for Christmas last year, Sam?'

He paused, fork in mid-air.

'I went to Lizzie's. She invited me round for dinner. We were both at a loose end. On Boxing Day, we went to the Royal Oak for lunch. It was fine, although to be honest, Christmas has never been a big deal for me. Something to get through, if you know what I mean? It was fun when I was a kid, but even then, it was usually just Mum and me. She never had a lot of money, but she always made it special.'

It pulled at Abbey's heartstrings to hear Sam talk about his childhood, hearing the sadness behind his words. His dad hadn't played a part in his upbringing, so it had been just him and his mum, and they'd been incredibly close until her untimely death from cancer, soon after he'd finished university, an event which turned his whole life upside down.

'Christmas is really for kids, isn't it?'

'Yeah, although it's for big kids too. Like me! It's my favourite time of year.' As if Sam didn't know that already. 'And this year is going to be the best one yet, spending it with you, and Dad and Lizzie too.'

She was determined to make it special for Sam, to show him just how lovely a proper family Christmas could be. The first of many Christmases together, she hoped, her mind running away with her as she imagined the special traditions they'd adopt and follow for years to come.

'It'll be great,' he said, with a smile. 'Anyway, tell me how it went with the big boss today?'

'Oh, my goodness, absolutely fine. You know how nervous I was, but it went much better than I could have expected. Matt assured me he's not going to be making any major changes, apart from streamlining the reporting processes and implementing a rebrand, but overall, he was very complimentary about our management of the home.'

'See, what did I tell you?'

'I know. I'd been expecting a stuffy middle-aged man to turn up, but Matt couldn't have been more approachable. I'm sure you'd like him. He's a similar age to us, and was really friendly. He was wearing a ridiculous Christmas jumper which made everyone smile and he took the time to speak to a lot of the residents too, which of course they all loved.'

'Definitely sounds as though he was on a charm offensive.'

'He was. In fact, he's taking Lydia and me out for dinner in a couple of weeks' time as his way of saying thank you for all our hard work this year. That's a first!'

'That's great. It's about time you got some recognition for everything you do at the Lodge.'

Abbey smiled. She loved her job, working with her great team of carers, and admin and catering staff, to ensure the home ran as smoothly as possible. Most of all, she relished the relationships she built with the ladies and gentlemen of Rushgrove Lodge. Often when they first arrived to take up residence at the Lodge, they were vulnerable and afraid, made to move from their homes through illness or incapacity, and Abbey understood their fear and reticence at losing a level of control in their lives. She made it her priority to ensure each of the guests was treated with kindness and respect, taking the time to listen to their wishes and concerns, in a way that she would want for her own grandparents, if they'd still been alive. She liked to think of them all as one big happy family. She didn't do it for any accolades, or for the money. She did it because it brought her a huge sense of satisfaction, knowing that she was making a difference to the lives of the residents. She would do the job even if they didn't pay her. Still, Sam was right, it was lovely to be occasionally acknowledged for the work she did and going for a slap-up meal with Lydia, and her charming new boss who she was intrigued to know better, would be the perfect way to celebrate.

7

There was always a lively atmosphere in the Three Feathers, but on this particular evening, the last quiz night of the year before Christmas, the buzz about the place was even more special than normal. The quaint country pub looked extra cosy with the Christmas tree in the front bay window decorated in a myriad of glinting fairy lights. Gold stars and bows hung from the old oak beams, holly with red berries adorned the picture frames and mirrors, and sprigs of mistletoe were fastened above the doorways. The open fires in both bars were ablaze and there was a lovely background noise of chatter, laughter and bonhomie. The Primrose Fancies, who hadn't been together as a complete team for a few months now, were busy catching up around their table. Malc, the landlord, had to call order to gain everyone's attention.

'Come on, you motley crew. We've got to make a start or else we could all still be here at Christmas. Usual rules. Ten rounds plus the picture round in the interval. If you want to play your joker, please give your wooden spoon to my glamorous assistant before the start of that round.' Jan, his wife, gave a curtsy behind the bar. 'Right, first round, geography.'

There was a collective groan from virtually all the teams, well, apart from The Swots, who were sitting on the next table. It wasn't their real team name, but it was the one The Fancies had labelled them with, as they invariably won every time with their extensive knowledge of seemingly every single subject under the sun. Still, The Fancies weren't bitter, well, not really, and were much more interested in having a good time than coming first. The quiz was even more fun than usual, as all the questions had a seasonal slant and, for a change, The Fancies picked the right round to play their joker on. They opted for the music round, which was on the subject of Christmas number ones, and with their collective knowledge, spanning the years, they managed to score a very respectable nine out of ten, which was doubled up to eighteen.

'You know, I think we could even win tonight,' said Lizzie, beaming, ever the optimist.

'Hmmm, I'm not so sure about that. The Swots have scored highly on all the rounds so far and haven't played their joker yet. Might be a close-run thing, though.' Luke kept a running total in his head of the team's scores and those of all the other teams too. When, at the end of the evening, Malc announced the results in reverse order, The Fancies became more and more excited as they waited to hear their name called.

'And in third place we have The History Buffs. Very well done!'

'This is it. I think we've done it.' Abbey, Lizzie and Rhi held hands across the table and stilled themselves to hear the result.

'So that leaves two teams and there were only a couple of points between them. But in second place, with a valiant attempt this time around, it's The Primrose Fancies.'

The team groaned before breaking out in laughter.

'So near and yet so far,' sighed Lizzie.

'Well, it's our best effort yet. The win can't be that far away,' said Bill.

After the post-match analysis on where they went wrong and how they might have picked up more points, they leaned across the tables to congratulate The Swots, who were very gracious in their win, and only the tiniest bit smug.

'Ah, well, there's always next year,' said Abbey with a resigned shrug.

Rhi glanced across at Abbey, her throwaway remark reminding Rhi that Luke wouldn't be part of their team next year. She suppressed a sigh, knowing it wouldn't be the same without Luke at her side. Quiz nights were always fun, but it was seeing Luke that made them special for her.

'Let's have another drink to celebrate being runners-up,' Sam suggested.

'Great idea,' said Luke and Rhi almost in unison, prompting a smile as their eyes locked across the table for the briefest moment.

'I'd love to stay, but I can't,' said Lizzie, gathering up her handbag. 'I need to get home and see how Katy is doing. Hopefully the children will have stayed asleep all evening and she's had a few hours' peace and quiet.'

'Before you go, Lizzie, I wondered if we all fancied going along to the Carols by Candlelight event at Primrose Hall? It's next Saturday. I'm desperate to have a nose, actually.' Abbey turned to Luke. 'I don't know if you've seen, but they've refurbished the old manor house that's been derelict for years. They've completely transformed it, and apparently the new owner has just moved in. Sam was saying that he's a local guy. Anyway, he's holding this event in the grounds of Primrose Hall and they're opening up the stables for mulled wine and mince pies. It sounds like it could be a fun evening.'

'Yes, I caught a glimpse of the renovations when I last walked through the woods. As you say, it would be good to get a proper look.'

'Shall we all go, then? I think Katy and the children would enjoy it too,' said Lizzie. 'Oh, and that reminds me, another date for your diary, if you'd like to come, of course. Christmas Eve at mine for a drink and a mince pie?'

'Sounds lovely,' said Abbey, taking a sideways glance at Sam, who nodded his agreement. 'That's if you don't mind having us for two days on the trot.'

'Not at all. I love having a full house at any time of the year. I've had far too many quiet Christmases in recent years, and I definitely know what I prefer. I'll have plenty of food and drink, so it will be lovely to have a little celebration. I still find it hard to believe that this time last year I didn't know most of you. It's the best thing that's happened to me, making such good friends with you all.'

She glanced across at Bill, who smiled at her fondly. Both of them had been resolutely single a few months ago, with no inclination on either of their parts to meet someone new, but when their lives came together at Primrose Woods, it was as though they were long-lost friends meeting up again after several years apart. They had so much in common, having lost their beloved spouses around the same time, and they'd hit it off from the start, quickly becoming friends before their relationship developed into something more serious. They hadn't put a name to it, or moved in together, but both of them realised that what they had together was something special.

'Aw, that's lovely,' said Rhi. 'I feel exactly the same. I think we'll all be friends for life now. Thanks for the invite. I'll definitely be there.' It was a relief to have something planned for Christmas Eve. Her mum and Robb were going to the carol concert in the High Street and although she'd been invited, she didn't much fancy tagging along with them, being a third wheel again. Spending time with Lizzie and her friends was a much more attractive proposition, especially if Luke would be there too. She looked across at him expectantly.

'Sounds good to me, I've no plans for that day.'

Rhi smiled, hoping she was doing a good job of hiding her feelings, but who was she kidding? Only herself. Luke must have known how she felt about him. She'd given him enough signals, the sly looks, the way she giggled at his terrible jokes and how she couldn't stop herself from laying a hand on his arm whenever he was within touching distance. Would Christmas Eve be the last chance she'd get to see him before he moved away? Perhaps she could organise something for New Year's Eve, just the two of them, although the thought made her sad. The new year was meant to herald new beginnings, but for Rhi and Luke, it could mean a farewell party.

'That's perfect then.' Lizzie smiled. 'We'll look forward to them both, won't we, Bill?'

After they'd left, Sam went up to the bar to order another round of drinks and Rhi excused herself, wending her way through the tables towards the back of the pub. She stopped to chat with Jan and Malc, her lovely bosses who she now considered as friends, and then to several of the locals she'd come to know through working at the pub over the last few months. They enjoyed having a laugh and a joke with her, teasing and pulling her leg, but it was nothing she couldn't handle. Rhi was confident and sassy and could give as good as she got. After Christmas, she would cut her hours right down so that she could concentrate on building her business, but she would miss the camaraderie that came from working behind the bar on a regular basis.

In the loos, she washed her hands and then zhuzhed up her

hair, teasing out her abundance of dark curls with her fingertips. She felt the glow in her cheeks as a mix of emotions ran through her body. A delicious sensation of giddiness coursed through her veins, helped no doubt by the couple of glasses of Prosecco she'd enjoyed, but she suspected it had more to do with simply being in the company of Luke. What was it about him that got beneath her skin so? Disregarding the fact that he was undeniably gorgeous with his shock of blond hair, intense blue eyes, and a fit and toned body, it was the way he made her feel about herself that was most surprising of all, as though she was something really special. *Uggh.* Why exactly was she acting like a lovesick teenager? It was all Luke's fault. Maybe it was for the best that he was moving away after all.

She shook her head and gave a rueful look at her reflection before taking a deep breath, putting on a rallying smile and waltzing out the door. Christmas tunes were playing now, making her smile, and she couldn't help but sing along, 'Merry Christmas Everyone', as she walked jauntily along the back corridor towards the main bar, round the corner and straight into...

'Luke!'

'Hey,' he laughed, taking a step backwards, his hand reaching out for her waist and pulling her forwards as someone else tried to squeeze past. They were so close she could smell his after-shave, the faint aroma of Belgian hops wafting around him. She was so close she could press her lips against his, but she remembered the last time she'd tried that and how badly it had ended. Luke had recoiled and asked her what she thought she was doing. She wouldn't make the same mistake again.

She often wondered how she could have misread that situation so badly? Especially when she'd known that he'd liked her in that way at one point in time. He'd even asked her out once and she'd flatly refused. Then, at a much later date, at Lizzie's party before her trip to Australia, he'd kissed her unexpectedly. *Oh so memorably*. Before she'd been able to make sense of what was going on, it was over, the moment lost, and she'd been left wanting so much more. Her imminent trip abroad had ruled out a repeat of that lovely moment, but she'd hoped that it might have meant as much to Luke as it had to her, and that he would be waiting for her when she returned from her travels.

Now they were here together and he was making no attempt at removing his hand from her waist. Was she imagining it, or were they were standing much closer now, as though there was an invisible magnetic pull between them?

'Everything okay?' Luke asked, his piercing blue eyes locking onto hers, refusing to budge.

'Yes, great,' she said, her voice not sounding like her own, her gaze drifting, unable to stay on his, knowing she would be utterly lost there.

'Good, it's just that you've seemed a little quiet tonight, distracted maybe...?'

Trust Luke to notice. She'd thought she'd done a pretty good job at hiding her feelings, but obviously not a good enough job.

'Really, I'm fine. I just have a lot on my mind what with Christmas, the new business. Well, you'll know what it's like. It's great to be back with everyone, though, we always have such fun on these nights.' Her voice trailed away and he looked at her expectantly. 'It's sad to think this will be the last quiz night for the six of us.'

'Yep,' he said, with that boyish smile of his. 'So you're going to miss me, then?'

She shrugged off his question nonchalantly, annoyed and amused at the same time.

'Maybe, but don't worry, I'll get over it. Guess I'll just have to find myself another handsome guy to fill your spot on the quiz team.'

'Is that even possible?' he asked, tipping up her face with a finger so that she had to look into his eyes. 'You don't really mean that, do you, Rhi?'

'Oi, you two, you're not still blocking the way, are you? Come on, move along.' Gerry Fisher, a big bear of a man, who was a regular at the pub and one of Rhi's favourite customers, scooped the pair of them up in the width of his arms and bowled them along back towards the main bar. 'There you go!'

Luke grinned and raised his palms to the air, his gaze glancing upwards, a suggestion in his raised eyebrow.

'Well, it would be rude not to. Don't you think, Rhi?'

It took a moment for her to cotton on, but she glanced up too, spotting the mistletoe above her head. She laughed at Gerry's playful interference. A shiver ran across her shoulders and a rush of thoughts bombarded her head, making her giddy. So what if Luke would soon be moving to another part of the country, so what if their lives were about to go in opposing directions, so what if they'd missed their chance at a proper relationship, did any of that matter right now? After all, Christmas came but once a year! She scrunched her eyes closed tight, pursed her lips and waited for Luke's touch. When it came, the sensation of his lips upon hers was every bit as electrifying as she had imagined. His hands cupped her face, creating an intimacy that shut out all the noise around them. It was just the two of them alone in the busy pub to the sound of Shakin' Stevens doing his stuff. In that moment, she thought it the most romantic moment ever, and she knew, deep in her heart, despite her internal protestations, that it was so much more than just a cheeky Christmas kiss under the mistletoe.

If only Luke might realise it too.

8

'Remember, you'll need to fend for yourself tonight. I'll be going straight out to dinner from work. I'll get a taxi home, so you won't need to worry about picking me up. I'll text you as I'm leaving.' Abbey had her sparkly dress and some strappy heels in a separate holdall ready to go. She'd decided to make an effort, especially when she realised where they would be dining. Her suggestion for the meal had been the local carvery, which always offered a lovely roast along with lots of other choices, but Matt had politely suggested another restaurant, Chez Michel's, on the Stockmere estate. Did she know it, he'd asked. Of course she knew it. It was a renowned restaurant locally and beyond, with two Michelin stars and a fabulous reputation. Somewhere she'd always wanted to visit, but had never had the opportunity, or the funds, until now. Lydia had been overcome with excitement.

'I can't believe he's really taking us there. It will cost him a fortune! What a treat!'

Abbey smiled at the reminder, knowing that Lydia wouldn't be able to settle to anything today, but then who could blame her? Abbey would probably be in the same state of giddiness all day long.

'Ah, yes, of course!' Sam said now, refilling Lady's water bowl. 'Dinner with the boss. In that case, I might give Luke a call and see if he fancies a game of squash or even just a pint at the pub. Have a great time, won't you? I can't wait to hear all about it.'

'Oh, God, Sam,' she released her hand from the front door and dropped her bags on the floor, 'I love you so much.'

He looked at her, bemused, and grinned, his dark chestnut hair curling at his collar and his brown eyes crinkling at the sides as they always did when he smiled.

'Well, that's very good to hear because I love you too, Abbey.'

She dashed to his side and threw her arms around his neck, kissing him urgently, feeling a pang of regret at having to leave him, at not seeing him again for at least another fourteen hours. It was ridiculous, she knew, but she couldn't help the way she felt.

'I don't know what's brought on this sudden display of affection, but I approve wholeheartedly,' said Sam, laughing.

That was the thing, she realised, as she drove to work. Sam had no idea. His easy-going undemanding nature continued to surprise her on a daily basis. Too many years spent with Jason had made her wary and cautious about making her own plans and needs heard. Jason would have asked her a dozen questions about where she was going, who she was going with and what time she would be back. He would have sulked and given her the silent treatment and she would have spent the entire time when she should have been enjoying herself feeling anxious, glancing at her watch, thinking about the reception waiting for her when she got home.

She had no such worries being with Sam. He was encouraging and supportive, where Jason had been critical and demeaning. Sam told her all the time how much he loved her and how he just wanted to make her happy, and she had to pinch herself at times to realise how lucky she was.

At work, the hours rushed by as they did every day at Rushgrove Lodge, and when they finished their shift, Abbey and Lydia had a well-deserved cup of tea before changing into their party gear.

'Oh, my goodness, you look amazing.' Lydia swooned when she saw Abbey in her finery. The velvet smoke-coloured dress skimmed her body in all the right places and the tiny sequins across the bodice shimmered as she moved. Her auburn hair, usually worn in a smooth bun on her head, fell onto her shoulders in loose, big curls. 'Like a Hollywood movie star!'

'Stop it,' chided Abbey, embarrassed by the compliment. 'You look pretty fantastic yourself.'

Lydia gave a twirl, showing off her black wide-leg satin trousers and plum-red halter neck top, her blonde bob shiny and glossy after a trip to the hairdresser's during her lunchtime break.

'Thank you! Well, it's not often I get to go out to a posh restaurant with a very eligible, good-looking and successful man, oh, and with you, of course.'

Abbey shook her head, laughing.

'Yeah, well, don't sound too excited about that! I'm sorry that I have to be there tonight as well. I'll try to keep a low profile and not cramp your style too much.'

'Yeah, could you? Maybe, you could leave early,' Lydia teased. 'Say half past seven or something? I just have to hope that the divine Mr Walsh is into older, sophisticated and curvy women,' she said giggling.

'You're terrible, do you know that? We don't actually know that he's single, only that's he's divorced. Try to remember, Lydia, that this is effectively a business meeting and not a date. So please don't give the poor man the third degree on his relationship status. We need to be on our best behaviour.'

'Aw, shame, but you can't blame a girl for indulging in a bit of romantic fantasy. I'm sure you might have done the same if you weren't completely loved up with Sam.'

Abbey smiled sweetly, raising her eyes heavenwards, as though the thought hadn't even occurred to her, before bursting into laughter.

'Okay I might have done, but, you know, I only have eyes for Sam these days,' she said, batting her eyelashes exaggeratedly.

She couldn't deny that Matt was a very attractive man, charming and clearly successful too, and if she'd met him in other circumstances, where he wasn't her boss and she wasn't madly in love with Sam, then she might have considered him in a different light entirely. Still, that's what made the prospect of the night even more tantalising than it might have been. A dinner date with a gorgeous-looking guy without any complications whatsoever.

* * *

Chez Michel's was a manor house situated in the depths of the glorious English countryside and was approached by a long, sweeping drive through beautifully tended lawns. As the taxi pulled slowly onto the gravel turning circle around a classical three graces water fountain, Abbey's gaze was taken by the beauty of the building illuminated against the dark night sky. She spotted the orchard to the left of the house and then the kitchen gardens signposted to the right. She wondered why it all seemed so familiar to her before remembering she'd read an article in one of the Sunday supplements about Michel Arnaud and his passion for the vegetable and herb gardens which provided the restaurant with all its organic produce.

'I can't believe we're actually here,' said Lydia, echoing Abbey's thoughts exactly.

Inside, the central hallway was every bit as charming as the exterior, with its huge stone fireplace, comfy armchairs in tartans and faded florals, and photos and paintings of the manor house through the seasons adorning the walls. Abbey and Lydia looked in awe around them, taking in the stunningly beautiful Christmas tree aglow with warm candle lights and red velvet bow decorations. They were welcomed warmly by the house manager, who led them through to the lounge where Matt was waiting. He stood up, looking very smart but relaxed in a navy suit and open-necked white shirt. He greeted them both in turn before inviting them to sit down.

'I took the liberty of ordering a bottle of champagne. I hope that's okay with you both? We can get some soft drinks if you prefer?'

'Champagne is always my preferred choice of drink,' said Lydia, laughing, already giddy from the swishness of the occasion.

They chatted about the Lodge and Abbey told some entertaining stories about the residents, with Lydia chipping in with some funny asides. It was clear to Matt that Abbey was dedicated to making the lives of the residents at the care home as fulfilling and happy as she possibly could. Abbey and Lydia were a great team and Matt considered himself lucky to know that Rushgrove Lodge was in such capable and dedicated hands. He raised a toast to all their hard work over the year, but the talk didn't linger on work for very long. With the champagne flowing freely, soon they were discussing their plans for Christmas.

Matt was visiting his parents for the day, along with his

siblings and their families, Lydia was going to her mum's and Abbey spoke about her planned visit to Lizzie's house with her dad and Sam. Despite Abbey's warning words to Lydia about not pressing Matt on his personal life, a turn in the conversation led to Matt revealing details of his short-lived marriage.

'I was very young when we got married. Just twenty-one. We met at uni and we got swept away by the idea that we were in the midst of this huge love affair. She proposed and it seemed like a wild, fun thing to do. We married and went travelling around Europe for six months. I knew even before the trip was over that I'd made the wrong decision. We stayed together for another couple of years because I think we were both desperate to make it work, but in the end, I knew for both our sakes I had to walk away.'

'That must have been so hard. Any break-up is difficult, even when you know the relationship is not right for you.' Abbey, emboldened by Matt's openness, felt equally willing to open up about her own relationship history. 'I'd been with my fiancé for nine years and we were due to be married this year, but it all fell apart at the last moment. I was devastated at the time, but I realise now it was the best thing that could ever have happened to me. It would have been a huge mistake to marry Jason.'

'You wouldn't be with Sam now, if you had,' said Lydia. 'And you're just perfect together, the pair of you.'

'That's true. I certainly wasn't looking to find anyone else, but it just happened. Funny how these things work out.'

'You're much braver than I am,' said Matt ruefully. 'It's a case of once bitten, twice shy, for me, I think.'

The meal was every bit as exquisite as Abbey could have imagined. From the delicious canapés to the starter of scallops with a truffle vinaigrette and the main course of goose breast with a cranberry relish, every mouthful was absolutely sublime. The pudding, a pineapple upside-down cake, was a lovely touch of nostalgia with the accompanying spiced rum caramel sauce and Devonshire clotted cream offering a contemporary twist. Every mouthful elicited a groan of delight from around the table.

'That was the best meal I've ever had,' said Lydia, swooning, sitting back in her chair.

After dinner, they retired to one of the lounges for coffees and petit fours and when Abbey sank into the large squashy armchair, she thought she could quite happily sit there all night long, revelling in her surroundings. She was relieved that there had been no awkward moments with Matt, and instead it had been like meeting up with an old friend, with the conversation flowing naturally amongst the three of them.

'Are you going back home tonight?' she asked, glancing at her watch, realising that their taxi would be arriving at any moment, bringing the evening to a reluctant close.

'No, I'm staying at the Three Feathers in Wishwell,' said Matt. 'It's just a short car ride from here. I've got a meeting tomorrow over this way, so it made sense to stay over.'

'The Three Feathers? That's my local. It's literally just down the road from where I live.'

'Really?'

'Yes, we'll have to drive past it on our way home. You're welcome to share our taxi if you'd like to?'

'Great, I was just about to get that organised with reception, but if you're going my way, then so much the better.'

Walking out to the beautifully decorated hallway, Abbey's gaze ran around the room as she soaked up the atmosphere for the final time, trying to consign every detail to her memory so that she could tell Sam all about it. One day, she would bring him here, maybe for their first anniversary, even if she might need to start saving her pennies straight away. Abbey turned to Matt.

'Thank you so much for tonight. It's been a wonderful evening.'

'It really has,' agreed Lydia, who had to steady herself on the chair when she stood up, as the effects of the champagne rushed to her head and to her legs.

'It's been my absolute pleasure. Just a small way to show my appreciation for everything you both do at the Lodge.'

Hardly a small gesture, thought Abbey, as the taxi made its way along the country lanes back to Wishwell. In her warm fuzzy state, she felt so grateful for Matt's kindness and generosity. She stared out of the taxi window, mesmerised by the familiar villages transformed by white shimmering lights along the roof lines of the stone cottages, Christmas trees sparkling through the house windows and beautiful wreaths upon the doors. Lydia, beside her, rested her weary head on Abbey's shoulder.

'I might have a nightcap in the pub before I retire for the night,' Matt said from the front seat. 'You're welcome to join me if you fancy it?'

Abbey gently nudged Lydia, who was perilously close to snoring. She could tell by the change in her breathing.

'What? What is it?' Lydia jolted awake and Abbey laughed at her friend's bewildered response.

'A drink? At the Three Feathers?'

'Oh, I couldn't,' said Lydia, yawning repeatedly. 'I've had such a lovely evening, but I really need my bed. I'll never get up in the morning otherwise.'

'I'll join you for one,' said Abbey to Matt, not really wanting the evening to end, 'and then I'll get Sam to walk down and collect me.'

After they dropped Lydia off at home, they directed the taxi to the pub and as they drew up outside, Abbey could see that the place was full to the rafters with revelling customers. Pushing open the heavy oak door, the sound of conversation and laughter welcomed them indoors. Matt went up to the bar and ordered the drinks, a whisky for himself and a gin and lemonade for Abbey. She spotted Rhi behind the counter and gave her a wave, although there wasn't a chance to chat as Rhi was clearly rushed off her feet, managing the bar in her usual efficient and friendly manner.

'Shall we try and find a seat?'

Abbey turned round to speak to Matt, not realising he was right behind her and she bumped straight into him, jogging the drink in her hand and spilling the contents over the top of her glass and all down her lovely frock. For a moment, she was frozen to the spot, trying to make sense of what had just happened. Matt's gaze hooked on her dress, which now had a fetching wet patch over her chest, clearly at a loss as to how he might be able to help, quickly returning his gaze to her face.

'Oh, God, I'm so sorry,' she laughed, brushing down the liquid from her dress, relieved she'd managed to avoid drenching him too. 'At least it didn't happen at the beginning of the evening.'

What was she thinking? Why did she agree to have one last drink with Matt? It was definitely one too many. Her head was fuzzy, tiredness washed over her, and she really needed to be tucked up in her bed now. She didn't want her boss thinking she couldn't handle her drink. *Sober up, Abbey*, she told herself.

'Let me get you another one,' Matt gallantly offered.

'No, please don't. This will be fine. I'll take it as a sign that I should probably stop drinking at this point,' she laughed.

Abbey laid a hand on Matt's arm, gesturing to him to follow her, as they negotiated the huddles of people until they reached the back bar, which was thankfully a little quieter. They found a table for two in the corner and pulled out the wooden chairs to sit down. Abbey was still dabbing at her soggy dress with a tissue when something made her stop. An unnerving sensation swept over her entire body. She was being watched, she could feel it in her bones, but who by and why? Abbey lifted her gaze and looked around, her heart picking up momentarily when she spotted Sam standing beneath the architrave, a sprig of mistletoe above his head. Involuntarily her face broke into a wide smile, as it always did when she saw Sam, but her joy was short-lived when she noticed the expression on his familiar features. It was a look she had never seen before, one that unnerved her with its dark intensity.

'Sam, hi!' she said brightly, over-compensating. She stood up, trying to catch eye contact with him, but his gaze was fixed firmly elsewhere. 'Is everything okay?' She mouthed to him from across the room.

'No, Abbey, it's not okay. It's not fucking okay at all.'

9

'Sam, what on earth's the matter?'

But Sam wasn't listening. His sole attention was fixed on Matt, for some reason. A cold feeling of dread filled Abbey's chest. Something was wrong, but she had no idea what. Had Sam been fooling her this whole time? Was he really the jealous type after all? He'd seen her and Matt laughing together over the spilt drink, and he'd got the wrong end of the stick entirely? Annoyance prickled at her skin. This was embarrassing. She could sense people were staring, heard the hushed whispers rustling around the room. What the hell did Sam think he was playing at? He knew how important tonight was for her. She turned and uttered an apology to Matt before walking the short distance across to the other side of the small snug bar to Sam, but he physically moved her to one side without saying a word. He walked past her, heading towards Matt, who had finally cottoned on to the fact that something was amiss. He stood up and glanced from Sam to Abbey, as they both looked at him now, his forehead scrunching and his eyes narrowing as he took a closer look.

'Hey, bloody hell... Sam? Is it really you?' Realisation dawned on his features, as he tried to make sense of the situation. 'Wow, it's... um... great to see you.'

How on earth did these two know each other? Abbey was racking her brain for some kind of explanation. Despite what Matt said about it being great to see Sam, she wasn't convinced by his words and as for Sam, she'd never seen him less pleased to see anyone before. Anger bristled off his every fibre.

'I've got no idea what you're doing here, but I suggest you turn right around, walk out of this pub and never come back.'

'Sam! This is Matt, *my boss*,' Abbey hissed through gritted teeth.

'I don't need any introductions. I know exactly who this lowlife is.' Abbey's mouth dropped open, as she glared at Sam, feeling the heat of embarrassment fire in her cheeks. By now, the altercation had spiked the interest of the other customers in the back bar and the noisy hubbub had faded to a quiet rumble.

'Sam, come on, don't be like this,' said Matt, standing up, his palms held high in a defensive gesture. 'This is a shock, admittedly. It took me a moment there to realise it was actually you. Come on, let me buy you a pint and we can talk, catch up.'

'I've got nothing to say to you. Not now. Not ever. So if you've got any sense, you'll walk straight back outside again. You're not welcome here.'

There was a steeliness to Sam's words that Abbey had never heard before. What was going on? With Matt looking bemused, showing no inclination to go anywhere, Sam lunged forward and grabbed a fistful of Matt's lapel in his hand, physically manhandling him up against the wall so that they were soon grappling with each other in the middle of the bar.

'Stop it!' Abbey shouted, hardly believing what was happening, wondering how events had spiralled out of control in such a short space of time. 'Sam!' This time, she grabbed hold of his arm, but he shook away her touch and her words went unheeded. Tears gathered in her eyes, not that Sam would have noticed, his focus was fixed on only one person at the moment.

'You're lucky I don't bloody murder you.' His finger was stabbing at Matt's chest and Abbey, seeing Sam's eyes flaring wildly, was petrified he might do just that. A couple of the locals jumped in to pull the men apart, steering Sam to one side. Poor Matt, who had been as shocked as Abbey by the unexpected turn of events, brushed himself down, shaking his head ruefully as he looked at Abbey apologetically.

'Look, it's best if I make a move.' He raised his eyes to his waiting bedroom upstairs. 'Will you be all right getting home?'

'Yes, don't worry. Thanks for tonight, and sorry,' she said, wincing, at a loss for anything else to say. She had one eye on Sam, who was over on the other side of the room, being placated by a couple of the regulars, but she was still worried that he might come back to have another go at Matt. She couldn't understand it. She'd never seen this side to Sam's personality before. Part of her wanted to rush over there and demand to know what was going on, but another part of her wanted nothing to do with Sam, not when he'd embarrassed and humiliated her in that way.

'Goodnight, Abbey, I'll… um… catch up with you soon.'

'Night, Matt,' she said, feeling desperately sad that right at this moment, Matt was showing more concern for her than Sam, who had a face as dark as the December night outside and was completely lost in whatever it was that was going on inside his head.

'Abbey, are you okay?' She felt Rhi's arm on her shoulder and turned to see her friend's concerned face looking into her own. 'What the bloody hell was that all about?'

'Honestly, Rhi, I have no idea.' Abbey shook her head, as she slumped down onto the nearest chair. Now the main event was over, people had returned to their conversations or were getting ready to leave. Last orders had been called and the pub had thinned out. Luke came over to check how she was doing.

'Sam has been persuaded to go home. It's probably for the best. I told him I'd make sure you got home safely.'

'Really?' Abbey dropped her head in her hands. 'He didn't even wait for me? What is that man's problem? I don't understand. I had such a lovely evening tonight with Lydia and Matt, *my boss*,' she emphasised, 'and then Sam comes along and spoils it all. What did I do wrong?'

'You haven't done anything wrong,' Rhi reassured her. 'He's a bloody idiot.'

'Look, Sam lost it tonight, admittedly, but we don't know what it was about. Those two guys obviously have some history. Give Sam some space tonight and I bet tomorrow he'll be in a better frame of mind.'

'Huh, don't defend him, Luke. Whatever it was about, there was no reason for him to act like that. He was totally out of order,' snapped Rhi. 'Look how upset Abbey is.'

'I'm not defending him. I'm just saying that there's obviously more going on than we know about. You know what Sam's really like, Abbey. That was totally out of character for him.'

She breathed out a heavy sigh.

'I thought I knew what Sam was like,' said Abbey sadly, 'but after seeing him tonight, I wonder now if I really know him at all.'

10

It was closing time at the Three Feathers and Rhi saw the last of the customers out of the front double doors, waving them goodbye and locking up after they'd left. By the time she'd finished clearing up inside, Luke was back from walking Abbey the short distance home, and had slipped in through the back door of the pub to wait for Rhi.

'Was she okay?' Rhi asked, still concerned for her friend. 'What about Sam, was he there?'

'Yeah, I think she was just confused as to what had happened. I didn't see Sam, I didn't go inside, but I assume he was there. They'll work it out, whatever it is, when the emotions have died down a bit.'

'I hope you're right. They adore each other, those two. I'd hate for anything to come between them, especially after what happened with Abbey and her ex, I wouldn't want to see her hurt again.'

'It was probably just a spur of the moment thing on Sam's part. He'd had a few beers. He'll probably wake up tomorrow with a sore head and a guilty conscience.'

'And you really don't have any idea what it was all about?'

'Not a clue,' said Luke. 'I was sitting with Sam all night long and he was his usual upbeat self. We saw Abbey come in with the guy, Sam said something about him being the new owner of the care homes, and then something changed in him. It was like a light switch flicking on. I could tell he was really riled up. It was a bit of a shock, to be honest with you, I've never seen him like that before.'

'Me neither. Poor Abbey. I hope she's okay. I'll give her a call in the morning to see how she's doing.'

Rhi collected her jacket from the row of coat hooks in the back corridor and called goodbye to Malc and Jan on her way out, following Luke out of the back door of the pub to the car park.

'Thanks for waiting for me,' she said, as he held open the door for her.

'No problem. It's what mates are for, right?'

Rhi's car was in the garage for a couple of days and Luke had offered to drive her into work and collect her too, which was really kind of him when it was out of his way, and how had she repaid him? By snapping at him over the way Sam had acted tonight. It wasn't Luke's fault and he'd only been trying to reassure Abbey.

Mates, though? Her heart sank a little. Was that all he wanted from their relationship? She was still holding much higher hopes for them both, but there was no denying that Luke really was a good friend and a sweetheart too.

As he pulled out from the pub car park and turned left onto the country road that led to home, she couldn't resist gazing at his handsome profile, lost in thought for a moment as she replayed the events of the evening. It was only when he turned and grinned at her that she realised she'd been gawping for far longer than was probably polite.

'So, what time are you finishing work tomorrow?' Luke asked.

'I'm on an early shift so I'll be finishing at six, but don't worry if you can't pick me up. I can make other arrangements.'

'Actually, I was going to suggest going for something to eat, if you fancy it? There's a lovely little Italian on West Street in town?'

'Oh?' Luke's casual invitation took Rhi completely by surprise and momentarily she was lost for words. He snuck a friendly glance at her as he steered the car around a windy bend.

'Only if you want to, of course. No pressure.'

Rhi hadn't intended to appear rude. She'd been dreaming of a date with Luke for months now, just the two of them together, but over recent days, she'd been tempering her expectations. They might have shared that steamy kiss under the mistletoe, but with Luke moving away soon, she might have to accept that their friendship would never develop into anything stronger.

She was beginning to think that was the way Luke wanted it, keeping her very much in the friend zone, but now he was inviting her out to dinner. Mixed messages or what? Maybe she'd need to alter her expectations again? A Christmas romance with a good-looking guy, one she considered a really good friend, might be just the boost she needed right now. A no-strings attachment that would satisfy her attraction and fascination for Luke. Other people managed romantic flings, so why couldn't she? She would just have to make sure that she didn't do anything silly, like fall madly in love with Luke. Which might not be as easy as it sounded.

'Oh, my god!' It happened in an instant. One minute, she was indulging in a bit of romantic fantasy, the next, she was pinned back in her seat, slamming on the non-existent brake in the passenger well with both feet.

'Shit!' cried Luke.

The deer appeared as if from nowhere but had obviously

come galloping out from the bushes into the road in front of them. It stopped dead still, its eyes wide, mesmerised by the glare of the headlights, clearly ready to bolt again at any moment. Luke jammed on the actual brakes, not knowing which way the animal was about to dart, and veered the car off to the left-hand side of the road.

'Look out!' yelled Rhi, but it was too late. The animal had decided to head straight for the bonnet of the car and they collided with a heavy thump, the impact reverberating through the car. Somehow Luke managed to point the car in the direction of a muddy cutaway on the side of the road, narrowly avoiding a ditch and then a huge redwood tree too. They both gasped at their lucky escape as the car skidded to a halt on the rough ground while the deer, legs flailing on the bonnet, slid off the front of the car, landed on his feet and then dashed off into the darkness.

Immediately Luke turned off the ignition, flung off his seat-belt and leaned across to Rhi.

'Are you okay?' he asked, his face a picture of concern.

'I think so,' she said, her voice wobbling as she wriggled her fingers and toes, realising she was okay, well, physically at least, she was still in one piece, but knowing that it could have ended so very differently.

'I just didn't see it coming,' said Luke, collapsing back into his seat and running his hands through his hair. 'That was too bloody close for comfort.' He puffed out his cheeks and blew out some air. 'Are you sure you're all right?'

'Fine,' she said, able to force a small smile for the first time since the collision, relief washing over her. 'What about you?'

'Yeah, okay, just shocked, I guess. That was pretty scary.'

'I know, but you did brilliantly. I'm not sure I would have been so composed in the circumstances. It was your driving that saved us from an even worse accident. That poor deer, though, do you think it was okay?' she asked, the memory of its stricken face still on her mind.

'Well, it went running off and, to be frank, I think it's fared much better than my car,' he said, wryly, peering over the top of the steering wheel to examine the huge dent made by the animal.

'I'm so sorry, Luke. Look at the state of it! This is all my fault. If you hadn't been driving me home, then this would never have happened.'

'You can't think like that. It was an accident, that's all. And we're both okay, so that's the main thing. Come here.' He held open his arms wide and she fell into his embrace and they hugged each other so tightly, as though they might never let go, both knowing how close they'd come to a very untimely end together.

11

Abbey waved to Luke from the doorstep, grateful to him for walking her home. At least her friends had rallied round to support her, but now as she fumbled with the key in the door, she was suddenly hesitant at seeing Sam again. What would she say? Where on earth would she even begin?

'Hello, you!' Someone was pleased to see her. As soon as she was through the door, Lady was there, running circles around her feet, wagging her tail excitedly.

'Sam!' she called.

He appeared from upstairs with his big jacket on, refusing to look at her, focusing his attention instead on pulling up his zip.

'Sam, look at me! What's going on? What was that about exactly?'

'Forget it. It's not important.'

'You can't say that. Not after the way you reacted. It's important to me. You embarrassed me in front of my friends and my boss, for Christ's sake. I deserve some kind of explanation. I'd had such a lovely evening up until that point.'

'I could tell,' said Sam dryly. 'And excuse me for cramping your style and spoiling your perfect evening.'

'Sam! That's not what I meant! Is this all because I came into the pub a little bit merry with another guy?' Sam shook his head and rolled his eyes. 'You're not my keeper. I can do what I like, see who I like, but this was totally innocent, Sam. I don't see why you're getting so worked up. I had nine years of being in a controlling relationship. I won't do it again.'

'I wouldn't expect you to understand.'

'How can I when you won't talk to me about it!'

'I really can't do this now. I need to walk Lady and get to bed.'

Sam clipped Lady onto the lead and headed out of the front door, without giving a backwards glance.

Where was the Sam she knew and loved? The one who looked at her with such tenderness and fondness, the one who put her feelings above his own all the time. Although he hadn't tonight, had he? He was right, she didn't understand. What had happened to create this huge, immovable barrier between them?

'Come back now! We need to talk.'

But Sam wasn't listening, and Abbey was fizzing with anger. From the front window, she watched him stride down the path, helpless to know what to do.

'Aargh.' She let out a strangulated cry to the walls of her cottage.

Clearly, Sam was in no mood for talking and she would become so agitated in his absence that no good could come from having any kind of conversation tonight. Besides, Sam was due to visit the care home the following morning to give a talk to the residents and she knew how much everyone was looking forward to it. She shouldn't do anything to jeopardise that. *What a mess!*

Deciding not to wait up for him, she hurriedly ran up the stairs, shrugging off her clothes, the memory of her lovely meal with Matt long forgotten. She climbed into bed without any real hope of falling asleep as the scene in the pub replayed over and over in her head.

She hugged her side of the mattress, steadying her breathing so that later, when Sam finally came upstairs, she could pretend she was fast asleep. Her ears strained to his every movement as he paced from the bathroom to the bedroom, listening as he undressed and discarded his clothes on the chair in the corner of the bedroom, his suppressed emotions charging the air.

This was new territory for their relationship. They didn't argue, not really. They might occasionally bicker over something inconsequential, but they'd never had a big bust-up until now. And she was still at a loss as to what they'd exactly fallen out about. Although obviously Matt had a big part to play in it.

Most frustratingly, Sam fell asleep almost as soon as his head touched the pillow while Abbey thrashed about restlessly, half hoping her fidgeting might stir Sam and force him to talk. No such luck, she thought, staring at the ceiling morosely.

In the early hours of the morning, she must have finally fallen asleep, only to wake with a start a couple of hours later to find that Sam's side of the bed was completely empty. She felt bereft and hurriedly climbed out of the bed and padded over to the window, peering outside. There was no sign of Sam's Jeep and that discovery made her very sad.

Sometimes Sam left for work early, creeping down the stairs, being careful not to wake her, but he would always kiss her gently on her forehead before going on his way, and she would stir and turn over with a smile on her face, spreading out onto his side of the bed. Sam was clearly still as angry as hell if he couldn't even be bothered to kiss her goodbye.

* * *

All morning at work, Abbey was on tenterhooks, still thinking about Sam, her quiet and anxious mood easily explained away by the excesses of the previous evening. Lydia was similarly subdued, and Abbey decided now wasn't the time to tell her what had happened last night after she'd gone home.

A little while later, Abbey breathed a huge sigh of relief, seeing Sam pull into the car park in his Jeep.

'Thank goodness for that!' she said to herself, peeling back from the blinds of her office. She'd been worried that he might not turn up at all.

Seeing his familiar broad figure bowling towards the front door, her overriding emotion was one of relief. She loved that man more than she ever thought it possible to love another person and, despite her frustrations and confusion over what had happened last night, her heart still melted at seeing him again. She hated that he was upset when she still had no idea what was behind that fracas with Matt. They needed to talk urgently to get to the bottom of the problem and to clear the air, but that wasn't going to happen now. He had an audience of eager residents waiting to hear his latest talk on Primrose Woods at Christmas time. Any talking of their own would have to wait until they both got home this evening.

'Lydia, Sam's here. Would you mind taking him through to the guest lounge and getting the session started? I've a couple of calls I need to make first, but I'll be through in a few minutes.' She couldn't face him now, not one-on-one. She needed to get her emotions under control, and her business head on, if she wasn't going to burst into tears in front of all the residents. That would certainly cause a talking point and she would never hear the last of it from the guests who took more than a passing interest in her love life.

Earlier she'd emailed Matt to thank him, on behalf of herself and Lydia, for such a lovely evening. She'd hesitated over whether she should mention the incident in the pub with Sam and decided against it. If only she'd politely refused that last drink, then none of this would ever have happened. Hopefully it would be a case of least said soonest mended and when she saw Matt again, probably in the new year now, it would all be forgotten about.

A little later, with her thoughts and emotions in order, Abbey took a deep breath and opened the door to the guest lounge, slipping inside and taking a seat at the back of the room. Sam was holding court, as he had done on previous occasions at the home, as he was a firm favourite with the residents. Today's talk was about the history of Christmas trees and the types of trees grown and sold at Primrose Woods. He'd brought along some pinecones, some holly and ivy, and some mistletoe for the craft session which would follow his short talk. There was no sign of the angry man she'd witnessed last night. This morning, he was his usual charming self, entertaining the gathered audience with his breadth of knowledge and making funny little asides to keep the subject interesting and accessible to everyone. He was assisted in no small part by his faithful assistant, Lady, who lay on the floor in front of him, always proving a great hit with the residents. It was almost easy to imagine that there had been no falling out and he would saunter over, his eyes lighting up as he appraised her appreciatively.

Instead, when he'd finished his talk, and the teas and coffees had arrived, he spoke with the residents individually, as the tables were being set up for the craft session. When she could bear it no longer, Abbey wandered over to greet him.

'Sam, thank you. Another great session. You've definitely brought some Christmas cheer with you today.'

'I loved it,' said Stella Darling, patting Sam's arm fondly. 'I didn't know there was so much to learn about Christmas trees. We always had an artificial one at home. I couldn't be doing with all those pine needles falling off and having to vacuum them up every day. Mind you, it sounds as though that doesn't always happen now. That's one of yours, isn't it?' Stella gestured to the tree in the corner of the room.

'It is, Stella. Do you approve?'

'Oh, very much so!' she giggled. Where Sam was concerned, she was the most terrible flirt. 'It looks beautiful. Christmas is the best time of the year. I expect you two are going to have the loveliest of times, it being your first one together.'

'Yes, we're looking forward to it, aren't we, Sam?'

She'd hoped to see a glimmer of warmth in his eyes, but he simply nodded and smiled tightly, before moving on to talk to another of the residents, the moment lost. Now wasn't the time to discuss what had gone on last night, but couldn't he at least show her that he still cared? Instead, there was nothing but a cool breeze wafting in from his direction.

Later, after the morning's activities were over, Abbey caught up with Sam on his way out, away from the prying eyes of the residents, laying a hand on his sleeve.

'Sam! Don't be like this. I don't understand what's happened. We need to talk. I hate all this bad feeling.' She looked at him imploringly, hoping he would take her in his arms and explain, tell her how sorry he was, that he'd been overtired and hadn't meant anything by his outburst last night, but nothing like that was forthcoming. 'What was it about, Sam? Please tell me. Were you jealous, was that it? Matt is my boss, Sam, that's all.'

'Jealous, of him? You must be joking. You might have been charmed by his smooth-talking ways, Abbey, but you don't know what he's really like. Look, I can't talk about this now.' Distractedly, he ran a hand through his messy brown hair. 'I need to get back to work. We'll speak tonight, but I'll probably be late. Don't worry about dinner for me, I'll pick something up while I'm out.'

If she hadn't been at work, then she would have grabbed Sam by his strong arms, looked him squarely in the face and shook him until she got some kind of response, so that the Sam that she knew and loved would be back with her, but at the moment, there was no reaching him. She watched as he strode across the car park and jumped into the Jeep, Lady following his every movement. As they drove away, she sighed heavily, her frustration all-encompassing, but she couldn't let her bubbling emotions get the better of her now. She plastered on a smile and returned to the guest lounge where the residents were getting ready for their lunch. From across the room, she noticed Stella Darling waving, attracting her attention.

'He's a lovely man, your Sam, but when are you two going to get married? No point in hanging around. Especially after what happened with the last one. You don't want this one getting away too. And you're not getting any younger, Abbey. I would love to see you settled down at last.'

Stella patted Abbey's hand as she imparted her words of wisdom. Usually, Abbey would laugh off Stella's advice regarding her love life, she knew she only had her best interests at heart, but her words couldn't have come at a worse time. Not when she'd just witnessed a side to Sam that she'd never seen before. Did she really know him as well as she thought she did? Like Stella, she'd believed that her future was inextricably linked with Sam, but last night's events had showed her that their relationship was on much shakier foundations than she'd thought. And if Sam was unprepared to talk to her about this obstacle in their relationship, then what real hope did they have for any kind of future together?

12

On Wednesday evening, with Luke's car in the body repair shop, he arranged a taxi to collect both himself and then Rhi to take them the short distance into town, where they pulled up outside Lombardi's, the Italian restaurant on West Street. Stepping out of the car, Luke guided Rhi to the entrance, with a hand in the small of her back. She looked over her shoulder at him and smiled, loving the way that small and intimate gesture made her feel totally safe and valued.

In the authentic trattoria, they were shown to a table for two by the welcoming and effusive maître d'. He pulled out a chair for Rhi and shook out her linen napkin with a flourish before laying it across her lap. She revelled in the attention and took the menus offered and ordered a Bellini, while Luke plumped for an Italian beer and ordered a bottle of Prosecco for the table.

'So how have you been today after our close shave last night?' Rhi asked, leaning across the table. 'Honestly, I can't stop reliving that moment when the deer suddenly appeared out of nowhere and locked eyes with me through the windscreen. It gives me a cold shiver every time. Honestly, it was so scary.'

'I know and it could have been so much worse. We were lucky to get away with just a smashed-up car. I've spent pretty much the whole day sorting out the insurance and arranging quotes for the repairs.'

Rhi dropped her head into her hands.

'I'm so sorry, Luke.'

'Don't be. It wasn't your fault. Besides, we'll look back on that night in years to come and laugh. It will definitely be something to tell the grandchildren.'

She liked the idea that, at least now, Luke would have reason to remember her and that fateful night forever. She sat back in her chair, took a sip of her drink and allowed her gaze to drift around the room. With the exposed brickwork and scenes of the picturesque Amalfi Coast on the walls, it was easy to imagine stepping outside and seeing the dramatic coastline for herself, being amongst the terraced vineyards, and the sweet-scented olive and lemon groves. Her mind danced with images of Luke and her sharing a twilight stroll, walking hand in hand, soaking up the balmy heat, returning to their clifftop villa to enjoy a night of slow, sensual seduction. Well, it was a much more enticing image than the cold December night outside. All the time she'd been in Australia, she'd thought about how different it might have been if Luke had been at her side, sharing the experiences and scenery with her, seeing the unfolding landscapes through his eyes as well. Making memories.

Now, in the cosy restaurant, she waved the menu in front of her face to fan the heat coursing around her body. Tea lights flickered in the middle of the table, casting shadows across it, and Rhi smiled, locking eyes briefly with Luke. He looked even more handsome than usual tonight. His pale blue chambray shirt brought out the piercing blue of his eyes and his attentive open gaze was fixed firmly on Rhi, as though seeing her for the first time.

'Cheers!' He raised his glass in her direction. 'Here's to lucky escapes and great friendships. I can't believe we haven't done this before.'

'Cheers!' she said, raising her glass to his.

A romantic dinner with Luke was long overdue, although it wasn't for her lack of trying. She couldn't help thinking that they'd missed their chance to get together properly. If only she'd realised when they'd first met at work what a great guy Luke was, instead of wasting her energies on someone who hadn't been worth her time, who knew where they might be now? Instead, Luke was about to take a big step in a new direction, miles away from here. Was their friendship strong enough to survive the enforced distance? Already she missed him, and he hadn't even left yet! Still, now wasn't the time to dwell on those thoughts, she was determined to make the most of the moment, here with Luke, the memory of their kiss in the pub taunting her with possibilities.

She took a sip of her refreshing Bellini, the bubbles hitting the required spot immediately, relaxing the tension in her limbs. The waiter delivered their starter, a shared wooden platter of antipasto with cured meats, olives, stuffed peppers and artichoke hearts, accompanied by a basket of bread. It was delicious and wholly intimate to eat off the same plate, especially when she lifted her gaze from the food in front of her and up into Luke's turquoise blue gaze from across the table. They talked about their preparations for Christmas, deliberately avoiding the subject of Luke's impending move. Was Luke feeling the same as she was? Or was the sizzling chemistry and sexual attention radiating around their table just a figment of her imagination?

'Well, this all looks very cosy.'

Rhi had been so caught up in the moment she hadn't noticed the approach of someone who was now standing beside their table. At first, she thought it must be the waiter, but the familiarity of the voice gave the game away and it took her only a nanosecond to realise exactly who it was standing there.

Jason? Her heart plunged. She'd only seen him once since she'd drenched him with a cup of ice-cold water, walking out on her job and the relationship in the same moment, never wanting to set eyes on him ever again. A few weeks later, he'd turned up at the pub and tried to wheedle his way back into her life, but she'd been determined not to have anything to do with him again. She'd managed to avoid him since but now he was here, bringing with him a whole raft of bad memories.

'So, you two are an item now?' He had that smug, self-satisfied look on his face, the one that she'd once found so attractive. The one that she now wanted to punch. What on earth had possessed her, she thought, with a cold shudder. 'Who would have thought it?' he chuckled.

'We're not. Not that it's any of your business,' said Luke, sharply.

Rhi felt half inclined to throw her glass of fizz over Jason, but that would be a waste of good wine and besides, she wouldn't give him the satisfaction. His continuing presence, though, looming over their table, was severely spoiling her previous good mood. Clearly Jason had something to say, and he wasn't about to leave until he got it off his chest.

'Probably a good move on your part, Luke,' said Jason. 'I wouldn't go there if I was you.' He tipped his head in Rhi's direction. 'She might seem like a sweet girl, but a word of advice, she's trouble.'

Rhi tucked her hands beneath her thighs, not trusting herself to not pick up the nearest object from the table and using it as a missile in Jason's direction.

'Stop it. You're toxic, Jason, do you know that? I wish I'd never met you.'

'The feeling's entirely mutual, love. If it wasn't for you, I'd be happily married by now. You couldn't help yourself, could you? Searching Abbey out, spreading lies about me. You had to interfere, when you had no right to, poisoning her mind against me.'

'You did that all by yourself, Jason, you didn't need any help from me. You're deluded to think that you could still be with Abbey. The best thing to come out of that whole sorry episode is my friendship with Abbey. She's a great girl who deserves so much better than you. She's happy now. She's found someone who treats her with the love and respect she deserves. We've all moved on, Jason. You need to do the same. Now, if you don't mind, you're spoiling our evening.'

How she managed to keep her voice reasonable and calm, she just didn't know. If Luke hadn't been with her, she wasn't sure what she might have done. She certainly wouldn't be hanging around here to listen to Jason's lies. Her cheeks stung with a mix of embarrassment and annoyance. How dare Jason suggest that she was in any way to blame? He'd lied to her and betrayed her, in the same way as he'd done to Abbey. The fault was all with Jason.

Luke pushed back his chair and stood up, putting his body between Jason and Rhi. He was a good inch or two taller than Jason, and broader too. He firmly placed a hand on Jason's arm, guiding him away from the table. The maître d', who until then had been oblivious to the tension in their corner of the restaurant, rushed across to the table to see if he could help, his face full of concern.

'Is there a problem here?'

'No problem,' said Luke with admirable confidence. 'Our friend here was just leaving.'

Jason smirked.

'Don't worry. I wouldn't want to hang around here. Very gallant of you to defend this lady's honour,' he said, looking over his shoulder, making eye contact with Rhi, 'but don't say I never warned you, Luke. I'd steer clear if I was you.'

'You...' Rhi stood up, about to lunge at him, but Luke warned her against it with a dark look, holding up a hand to stop her. He followed Jason out through the restaurant. She sighed heavily with frustration, slumping back down in her seat, furious with Jason but more annoyed with herself than anything else. Why was she allowing Jason to rile her like this? She'd decided months ago that he wasn't worth her time or energy, but seeing him again just brought all those feelings of powerlessness and vulnerability to the fore. What must Luke think? It wasn't long before he was back again.

'You'll be relieved to hear the idiot has left the building.'

'Thank god.' She shook her head crossly. 'I'm so sorry, Luke. We were having such a brilliant time until he turned up.'

'Well, I'm not going to allow him to spoil our evening. Don't give the creep a second thought. He was drunk, talking out of his backside. Look, why don't you finish your drink,' he suggested, gesturing to her Bellini.

'Yeah, you're right.' Rhi took a sip from the champagne flute, trying to recapture the mood before Jason had so rudely interrupted, but it wasn't easy. To think that she'd once been so infatuated with Jason that she'd barely given poor Luke the time of the day. She'd definitely picked the wrong man back then and tonight of all nights, when she was finally on a date with Luke, Jason had to rear his ugly head again.

'I am sorry, though.' As soon as she said the words, she smiled. 'I seem to be making a habit of apologising these days.'

'Well, I'm beginning to realise that life is never dull with you around, Rhi.'

Luke reached across the table and took her hand, smiling at her with those bright blue eyes. She returned his smile, grateful for his understanding, but embarrassed that she was something of a liability at the moment. No wonder Luke wanted to keep her very much in the friend zone.

They finished their meal, sooner than they might have originally expected, deciding to forego desserts and coffees. Rhi was relieved when they stepped outside, embracing the bitterly cold December evening, leaving all memories of Jason behind. She was wrapped up in her faux fur-lined black jacket, and dug her hands deep into her pockets, searching for warmth.

'Do you want to find somewhere to get a nightcap?' Luke asked, as they walked together, heads down against the wind.

'I should get home. Dinner was lovely, despite the unwelcome interruption. Thank you so much.' She'd offered to pay the bill, to thank Luke for ferrying her around for the last few days, but he wouldn't hear of it. The date hadn't turned out the way she'd imagined. It should have been a lovely intimate occasion, the two of them laughing and flirting together, when instead she'd had a run-in with her past, leaving her deflated and unsettled. She glanced at her watch. She'd taken up far too much of Luke's time already.

'Is that an invitation?'

She turned to look at Luke's profile, his mouth curling up at the corner, in that cheeky beguiling way of his.

'Come on, Rhi. We always grab a coffee at yours. I haven't seen your mum in months.'

'Well, she's out tonight with her new man, so you'll be disappointed on that front.' The irony of her mum's love life going much more swimmingly than her own wasn't lost on Rhi. 'But you're very welcome to have a nightcap at mine... if you'd like to?'

Now she was second-guessing her own choices. When had she ever been so hesitant? Only yesterday, Luke had made a comment about them being friends, it was why he was helping her out. But was that really *all* she was to him? She remembered those other occasions when she'd invited Luke home, expectant and full of anticipation, and that godawful time when she'd misread the situation and kissed him. It still made her shudder even now.

So much had changed since then. She hadn't imagined the intensity of that enticing kiss beneath the mistletoe, nor the way that Luke was looking at her right now, with those deep blue sparkling eyes, as though he might even want to kiss her again.

'I'd love to, Rhi. Come on,' he said, putting an arm around her shoulder and pulling her in to his embrace. 'Let's get you home.'

13

'Bill! Come in!' Lizzie's face lit up in a broad grin and she held her arms wide to greet him, wrapping him in a warm hug. 'Ooh, I have missed you,' she whispered conspiratorially.

'It's only been a few days,' he said with a bemused smile.

'I know, but it feels much longer. Good timing, though. We've just made some shortbread cookies. You'll have to have one.'

Since Katy's arrival, Lizzie hadn't seen as much of Bill as she might have liked. He'd been keeping a low profile, insisting that she needed some one-on-one time with her daughter and grandchildren. It was typically thoughtful of Bill, but in the space of a few months she'd become so used to his constant and reassuring presence in her life that she'd felt adrift without him at her side.

'Goodness me,' he said, shaking off his coat. 'Something smells delicious!'

'Bill, Bill!' Rosie, who despite wearing a little pinny was covered in a dusting of icing sugar, clambered off the kitchen chair and ran up to their visitor, throwing her arms around his legs, leaving a cloud of dust on his dark navy trousers.

'Hello, you!' he said, putting an arm around her shoulder,

unperturbed by the mess. 'It looks as though you've been very busy.' Bill looked attentively at the plate of biscuits which had been iced in varying degrees of proficiency. 'Am I allowed to have one?'

Rosie squealed.

'This one, this one! I make this one.' Her fingers scrabbled to pick up the biscuit before handing it over proudly to Bill. Lizzie looked on fondly, delighted by the bond she'd seen develop between her granddaughter and Bill. If Abbey ever had children, then they would be very fortunate indeed to have Bill as their grandfather.

A little later, with Rosie worn out from her baking efforts in the kitchen, she settled on the sofa with a couple of her biscuits and a glass of water in front of *The Snowman* on the telly with little Pip on the floor in his rocker, cooing contentedly. Lizzie made a coffee for Bill, and they sat at the dining room table in sight of the children.

'So where's Katy today then?'

'She's gone to have her hair cut. I thought a little bit of pampering time might make her feel better.'

'A well-deserved break from the children. It's probably just what she needs right now. How has she been?'

'Up and down, I'd say. She has some good days and some not-so-good ones. I managed to persuade her to go and see the doctor yesterday and he's told her she is suffering from post-natal depression.'

Bill's face creased in concern.

'In a way, I think she was relieved to find out that she has an illness that needs to be treated in the same way as any other illness. The doctor reassured her on that front and has arranged some talking therapy sessions. I'm so pleased, I think it's just what she needs. Speaking to someone outside of the family will help her realise that what she's feeling isn't anything to be ashamed of.'

'Of course not.'

'I'm just glad that she's here now so that I can keep a close eye on her. All she needs to do is concentrate on getting herself better. I can help her with the children and anything else that needs doing. I think she feels guilty about Brad, leaving him behind in Australia, but I've heard them FaceTiming and he's always reassuring and supportive of her. I know once he's home for good in the new year and they're living in their own place, things will seem so much more manageable.'

'She's lucky to have you, you know?'

'I'm only doing what any mum or grandma would do. You'd do anything to make your kids' and grandkids' lives a bit better, wouldn't you? I know you're the same, Bill.'

He nodded, knowing only too well. With Abbey having lost her mum, he knew he could never fill the huge gap she'd left behind, or replace the closeness between mum and daughter, but he did whatever he could to be there for Abbey, and to provide support.

'You never stop worrying about them, that's for sure. I spoke to Abbey early this morning and she was in a bit of state. She said something about her and Sam having a row last night. She was rushing off to work so we didn't chat for long, but I told her it would no doubt blow over. I certainly hope it will... All couples have their disagreements, don't they?' he said with a plaintive tone to his voice.

'Oh, yes... I'm sure they'll sort it out,' said Lizzie, contemplative for a moment. 'I wonder what that was all about, then? I can't imagine the two of them falling out. They're so good together.'

'Yep, that's what I thought too.' Bill shrugged. 'Not the best start to the day, for either of us,' he said, forcing a chuckle. 'Things can only get better.'

Lizzie laid a hand on Bill's arm.

'So, what else has happened, then?'

'Ah, well, I had a bit of a rude awakening this morning. I woke up to find water gushing up through the kitchen floor.'

Lizzie's eyes grew wide and her mouth gaped open.

'Oh, you should have seen it, Lizzie. It was like Niagara Falls. I managed to turn the water off at the mains, but the damage had been done by that stage. There were about two inches of water sloshing around the kitchen floor and in the bottom cupboards too. Most of the tiles have been lifted off the floor.'

'No!' Lizzie raised a hand to her mouth. 'What caused that?'

'I think it must have been a burst pipe. I've spent all morning on the phone to the insurers. They're sending someone out this afternoon to have a look at the damage, but it's going to take a bit of sorting out.'

'Well, you won't be able to stay there if your kitchen's out of bounds.'

'No, I think they'll probably have to get the dehumidifiers in, but I'll have a word with Abbey, she's got a spare bedroom,' said Bill.

'What? Don't be daft. You'll come and stay here.'

'But, Lizzie, you've got an awful lot on your plate at the moment.'

'Yes, and that's just the way I like it,' she said. 'Besides, having you here makes everything easier, not harder, Bill. You're coming for Christmas anyway, so an extra few days won't make any difference.'

'Well, I wouldn't want to intrude.'

'You wouldn't be. You know Katy and Rosie will love having you here as well. Although I can't guarantee you'll get any peace from Rosie. She'll have you reading all the books and playing all the games.'

'It will be a small price to pay,' said Bill, laughing.

Lizzie pushed back her chair and went across to Bill and wrapped her arms around his shoulders, kissing him on the cheek.

'So, that's all sorted, then.' It was a statement of fact rather than a question.

Bill stood up to face her, his gaze roaming hers before placing his lips gently on her mouth, both of them enjoying the intimate moment, until Rosie slid off the sofa dramatically, arms and legs flailing, landing with a thump on the floor. She scrambled to her feet, looking at her grandmother accusingly.

'Yuck, Nanna! Don't kiss Bill.' Little Rosie shook her head. She stomped across to the wicker basket and pulled out a box. 'Do puzzle, Bill.' She handed him the jigsaw puzzle box and clambered up on the seat next to Lizzie and Bill had no choice but to sit right back down again.

Lizzie chuckled to herself. So their romantic moments might be few and far between right now, but with Bill living under the same roof, things could only improve. For the time being, she was happy being at the centre of her family and providing all the support she could when they needed it the most.

Just then, they heard the front door open and, moments later, Katy appeared, sporting a new choppy hairdo which framed her delicate features perfectly.

'Well, doesn't that look lovely,' said Lizzie. 'You look like a new woman.'

'Thanks, Mum.' She tilted her head from side to side, showing her new hairstyle off to its full effect, a smile on her face. 'I feel like a new woman! I popped into the estate agent's too while I was in town and picked up some details on available properties, so I might arrange some viewings soon.'

'Good idea,' said Lizzie, relieved to see this new sense of purpose in Katy. 'I'll look after the kiddies, if you'd like me to, so you can have a proper look around without being distracted by the little ones.'

'Thanks, Mum,' said Katy. 'In that case, would you mind coming with me, Bill? I could do with a bit of moral support. Brad has a long shopping list of requirements so it would be good to get a male perspective on any properties.'

'Of course.' Bill smiled from the table, a large puzzle piece in his hand. 'Just say when. I'll make sure there's enough space for Brad to have his man cave and anything else he needs,' he said, chuckling.

'Let me make you a coffee,' said Lizzie, heading for the kitchen with a smile on her face.

She felt lucky to have all her loved ones under the same roof this Christmas, especially now Katy's mood looked to be picking up. Lizzie would do all she could to make Christmas special for everyone, especially Katy and the children. She knew that Katy wouldn't be totally happy until Brad was back at her side and they could resume a proper family life together. Lizzie only hoped there would be no hiccoughs that might keep him away longer than absolutely necessary.

14

Abbey glanced at her watch for the umpteenth time that evening. Sam had told her he would be late home, but she hadn't expected him to be this late. He was never this late. The Christmas tree yard closed at seven, so even after cashing up and getting everything prepared for the following day's business, she would still have expected him home by nine. Perhaps he'd called in at the pub, deliberately avoiding her so that he might put off, for as long as possible, that awkward conversation they needed to have.

She was reminded of those last few months with Jason when he was often late home, claiming he was working hard on a project, when in fact he'd been doing something else entirely. She sighed heavily, peering out of her bedroom window into the dark of the December night, hoping for a glimpse of Sam's Jeep driving down the lane. All she could see was the sparkle of Christmas decorations lighting up the village in the distance, but even those couldn't lift her mood. A ripple of unease ran along her body. Sam wasn't Jason. She trusted him implicitly, but still she couldn't help worrying. Perhaps he'd been involved in an accident, or perhaps... An awful thought occurred to her. Maybe Sam had had a change of heart, something to do with Matt last night, and had decided he didn't want to be with Abbey after all. The idea struck her with a sharp pain in her chest, her breath coming in short gasps.

She yanked open the wardrobe, relieved to see his shirts still hanging there. She fell down onto the floor in search of his holdall beneath the bed and scrabbled around to find it, pulling it out from its hiding place. Thank goodness. She thought he might have left, taken his belongings with him and gone back to his small cottage in the woods. The very idea made her stomach twist in pain. She couldn't imagine life now without Sam and Lady in it. Even if she was still angry with him at his behaviour last night. Whatever it was that was so troubling Sam, it had to be sorted and soon. She shifted her weight onto her hands to lift herself up from the floor when she noticed something else beneath the bed, a carrier bag, one that she hadn't seen before. She didn't pause to think. Instinctively, her hand reached out to grab it, her heart in her mouth as her fingers ran over the smooth, glossy material of the bag as she retrieved it from its hiding place. Momentarily, she wavered, but she couldn't stop herself now even if she wanted to. If Sam was hiding something, then Abbey needed to know about it. Jason had managed to lie and keep a huge secret from her for months on end. She wouldn't allow it to happen to her again.

Abbey peered into the bag and her heart lifted when she spotted a cookery book, the one she'd been dropping none-too-subtle hints about to Sam for the last few weeks. Relief washed over her. It was his Christmas shopping and she wondered now how she could ever have doubted him. Their first Christmas together and she honestly believed he would be the type of man to rush out on Christmas Eve to do his shopping, wrapping up his gifts late into the night, but she was surprised to discover that he was much more organised than she gave him credit for. Now she felt guilty that she'd been nosing around where she shouldn't and she'd spoilt the surprise of one of her presents. She wouldn't look at the others, although she caught a glimpse of some white and red tissue paper wrapped around something soft and squishy, perhaps an item of clothing, a jumper, she would guess. Nestling at the bottom of the bag was a small black velvet box. She gasped, a thrill of excitement bubbling in her chest. Some jewellery, she loved jewellery. She held her breath, knowing that what she was about to do was very wrong, but she couldn't help herself. Her hand clasped around the box, the smooth rich fabric sending a shot of electricity through her arm. She prised the top off, her eyes growing wide as her gaze alighted on a huge, sparkling diamond ring inside. In the lined lid of the box, the words 'Christmas 2022' were engraved in gold lettering.

'Oh, my god!' she said aloud, resting back on her heels, trying to make sense of what she was holding in her hands. It was a ring. A present for Christmas, but for her? Really? Who else could it be for, and was it really what she thought it was? With a rock that size, it could only mean one thing. A whirlwind of thoughts rushed around her head, her skin prickling in anticipation, but she couldn't make sense of any of them. Of course! That was why Sam had suggested staying at home for Christmas, just the two of them. He had plans, he was intending to propose.

Just then, the familiar sound of Sam's Jeep pulling up outside the cottage brought her back to her senses, and a panic washed over her as she hurriedly but gently put the lid down on the box, her fingers trembling as she returned it to the carrier bag, sliding it back beneath the bed. She stood up, looking all around her, checking that everything was back where it should be. She took a deep breath, her emotions a mix of excitement and apprehension. She heard Lady scooting around downstairs, clearly looking for her, and Sam opening up the fridge in search of something else, a beer more than likely. She gathered herself, taking a moment, brushing down her clothes to get rid of any debris she might have picked up from the carpet. She checked her reflection in the mirror, seeing the flush of colour in her cheeks, feeling guilty at what she'd done, but she couldn't worry about that now. It had happened and there was no going back.

'Hello, you!' she said brightly when she reached the bottom of the stairs. At least Lady was pleased to see her. The dog rushed around her feet, wagging her tail furiously. Abbey bent to greet her, grateful for the distraction allowing her to avoid Sam's gaze.

'Hey.' He turned to look at her, his welcome not so nearly as effusive as Lady's. Her emotions were soaring up and down. Should she still be angry with Sam over what had happened last night, or thrilled, knowing what she'd just discovered beneath the bed?

'Drink?' he asked, holding up his beer bottle in her direction. She'd had far too much to drink last night and her head had been muddled all day, although how much of that was due to her confusion over what had happened at the pub, she still didn't know. Tonight, she needed to keep a clear head.

'Just a water please,' she said, trying to gauge his mood, as his gaze appraised her.

'What were you doing? You look guilty.'

'Sam! Nothing happened. It was a work do, that's all. I don't know what's got you so riled up about all of this.'

He shook his head, his expression stern.

'I meant, what were you doing upstairs?' He pulled a glass out from the cupboard and ran the tap. 'You look furtive. I was making conversation, that's all.'

Abbey breathed a huge sigh of relief. Of course, it was a throwaway comment. When had it become so difficult for the two of them to communicate properly? No wonder she looked guilty.

She was guilty. Of nosing around in Sam's personal belongings when she had no real reason to do so, and now she wished she hadn't. It had only filled her head with so many questions that she wouldn't be getting any answers to anytime soon.

She took the glass of water proffered and put it to her lips, taking a sip as she perched on the arm of the sofa. Until they cleared the air over what had happened last night, they wouldn't be able to move forward.

'Sam...' She looked at him imploringly. 'Tell me, please, what was it all about? I can't bear this. We never fall out.'

'Christ.' He ran his hand through his hair, leaning against the doorframe to the kitchen. 'I haven't fallen out with you. I don't want that either. Look, I'm sorry for my behaviour last night. It was just a shock after all this time, seeing Matt again.'

'I didn't realise you two knew each other.' She'd been racking her brains as to how they did. Someone he'd met through his work, she suspected. Someone he'd obviously had a huge falling out with, even though she couldn't fathom why Sam would take so vehemently against anyone. He was the most laid-back, easy-going guy she'd met. If there was ever anyone he wasn't keen on, then he would just take a backwards step and never let his true feelings be shown. He was too polite for that. But last night, there had been no disguising his real emotions.

'Matt? Oh yeah! We met at sixth form college, best mates, we even chose to go to the same uni together.'

Abbey's hand flew to her mouth.

'Oh, Sam!' In that instance, everything fell into place. 'Matt who went off with your girlfriend, Sophie?'

'The very same. Funny, I thought I'd got over that whole episode a long time ago. It was just seeing him again, so unexpectedly, and with you too, it brought back a rush of emotions that I could never have anticipated.'

'I didn't realise,' she said, going straight across to wrap him in her arms. The relief she felt at hugging him again was huge. They could work through this. She'd been torturing herself with the idea that Sam was controlling and possessive in the same way as Jason had been, when all along, he'd been hurting inside. Sam had opened up to her once before about how his best friend had gone off with his long-term girlfriend just as they were planning on moving in together. He'd been devastated by the double betrayal, his hurt only compounded when his dear mum died soon afterwards. Now Abbey understood why Sam had reacted so angrily. She breathed in his familiar scent, her arms aching to comfort him. What a mess. And what about Matt? How was she ever supposed to interact with her new boss again knowing exactly who he was?

'There was no reason why you should. I shouldn't have reacted the way I did, but I wasn't thinking straight. Seeing Matt again...' Sam shook his head, drawing his lips tight across his mouth. 'I could have killed him.'

'That's understandable. I'm so sorry,' she said, holding his face in her hands, seeing the pain behind his eyes. 'If I'd known, then I would never have gone out to dinner with him, obviously.'

'You've nothing to apologise for. And he's your boss, you're going to have to see him. Just don't ask me along to any of your work dos, or expect me to be civil to the guy.'

He gave a forced half-smile in an attempt to soften his words, but Abbey could tell how much Matt's sudden reappearance had affected Sam. It was awful what had happened, but it was years ago, when they were much younger. Maybe it was time to consign all those bad feelings to history. With Abbey's help, perhaps Sam could finally come to terms with what had happened back then and possibly even forgive Matt.

'I mean it, Abbey. Don't bring that guy anywhere near me again or I won't be responsible for my actions.'

'No, I won't,' she reassured him quickly. So much for Sam's attitude thawing towards Matt. 'There's no need for you to see him again. And I'm guessing Matt won't be rushing back to the pub anytime soon.' She raised her eyebrows, the tiniest of smiles hovering at her lips. 'I won't mention his name again, how about that?' She grabbed him by the wrists, looking in his eyes imploringly. 'Can we just forget any of this ever happened? And get back to how things were before?'

'Yeah.' Sam reached up and traced a finger around the contours of her face. 'Hey, I'm sorry. I should never have taken it out on you. None of this is your fault.'

Abbey breathed a huge sigh of relief. It was no one's fault. Just an unfortunate run-in with the past. But she sensed something had shifted between them. She just hoped they'd be able to recapture the special bond they'd created before Matt had waltzed into their lives and bulldozed a huge wedge through their relationship.

15

The taxi dropped them off outside Rhi's house and Luke put his arm around her shoulder as the pair of them hurried up the path, rushing indoors away from the cold of the night. Inside, Rhi shrugged off her coat and hung it up on the peg in the hallway, turning to take Luke's jacket from him, running straight into the immovable force of his body. Her gaze locked onto his deep blue eyes, before travelling down to his mouth, which was within touching distance, or more pertinently, kissing distance. Rhi shivered exaggeratedly, as a ripple of anticipation ran down her spine.

'Brr, it's so cold out there,' she said, to break the tension, although she suspected the shivers taunting her body had more to do with Luke's proximity than the temperature outside.

'Here, let me warm you up.' Unexpectedly, Luke took her in his arms, and wrapped her in his embrace and she melted into his firm, strong body. She hadn't had time to think whether this was what she wanted, but even if she had, there would have been absolutely no hesitation on her part. Her head might not know what it was she wanted, but her body was working to its own agenda, and knew exactly what it was she desired.

'Let me make you a drink. Would you like a glass of wine or maybe a warming tea or coffee?' she asked, laughing, extracting herself from his embrace, trying to regain her equilibrium. Bumping into Jason had brought back all those old feelings of rejection and humiliation. She thought she'd put that whole episode behind her, but tonight had showed just how much the experience had scarred her. Tonight of all nights, when she'd been hopeful of an exciting and romantic time with Luke.

'Well, a glass of wine would be great. If you're going to have one too, Rhi?' His hand in the small of her back as he followed her into the kitchen was intimate and tender, and she felt light-headed from the atmosphere sizzling around them. There was definitely a frisson of something delicious in the air.

It wasn't too late for them. Maybe this was what their friendship had been building up to all this time. Perhaps they were only ever destined to have a short romantic fling. It had to be better than nothing at all. Luke had joked about the pair of them remembering their midnight run-in with a deer for years to come, a story to tell their grandchildren one day, but there could be another reason for her to recall Luke long into the future. If they were to share a whirlwind romance, a short intense connection, then she would definitely remember him when she was an old lady, looking back on this Christmas period with great fondness. Perhaps she would always think of Luke as *the one that got away*.

She busied herself now finding a bottle of Sauvignon in the fridge and some glasses from the cupboard, before pouring the wine. She reminded herself what had happened last time she'd acted on her hunch that Luke was feeling the same way as her. She'd ended up disappointed and humiliated. Surely this time she couldn't be misreading the signs, especially the way those deep blue eyes of his swept her body appreciatively or the flirtatious smile playing on his lips. Still, she wasn't about to make a fool of herself again.

She perched on one end of the sofa after inviting him to sit down at the other end.

'Well, here's to new beginnings,' she said, brightly. 'Wishing you every success in your new job, with the new flat and... well, with the rest of your life.'

'Thank you!' Luke raised his glass, smiling. 'You make it sound as though this is a final farewell. I'm not completely disappearing off into the wilderness. I will be back again at some point.'

Rhi laughed, but that was exactly how it felt to her. Once Luke moved away and was settled into his new life, meeting new friends and putting down roots, she suspected he would quickly forget about her. Perhaps, to save a broken heart, she would need to do the same, but she'd tried that already. Three months away in Australia hadn't made an iota of difference to her feelings. She couldn't get him out of her head so easily, no matter how hard she tried.

'Well, The Primrose Fancies will certainly miss your sporting knowledge at the monthly quiz evenings, that's for sure.' It was true enough, but much more than that, she would miss knowing that he was just around the corner, that he might at any moment pop into the pub, that she could call him up and invite him for a walk over at the woods.

'My folks are still here. I'll be coming back regularly to visit.' In a way, she wished he wasn't. It would be much better if she could get some final closure on their relationship. So that she knew with a certainty that there could be no hope for a future together. Instead, seeing him, however infrequently, might keep a hope and a fire burning between them. 'I'll make sure to check in with you when I'm home.'

She gave a tight smile, biting back the sarcastic retort on her tongue, but she couldn't allow her frustration and disappointment to sour her mood. It wasn't Luke's fault that he was going off to pursue his dreams. She'd done the same when she'd headed off to Australia. If she hadn't disappeared off to the other side of world then maybe their relationship would have stood a chance.

'Hey, come on. I thought new beginnings were supposed to be cause for celebration.' Luke appraised her over the top of his glass and she mentally shook herself to rid herself of the negative thoughts that were swirling around her mind, spoiling the moment.

'Definitely,' she said, raising her glass in his direction. 'Exciting times ahead for both of us.'

'Come here.' Luke put his glass down on the coffee table before shuffling up the sofa to sit alongside Rhi. He took her wine from her grasp and popped it on the table, turning to gently take her face in his hands. His intense gaze on hers sent a trickle of anticipation along her spine. There was no mistletoe, no cheesy music, and no gentle teasing from the guys in the pub. There was nothing to distract them, only the intensity of the magnetism sizzling between them, their mouths on a collision course with each other. He pulled her closer, pressing his lips against hers as a million sparks ignited every nerve ending in her body. Her mouth parted involuntarily, the sensations shooting around her body every bit as delicious as she'd imagined they would be. Locked in his embrace, inhaling his natural masculine scent, she fell back onto the squashy sofa cushions, Luke's body firm against hers. She lost herself in the moment, his kisses all-encompassing and intoxicating, her body weightless, until a rogue, stray thought popped into her head.

'Why now?' she said, coming up for breath, gently pushing Luke away, putting some distance between them, although their eyes remained locked, neither of them wanting to break the spell they'd created. It did nothing to dampen the heat coursing around Rhi's body.

'What?' Luke's expression creased in confusion, his own breath raspy. 'How do you mean, Rhi?' His hand continued to stroke her face as his gaze scanned it for answers.

'We've had plenty of opportunities before tonight, but it never happened. You always said that we were fine the way we were, as friends. I had to accept that, but I didn't understand why. I thought you didn't like me in that way.'

Luke shook his head slowly, a smile hovering at the edge of his lips.

'The time wasn't right for us, that's what you told me.' She sighed, her frustration palpable in the air. 'I thought about you every single day on my trip to Australia. I missed you so much. I couldn't wait to get home and see you again.'

'I missed you too, Rhi.'

His eyes seemed to penetrate her soul. Had he really missed her? In the same way she'd missed him?

'I don't understand what's changed, though? You're about to move to another part of the country. So what is this? A last-minute fling?' She sounded needy to her own ears, but for her own peace of mind, she had to know exactly where she stood with Luke.

Luke took a deep breath and held his hands up in a defensive gesture, subtly edging sidewards on the sofa, giving her some space. 'I'm sorry if I've misjudged this, if this isn't what you want. The last thing in the world I want is to make you feel uncomfortable.'

'No, it's not that.' He didn't understand. How could he possibly understand when she was struggling to put into words her own conflicting emotions? 'I do want this, more than anything, but I'm confused. I guess I don't know what it is you're feeling. What this is for you, Luke? A fling? A Christmas romance? Something to see you through the holiday season?'

She was jeopardising the one thing she'd hankered after for months now. Was it her run-in with Jason tonight that had heightened her emotions, bringing her vulnerability to the surface? Even though Luke was nothing like Jason, she wasn't sure her heart could cope with being carelessly discarded by Luke.

'Rhi, you've always meant a lot to me. Ever since I first set eyes on you at Jansens. You know that.' He reached across and took her hand, interlacing his fingers with hers. 'I hated seeing the way Jason treated you, but I couldn't make any kind of move then because I could see how hurt you were. I didn't want to take advantage of you when you were so low and vulnerable. Then when you announced you were going travelling, I didn't know if or when you'd be coming home. I thought you probably didn't need the distraction of a new relationship. Maybe I assumed too much?'

'You did. You were so kind to me over that whole Jason thing that it made me see you in a completely different light. I really wanted you to make a move, but you kept insisting we were just friends. God, it was so frustrating. So I thought I just had to take matters into my own hands, but when I kissed you here that night, you reacted as though it was the worst thing in the world to ever happen to you. You were repulsed!'

'No, I really wasn't! You completely misread that whole thing.' Luke gave that lopsided smile that did funny things to Rhi's tummy. 'You have no idea how much I wanted to kiss you back, but I was forcing myself to keep some distance. We'd become friends and, despite your protestations that you were over Jason, I wasn't sure if you still had feelings for him.' He gave another wry smile. 'I didn't want to be your rebound romance.'

'It wasn't like that!'

'I realise that now. Look, I know I'm moving away, but it's not to the ends of the earth, Rhi. We could still see each other. We could make things work if that's what we both really want. Let's just see where this takes us. If the other night in the car has taught us anything, it's that we need to make the most of every moment because who knows what fate has in store for us around the corner?'

A silence fell between them. Even the gentle sensation of his thumb tracing circles on the palm of her hand was enough to send her body and heart into freefall. She'd been infatuated with Jason, but what she felt for Luke was something else entirely. Her whole body reacted to his proximity, her skin tingling from his touch. Just being with him was intoxicating and if she didn't know better, she could even believe that she was rapidly falling in love with him. Ha! Who was she kidding? She'd fallen for him months ago. Perhaps that was her fate?

'Yes, you could be right.' She edged towards him on the sofa into his waiting arms, knowing she didn't need any persuasion. 'Let's see where this takes us,' she breathed, repeating his words, before succumbing to his delicious kisses all over again. Luke was right, they should live for the moment. She was happy to go where the mood was taking her, to have some fun and enjoy Luke's company while she could. Who knew what the magic of Christmas might bring?

16

'Knock, knock...' The words, from a familiar but not immediately recognisable voice, immediately set her senses alight. They were accompanied by a tapping on her office door. Abbey looked up from the timesheets on her desk to see Matt standing in the doorway, a tentative smile on his face. 'I hope this is a good time?'

'Hi, come in,' she said brightly, masking her own hesitation. She hadn't received a reply to her email to him yesterday, and she'd wondered what on earth he must have thought after their wonderful evening together had ended on such a sour note. She hadn't dwelled on it for too long, though, because her head had been entirely focused on Sam and what was going on inside his brain. She'd almost, although not quite, forgotten all about Matt. Now he was here, and she suddenly remembered her manners. 'Can I get you a coffee?'

He held up a hand. 'No, really, it's fine. I just wanted a chat, if that's okay?'

How could such seemingly innocent words fill her with dread? There was only one topic of conversation he could possibly want to pursue, and she was pretty certain it had nothing to do with the Lodge. Fortunately, it was Lydia's day off, so at least they could speak in private. She invited Matt to sit down, taking the opportunity to observe him anew in light of the information she'd recently discovered about him. Stella was right, Matt bore more than a passing resemblance to Sam; they were of a similar age and shared the same rangy build. Both were undeniably good-looking in their own right too. Fleetingly, she wondered if the same thought had once occurred to Sophie too.

Now, Matt shifted in his seat, his awkwardness evident as he crossed and uncrossed his legs, and his fingers toyed with the collar of his shirt.

'Look, I felt I ought to clear the air. I'm guessing Sam will have told you what that...' he paused, searching for the right word, '... scene was all about the other night.'

'Yes.' She nodded sympathetically. 'He'd already told me about you and...' she stopped herself, not wanting to say Sophie's name aloud, '... and what happened, but of course I could never have known that it was you.'

'You'd have no reason to.' He steepled his fingers together, resting his chin on his clasped hands, looking across at her. 'It was a pretty big shock all round. You know, I've tried finding Sam on several occasions over the years, with no joy whatsoever, and then when I least expected it, I come face to face with him.'

It was hardly surprising that Matt had been unable to track Sam down. Abbey had discovered in the months that she'd known Sam that he eschewed all social media, saying he had no desire to broadcast to the world what was going on in his life. Now Abbey had to wonder if he'd been deliberately keeping a low profile, not wanting to be found by any ghosts from his past.

'Look, if that offer of a coffee is still available, I think I could probably do with one after all.'

Abbey jumped up, relieved to have the distraction. She

needed a coffee too. She went across to the kitchen workstation in the corner of the room, turning her back on Matt, taking the opportunity to take a couple of calming deep breaths, before filling two mugs from the cafetiere. When she was back behind her desk, Matt continued talking.

'I told you about my ill-fated marriage the other night. That was Sophie. When I look back now, it's as though that whole episode happened to someone else entirely. It was a real whirlwind romance, and we were both guilty of not stopping to think about Sam, we were just so caught up in our own crazy world. We honestly believed that we were doing the right thing, that our love for each other was more important than anything or anybody else.' He shook his head sadly. 'We were young and selfish, not that it's any excuse.'

'But your best friend's girlfriend?'

'I know.' His mouth twisted and his eyes fluttered closed for a moment. 'Probably right up there as one of the shittiest things anyone can do to their best pal. That's why Sophie and I were both so keen to marry. It was a way of justifying our actions. Proving to everyone that what we had done was worth all the pain we caused. The arrogance of youth, huh? When we heard shortly afterwards that Sam had lost his mum, we both felt terrible and tried to reach out to him. My mum went along to the funeral in our place, as Sophie and I were travelling around Europe at the time. We called him and sent messages, but I guess we were the last people in the world he wanted to hear from.'

'I suppose,' said Abbey noncommittally. Why was Matt trying to justify his actions to her? He must realise that she would have little sympathy for what he and Sophie had done all those years ago.

'I turned up at his flat some months later, when we got back from our travels, but I found the place empty. I was told by one of the neighbours that he'd moved away and that's when the trail went dead. I've never stopped thinking about him over the years, though, wondering how he's been getting on.'

'It was a long time ago now. I guess you've all moved on with your lives. Do you still see or hear from Sophie?'

'No.' He shook his head ruefully. 'By the time we finally managed to disentangle ourselves from the relationship, there really wasn't any love lost between us. She met someone else and was as keen as I was to get the divorce finalised as quickly as possible.'

'That's sad.'

'Yep, but we didn't really deserve a happy ending, did we? You can't find happiness on the back of someone else's unhappiness.' He gave a resigned shrug. 'Sophie's remarried now and living in France, I believe.' He paused, his gaze running over her face. 'You and Sam are happy together, though? I hope what happened the other night won't have caused you too many problems? You seem like a really good fit for each other.'

'Thanks, and no, don't worry. We're fine.' Abbey bristled. She really didn't feel comfortable discussing her relationship with her new boss, especially when Sam and Matt had history together. She wasn't going to admit to Matt that his appearance had caused the first big argument in Sam and Abbey's relationship, and if she was being honest with herself, she wasn't sure that they'd really got back to how things were before that episode.

Sam had apologised to her for his behaviour, but she couldn't simply forget what she'd seen; a side to Sam's personality that she wouldn't want to see again in a hurry. The anger, coldness and unwillingness to even talk to her when he'd been so consumed by the red mist had unsettled her with its intensity and made her question if she knew Sam as well as she thought she did.

She suppressed a sigh. Why had Sam acted quite so strongly?

It was such a long time ago. Surely it all belonged in the past.

'What was she like?' The words had slipped out of her mouth before she had time to stop herself.

Matt looked up from where he'd been examining his clasped hands.

'Sophie?' He gave a wry smile. 'Beautiful. Vivacious. Clever. Funny. It's that old cliché, she really did light up the room. People gravitated towards her. I suppose I kind of basked in the reflected glory.'

Abbey nodded interestedly. What on earth had possessed her to ask? Of course she was going to be beautiful and vivacious. What was she expecting? That Matt would tell her Sophie had been fat and frumpy and dull? She'd had two men madly in love with her, after all. Is that why Sam had reacted so strongly to seeing Matt again. Was it possible that he'd never got over losing Sophie, that he was still in love with her?

The intrusive thoughts bombarded her mind, making her feel nauseous as a heat rose up her neck. There were so many questions she wanted to ask of Matt, but how could she? She felt disloyal even being here with him, and talking about Sophie and Sam, about a different point in time. Really, it was none of her business.

She spun her gold pen around in her fingers, before tapping it on the desk.

'Look,' Matt said now, taking the hint. 'I won't keep you much longer. I just wanted to clear the air after the other night, especially as we will be working together. I hope this won't get in the way of that.'

'Of course not. And I appreciate you coming to explain. Lydia and I both had such a wonderful evening at Chez Michel's. We can't thank you enough.'

'Really, it was my pleasure. Hopefully we might get to do it again next Christmas.'

'Yes,' she said, without conviction. She wasn't sure how Sam might react to that news, but at least she had another year to think about it before it would even be a possibility.

'This is awkward,' said Matt, examining the backs of his hands, 'but I'd really like the opportunity to speak to Sam, to apologise to him in person. I'm not looking for his forgiveness, or anything like that, but I really would like him to know how sorry I am. I know he's pretty angry at the moment, running into me again, unexpectedly after all these years, and probably doesn't want anything to do with me, but I wonder if with a bit of time for reflection, Sam might reconsider. Do you think that could be a possibility?'

'No!' Abbey had answered immediately and instinctively. The last thing she wanted was for the pair of them to be put together in the same room again after what had happened last time. 'Look, Matt, I can't speak for Sam, but he didn't seem to me as though he might want to talk to you anytime soon. Sorry, it's between you and Sam. I really don't want to get involved.'

'Yeah, that's fair enough.' He held up a hand in a defensive gesture. 'The last thing I'd want to do is to put you in a difficult position, but can I just ask you a small favour? Let me give you another one of my cards. I'm not asking you to give it to Sam now, but if there's ever a time when you think he might want to reconnect, then he'll have a way of finding me.'

Matt pulled out a card from the inside pocket of his jacket and handed it across the desk to her. She took it from him and ran her figures around it edges. She knew she wouldn't dare utter Matt's name in Sam's presence again, not unless he initiated that conversation, but there was no need to tell Matt that. If taking the card and putting it away in a safe place went some way to assuaging Matt's guilt, then where was the harm in that?

17

Rhi couldn't help wondering if she hadn't made the biggest mistake of her life. She sighed, rolling over in her bed, stretching her body out to its full length, inhaling the faintest traces of Luke's aftershave left lingering on the sheets and pillows. If she closed her eyes, she could recapture those delicious moments spent wrapped in his embrace, his strong firm limbs entwined with hers, the taste of his kisses on her mouth and body which had been deliciously addictive. She buried her head in her hands, goosebumps running over her body. Not that she regretted Luke staying over in the slightest. It was all she'd dreamed of for months, and with her mum staying out overnight at Robb's place, it had given them that one-time opportunity that had escaped them for so long.

It was every bit as wonderful as she'd imagined it would be, but if she thought spending one magical night with Luke would rid herself of those all-consuming feelings of longing, and get him out of her system once and for all, then she was very much mistaken. Ever since he'd slipped out of the house this morning, her head had been revisiting every single moment of the time they'd spent together, the feel of his body up against hers, the sensation of his breath upon her skin, the words whispered in her ears, and the laughter they'd shared. Had it really happened? At least she had the perfect excuse to see Luke again soon, at the Christmas event at Primrose Hall on Saturday and then at Lizzie's house on Christmas Eve, even if they didn't organise anything else in the meantime. So their lives might be going in different directions after Christmas, but that didn't mean they couldn't enjoy every moment together until then. She would worry about her broken heart in the new year, she thought with a dreamy smile.

Still, she couldn't lie there all day mooning over Luke, as much as she might like to. She had to get to work for eleven and she wanted to pop into town beforehand to pick up some last-minute presents. She wanted to buy something for Luke. Just a little something to say thank you for everything he'd done for her, ferrying her to and from work and generally being a good friend. Maybe something small and personal that would always remind him of her. He might take a look at it one day, hopefully not too far into the future and suddenly realise that he couldn't live without her. Well, she could live in hope.

After climbing out of bed and jumping into the shower, she quickly dried herself and started getting ready, a ridiculous smile on her face, as the memories of her night spent with Luke kept popping into her mind. She was just applying her make-up when she heard the front door open and heard her mum's familiar voice call out.

'Rhi! Are you up there?'

'Yes, I'll be down in a minute.' She gave her reflection one last check in the mirror before grabbing her handbag and coat, then skipping down the stairs. 'Hi, Mum, did you have a good time last night?' she asked, as she hugged to herself the secret of her own lovely evening with Luke which seemed to have plastered a permanent grin on her face.

'Yeah, it was good, thanks. We went to the Turkish restaurant on the High Street. It was lovely.' Her mum's expression didn't quite match her words and Rhi could sense something was amiss. She tilted her head to one side. 'Is everything all right, Mum?'

'Oh, yes, fine. It's just I need to have a chat with you about something, that's all. Let me make us a coffee. You've got time, haven't you?'

'Sure,' she said, intrigued. If she didn't get to the shops today, then it wouldn't really matter. She could always go tomorrow. Rhi sorted through her handbag on the sofa while she waited for her mum, who was busy in the kitchen. A few minutes later, she came through with mugs of coffee for them both, and took a seat opposite Rhi.

'Right, well...' Her mum proceeded to chat about the weather, what they'd had to eat last night, who they'd bumped into, and what she still had to do in preparation for Christmas. Rhi listened attentively, although if her mum just wanted a general chit-chat, then surely they could do that later. She glanced at her watch.

'So what was it in particular you wanted to talk about then?' she asked.

'Oh, yes! Well, the thing is, Robb and I were chatting last night... Oh, Rhi, I really do like him. He's such a lovely, down-to-earth guy and we laugh all the time. He treats me really well too, which is a revelation after...'

'Dad?' Rhi offered.

Her mum nodded sadly.

'Sorry, love, but it's true. Robb was cheated on in his last relationship too, so honesty and trust are very important to him as well. I know I said I'd never get into a serious relationship again, but this has taken me completely by surprise.'

'I'm pleased for you, Mum. Really, I am.'

'Good, it's just we were saying how ridiculous it is that we're both running separate houses with all the expenses that go with that, and we thought...' Lisa took a deep breath, '... it would probably make sense if we moved in together.'

'You're moving in with Robb?'

'Well, nothing's arranged as yet, we're just talking around the idea, but if we were, it would probably make more sense for Robb to move in here, and then he could rent out his flat, and we could pool resources.' Lisa paused, gauging Rhi's reaction. 'Nothing's set in stone, though,' she added quickly. 'It would only happen if you were happy with the arrangement. This is your home, so obviously you would have a say in any changes.'

'Sure, Mum, if it's what you want to do.'

Rhi couldn't help feeling sad. It had been just Rhi and her mum for years now, so Rhi wouldn't relish someone new moving in, however lovely Robb was. She would never stand in the way of her mum's happiness, though, especially as she'd been planning on finding a place of her own one day, somewhere she could use the spare bedroom as an office for her new business. She smiled, suppressing a sigh. She might need to find her own place much sooner than she'd anticipated.

'I think I do, love.' Lisa clasped her hands together, holding them to her mouth, her excitement palpable. 'We're spending as much time together as we can, and the funny thing is, when I'm not with him, I miss him terribly.' Rhi nodded, she could relate to that entirely, feeling exactly the same way about Luke, although she suspected her future with Luke wasn't as clear cut as her mum's was with Robb. Lisa went on. 'At our age, you realise that you don't have time to waste. If you love each other and want to be together, then there's really no point in waiting.'

That could be true at any age, Rhi thought, but she opted to keep her thoughts to herself. Instead, she smiled and said brightly, 'That makes perfect sense to me. If it's what you really want, Mum, then you should go for it.'

'And you wouldn't mind?' Rhi spotted the gleam of light in her mum's eye, suspecting she was more relieved than anything else at having told Rhi her plans. 'I'd hate for you to feel uncomfortable in your own home,' she added.

'I won't,' she reassured her mum. She could hardly admit how she really felt, that the idea of sharing their small home with someone she had no real connection with only emphasised that she needed to move out as soon as she could. Next year was going to be a big one for Rhi. She was starting her own business and there was no room for failure. It had to be a success if she wanted to achieve the independence she needed for her own happiness.

Her thoughts drifted back to Luke. Again. It was becoming a habit. She was ready for a new relationship now as well, and after the magical, intimate and heady night they'd spent together, she knew that she and Luke could be so good together. If only they had a chance. Ordinarily, she might have confided in her mum, but now wasn't the time, as her mum was far too wrapped up in her own romantic plans.

She looked across at her now and smiled. There was no way she could begrudge her mum her newfound happiness. She was right, if there was an opportunity for a chance of happiness, then she needed to grab it with both hands. And so should Rhi.

She would keep everything crossed that she might be able to build a relationship with Luke, even at a distance. That was if it was what Luke really wanted too. It certainly seemed that way last night when she'd been wrapped in his arms, but perhaps it wasn't as important to Luke as she hoped and he'd just been making the most of the Christmas goodwill in the air.

18

Abbey had been observing Sam from a distance for a good ten minutes now, watching as he effortlessly hoisted trees up on his shoulders and chatted with the customers, before netting up their trees and wandering into the wooden hut to process their payments. Dressed in dark cargo trousers, a Primrose Woods green sweat top and brown gilet, it was the image of Sam she carried in her head. Handsome, capable and innately confident in his natural environment. The realisation made her heart swell. To see him now, she wouldn't think he had a care in the world, and there was certainly no sign of the angry man she'd witnessed in the pub the other night. She could quite happily have stood there all day, given the opportunity, but she supposed she ought to go across and make her presence known. But just another moment or two.

It was her day off and, on the spur of the moment, she'd decided to come to Primrose Woods. Wrapped up in her cosy padded coat, her hands dug deep into her pockets, she'd turned right from her cottage in Wishwell and headed over to Breakspear's Pass. Then onto the familiar path that led to the kissing gate on Long Acre Lane, one of the many footpath entrances into the park. In the warmer months, she made a habit of visiting the woods almost every day, getting her daily fix of the great outdoors. There was something about the natural rugged beauty of the country park, over three hundred acres in total, that was magical and restorative. Whatever her mood, she would always feel lifted after a visit to the park; the towering trees, the still tranquillity of the lake and the sounds of the squirrels and birds busy in the trees all around acted as a soothing massage to her soul.

Now Sam's dark brown eyes lit up as he turned and spotted her, the surprise evident in his features, and he immediately came over to greet her.

'Hey, what are you doing here?' He leaned forward to kiss her on the cheek.

'I was going to pop into the café to grab some lunch and have a chat with Lizzie. Just wondered if you wanted to join me?'

He glanced at his watch.

'Great timing. I was about to take my break. Give me a couple of minutes and I'll be with you.'

At least he looked pleased to see her, she thought, as she watched him head back inside the hut to chat briefly to Rick, one of his fellow rangers. There was such a lovely festive atmosphere around the Christmas tree yard. As well as the huge selection of trees on offer, they were selling evergreen wreaths with red berries, mistletoe garlands, and a range of wooden folksy decorations. The scent of pine mingled in the air with the warming aromas of freshly brewed coffee and hot chocolate emanating from the mobile vintage coffee van that was doing a roaring trade with the visitors.

'Well, this is a lovely surprise,' said Sam when he came to join her, putting an arm around her shoulder and planting a kiss on her cheek this time. 'Just like old times.'

'Old times!' She laughed – what could he possibly mean by that? Before their big bust-up? She decided not to ask. 'We've only known each other, what is it, eight months?' she laughed. 'We're hardly old-timers.'

'I know, but sometimes it seems so much longer,' he said, with a cheeky sideways glance, as he jokily swayed on his knees.

'Hey!' she said, laughing, playfully digging him in the ribs. Abbey took hold of Sam's arm and they walked in the direction of the café.

At least Sam was in a good mood, which hopefully meant that any annoyance he'd felt at running into Matt the other night had evaporated into the brisk cold air. With any luck, they'd be able to put that whole sorry episode behind them and forget it ever happened. She took a deep breath, not really believing that to be true. Ever since Matt's visit to the office yesterday, she hadn't been able to stop thinking about Sam and if he could still have feelings for Sophie. From Matt's description, she sounded like someone you wouldn't forget in a hurry.

'I'm kidding, but in some ways it does feel like it was only the other day that we met, and other times it feels like I've known you forever.' His dark eyes shone, locking onto hers.

She'd felt the same when she'd first met Sam. He was so easy to be around and just being in his company made her feel alive and happy, and that feeling had only deepened in the months since. At first, having just come out of a relationship with her ex, she didn't trust her feelings and thought Sam would be a passing infatuation, someone to help her get over Jason and move her on to the next stage in her life. She would never have believed that a few months later, they would be living together in a loving and committed relationship.

'Yeah, I agree. I suppose in a way it's still early days for us and we're still learning new things about one another.'

'Do you think?' He tilted his head to one side, considering her words. 'I think we know each other pretty well at this stage, don't you? Unless you're hiding some big secrets about... oh, I don't know, a mafia past, a string of abandoned children, a career in sexy movies?'

She laughed. She was pretty much an open book. She'd been thinking more about Sam and if she knew him as well as she thought she did.

'Come on,' he said. 'Let's get inside.'

The Treetops Café was abuzz with visitors and every bit as Christmassy as it had been outside in the yard. Christmas carols rang out from the speakers, the aromas of warming soups and mince pies wafted in the air and Lizzie greeted them in a fetching pair of reindeer antlers and with a big smile on her face.

'Hello, my lovelies. What can I tempt you with today?'

Sam plumped for a toasted ham and cheese sandwich while Abbey went for the sweet potato and Bramley apple soup, with both of them opting for a cinnamon-flavoured latte too.

'How's things with you, Lizzie? You must be incredibly busy with work and having your daughter and grandchildren at home too,' Abbey said.

'Oh, it's chaos,' said Lizzie, laughing, 'but I wouldn't have it any other way. It's such a blessing to have them here again. Rosie and Pip have settled in really well and Katy is doing a bit better now too. She's had a case of the baby blues but she's getting some treatment for it and, fingers crossed, she's on her way to recovery.'

'That's good! And, of course, you have Dad staying with you now as well.'

'Oh, yes, but he's no trouble. In fact, he's a great help around the house and with Rosie. She's his number one fan at the moment! Doesn't give him a moment's peace, mind. Katy and Bill have gone off to look at some rental properties today for when Brad comes home, so I think she was pleased to be doing something proactive.'

'Yes, Dad told me about that,' said Abbey. 'I bet she'll feel much more settled once they've got their own place sorted and Brad's home.'

When Sam excused himself and popped to the loo, Lizzie sat down in his vacated chair and leaned across the table.

'I wanted to check, is everything okay between you and Sam? Your dad mentioned you'd had a falling out and I heard there was a bit of a problem in the pub the other night too. What was that all about?'

Abbey's shoulders sank. She didn't mind that her dad had told Lizzie about the argument, she would have expected him to. What she had hoped, though, was that the scene with Matt in the pub might have gone unnoticed apart from the few people who had witnessed the scuffle in the back bar. No such luck. She supposed it was hardly surprising. Any whiff of gossip and it was more than likely to spread through the whole community within a matter of hours.

'Well...' She took a deep breath. 'I went out to dinner with my new boss, Matt, which was fine. Sam knew all about it. What neither of us could have known was that Matt turned out to be Sam's friend from school, the one who ran off with his girlfriend!'

'Oh, good grief!' Lizzie's hand immediately flew to her mouth. 'That was just after he finished university? He told me all about it once. I know he doesn't really like to talk about that time. Fancy coming face to face with your past like that. It's not like Sam, though, to lose his rag.'

'I know, and of course I had no idea what it was all about until the following day. Sam wouldn't talk about it. He was so angry, Lizzie. I'd never seen him like it before. He seems fine now, but I know Matt won't be making it on to our Christmas card list anytime soon, that's for sure.'

Lizzie glanced over her shoulder, spotting Sam making his way back to the table. She tapped Abbey on the hand.

'Well as long as you two are okay, that's the main thing. Are you all ready for Christmas?' she said brightly, quickly changing the subject as Sam re-joined them at the table. 'I think I am, it's just the food I need to get now, but obviously that will be a last-minute thing.'

'I think we're pretty much set too, aren't we, Sam?'

'So I'm told,' he said to Lizzie, with a grin. 'Although I take no credit, Abbey's done all the hard work. Apparently my main job is to turn up and enjoy myself,' he said with a smile. 'I think even I can manage that.'

It was true, Abbey had taken charge of all the preparations. She'd wrapped all the presents, and written and sent all the Christmas cards too. She'd dressed the Christmas tree and decorated the entire house with evergreen garlands intertwined with fairy lights. When she wasn't working, she liked to potter in the kitchen, baking mince pies and gingerbread biscuits. She was no Mary Berry, and a lot of her batches, fresh from the oven, turned out looking wonky, dented or with the filling oozing out from the sides. Not that it mattered. They tasted delicious and she had a willing and appreciative guinea pig in Sam.

'You hung the lights up on the front of the house, which I would never have managed on my own.' Although she'd had a pretty good go. It was only because Sam had come home early from work one day and caught her up the ladder, stretching precariously to hang the white icicle lights over the doorway, and along the eaves, that he'd insisted on taking over, going up the ladder and finishing off the job himself. She'd been mightily relieved, to be honest, and the lights looked so pretty sparkling over the front of the cottage.

'Yeah, well, you know I'm happy to do my bit where I can,' said Sam.

Abbey needed to be organised. She would be working right up until Christmas Eve, as would Sam, but she didn't mind that because there was always such a lovely atmosphere at the Lodge over Christmas, and the festive season wouldn't be complete without the opportunity to see all her residents in person and to pass on her good wishes for the holiday to each of them in turn.

'Look, I shall have to go and do some work,' said Lizzie. 'But we'll see you at Primrose Hall at the weekend. I'm really looking forward to it.'

With Lizzie leaving them alone to enjoy their lunch, Abbey couldn't stop herself from taking sneaky peeks at Sam across the table, as though she was meeting him for the first time. He had been utterly charming with Lizzie, as he always was, but that was totally at odds with the personality he'd shown in the pub the other night. *Would the real Sam please stand up?*

'I know!' she said, as though the thought had only just occurred to her. 'I've thought of something that I don't know about you.'

'Go on,' he said, munching on his sandwich.

'You've never really told me about Sophie. What she was like?'

He stopped with his sandwich in mid-air and lifted his eyes, which suddenly seemed so much darker, a flicker of irritation in his gaze. There it was again, that subtle closing down, any time Sophie's name was mentioned.

'Really? We're here, having a nice lunch, and you want to talk about my ex?' He put the rest of his sandwich down on his plate as though he'd lost his appetite. 'What do you want to know?'

Okay, so this might have been uncomfortable for Sam, but it was uncomfortable for her too. Sam knew everything there was to know about her ex, so it was only fair that she should know about the people that had played an important role in his life too.

'What was she like as a person? What did she look like?' She threw out the questions casually, as though she hadn't been brooding about them for the last few days.

He sighed.

'It was a long time ago. I can barely remember. She was fun, I suppose. Outgoing.' He shrugged, the act of talking about her clearly painful. He didn't have to say any more. She knew by his reaction that Sophie was everything Matt had described her to be. *Beautiful. Memorable.*

It was like picking at a scab. Abbey couldn't leave it. She had to know.

'Are you still in love with her, Sam?'

'What?' He lifted his gaze to look at her, laying his hands down on the table, grabbing onto the edge. 'Are you serious? This is Matt, isn't it? Turning up and putting ideas in your head.'

'No!' she protested. 'It just got me thinking, that's all. After what happened the other night? Your reaction?'

'What, and you think my reaction wasn't justified? That I should have acted differently? What should I have done? Opened my arms wide and welcomed Matt back into my life? I'm sorry if I got that wrong. Thanks for letting me know.'

'No, please, Sam, don't be like that. I'm just trying to understand, that's all.'

He pushed his half-eaten sandwich away, the moment

spoiled, and she dropped her spoon in the soup. Her appetite had vanished too.

'I need to get back to work,' he said, brusquely, standing up. He pulled out his wallet from his trousers pocket and took out a twenty-pound note, dropping it on the table. 'And for your information, I'm not still in love with her. No. Okay?'

19

'My feet are absolutely killing me. We must have seen over half a dozen houses today,' said Katy. 'Poor Bill didn't know what he was letting himself in for when he agreed to come along with me.'

'Thank him for me, won't you?' said Brad, through the computer screen. 'You'll have to send me over the details.'

'I will. The trouble is, properties are being snapped up just as soon as they come on to the market. The agent says if there's something we like, then really we need to be putting in an offer there and then if we want any chance of securing it.'

'Honestly, Katy, I trust you to make that decision. If it's the right size and in the right location and within our budget, then go for it. It's only a stop-gap, somewhere to rent for six months or so, until we can find something more permanent.'

That was easy for Brad to say from the other side of the world, soaking up the sunshine. Didn't he realise just how stressful it was trying to find somewhere to live? If he was only here, then the task would be so much simpler. She found the responsibility overwhelming. What if she made the wrong decision and they ended up somewhere that didn't work for Brad or the children?

'How's work going?' she asked, masking her irritation. 'Do you have a date yet as to when you'll be able to get home?'

Well, it had been a couple of days since she'd last asked, even though she hated badgering Brad. She was anxious to have her husband back as soon as possible. Initially, when she'd returned from Australia, Brad had told her he'd be following in a couple of months' time, but that timescale hadn't changed at all in the intervening weeks.

'After Christmas, I'll have a better idea of when I can get away. I know it seems like a long time, but I promise you I'll be home just as soon as I can.'

It seemed like a lifetime away. She was cross with herself for feeling this way. For being so needy and impatient. She'd always wanted to be a wife and mother. It was what she'd dreamed of, so why couldn't she just take everything in her stride and be happy with her lot?

'Come on,' said Brad, picking up on her low mood from across the miles. 'You and the kids will have a great Christmas from the sound of things. Just concentrate on enjoying yourself and then we can worry about everything else in the new year.'

'I feel bad that you're out there on your own. I miss you so much.'

'I know that, and I miss you too, but it can't be helped. Besides, we'll still be seeing each other on Christmas Day. I know a Zoom call can't match seeing each other in person, but it's the next best thing and I can't wait to see the kids open their presents. Honestly, Katy, we'll be back together before you know it, and all this will be forgotten about.'

She forced a smile, but she felt hollow inside. She would go through the motions, she had to for the sake of her mum and the children, but she was acting on autopilot. When would she ever feel like herself again? When would things ever get back to normal?

'Yeah, it will all work out,' she said, trying and failing to inject a note of enthusiasm in her voice. 'Take no notice of me, I'm just having a moment.'

'It's okay, you're allowed to,' said Brad with a reassuring smile.

As Brad told her about the progress he was making on the paper he was working on, she realised she'd been having a few too many of those moments. Everyone must be sick to death of her moping about the place. Hearing Brad talk about his work with such passion and enthusiasm, she realised in a moment of clarity what it was that she was so missing in her life.

'So how is Brad getting on?' Lizzie asked later, when they gathered up the crockery from the dining room table and were loading the dishwasher together, while the children were settled in front of an episode of *Peppa Pig*.

'Great. His paper's coming together now, although he seems to think he'll have to work right up to the deadline for the conference to get it completely finished.'

'Sounds as though he's got a lot on.'

'He has, but it's not all work. He's got his departmental Christmas do this weekend, it's a barbecue on the beach, can you believe?'

Lizzie shook her head, an expression of mild bemusement across her features.

'I can't imagine spending Christmas in the sunshine. It wouldn't feel right to me.'

'No, I never got used to it,' said Katy. 'It made me realise how much I missed home and all the traditions we have here. I want the children to experience the magic of a traditional Christmas so they'll have the same lovely memories when they're older. You've seen Rosie and how excited she is participating in all the festive activities, making paper chains, and writing to Santa. There's so much for her to do and she's loving all the build-up, even if she's still adamant that it's going to snow when Santa arrives!'

'Well, I'm sure we'll be able to negotiate that tricky little dilemma when the time comes. She'll be so excited about hanging up her stocking and discovering that Santa has visited that she'll forget all about the snow. We can sprinkle some make-believe footprints around the fireplace.'

'I can't wait,' said Katy, excited at the thought of seeing the children's faces on Christmas morning.

Brad was right. She had to throw herself into the celebrations. Her mum had just reminded her why she'd been desperate to be home this Christmas, even if it meant being apart from Brad for a short while. It was one year, that was all, and next year they would be settled in their own place and everything would be perfect.

'Do you have a copy of the local newspaper, Mum?'

Lizzie retrieved it from the wicker basket by the dresser and handed it over to Katy. 'Are you having another look at the property pages?'

Katy paused, looking up from where she was idly leafing through the newspaper at the table.

'No, Brad said I should just go ahead and make an offer on any house that I think might be suitable. The one we saw today, the one I told you about, the three-bedroomed detached with the garage converted into an office, would suit us fine. Bill liked it too. I only hope it hasn't been taken already. I'll give the agent a call first thing in the morning.'

Lizzie peered over Katy's shoulder, heartened to hear the note of positivity in Katy's words. That video call with Brad today had clearly lifted her spirits. Having something positive to focus on was exactly what Katy needed at the moment. She gave a gentle squeeze of her daughter's arm.

'So what is it you're looking for in there?'

Katy closed the pages of the paper decisively, and looked up at her mum with a smile, lifting her hand to touch her mum's hand still resting on her shoulder.

'Just browsing. Do you fancy a glass of wine, Mum? I picked up a bottle of the fizzy stuff when we were out today.'

'Sounds lovely.' Lizzie gave a small squee of delight. 'We can watch the final episode of *Peaky Blinders* when the little ones are in bed.'

'Great idea, I'll pop them up now, and then we can get settled.'

'Nanna do story,' said Rosie, sliding off the sofa, clutching her patchwork dinosaur with one hand and rubbing her eyes with the other.

'Of course I will, poppet,' said Lizzie, feeling an immense sense of pride at her granddaughter's love for her. She cherished being at the heart of the family, providing support to her daughter and the grandchildren. There was no better feeling in the world. 'We'll put Pip down in his cot and then we'll read a story.'

'Snowy night one, snowy night!' Rosie sang, heading up the stairs, with Lizzie following behind, a sleeping Pip in her arms.

'You don't mind do you, Mum?' Katy called after her.

'Are you kidding?' Her laughter tinkled out as she climbed the stairs. It was these small things that she'd missed so much while her family had been living abroad. She was so lucky to have them back living under her roof and determined to make the most of every moment while she could. 'You get that wine poured and open that box of chocolates on the dresser. I'll be down in a little while.'

20

Despite the chilly temperature and a biting wind, Abbey felt nice and toasty wrapped up in her quilted jacket, woolly hat and mittens. The cold was invigorating and energising, prickling at her face, the only part of her body exposed to the elements. She looked up at Sam and smiled. Nothing could spoil tonight, not now they'd called a truce. They'd agreed that no good could come of talking about their exes. They were in the past and that's where they should stay.

She huddled up beside Sam now as they walked along the sweeping driveway that led to Primrose Hall. It was lovely to see so many familiar faces from the local community walking the same route up to the manor house and to be amongst her family and friends; her dad and Lizzie were up ahead, with Katy and the children, and Luke and Rhi were alongside them. There was an air of bubbling festive anticipation in the atmosphere and Abbey was entertained by little Rosie in front of her, holding hands with her mum and Lizzie, skipping in between them, her excitement all too evident to see.

'Look, Nanna, can you see the sparkly reindeer?'

'Ah, aren't they beautiful!' Lizzie exclaimed. The reindeer of different sizes decorated in a myriad of tiny lights gathered in small herds across the lawns, creating a magical sight. Like Rosie, Lizzie didn't know where to look first as they approached the glittering tunnel of twinkling lights that led to the sweeping frontage of Primrose Hall. The seventeenth-century building lit up by floodlights looked magnificent, and their group seemed to swoon as one.

'It looks amazing. What a brilliant job they've done here.'

Just then, music started playing, the familiar notes of 'God Rest Ye Merry Gentlemen' rang out in the air, welcoming the assembled crowd and beckoning them through the stone archway that led to a beautiful courtyard where the band was gathered along with a small group of carollers, entertaining the audience.

'Look,' said Abbey, pointing in the direction of the stables, 'don't they look inviting? We'll have to go and have a look round later.'

The renovated L-shaped stable block was lit up against the dark night sky, a huge Christmas tree standing on the front corner of the building, shining invitingly.

'That's a very big tree,' said Rosie, her neck craning to look upwards to its very summit.

'It is,' said Katy, scooping her daughter up in her arms and holding her aloft so she could get a better view, planting a kiss on her cold cheek as she did so. She took a moment, squeezing Rosie to her body tightly. Times like these reminded her how lucky she was to be here with her children and her mum. She couldn't wait to talk to Brad tomorrow and tell him all about it. She glanced down at Pip, who was happy in his buggy, his big trusting eyes looking up at her bright and expectant, beneath his snuggly hat.

'Oh, sweetheart!' In that moment, from out of nowhere, she felt a huge swell of love for her baby boy, as though she was experiencing it for the first time. She popped Rosie down on the ground, where she immediately latched onto Bill's hand, and Katy crouched down to peer into Pip's face. He rewarded her with a big and gummy smile that made her laugh with happiness. 'Oh, Pip! I do love you.' She kissed him on the cheek, his skin cold against her lips.

'Something smells good,' said Lizzie. 'It said in the local paper they're serving mulled wine and mince pies, if anyone's hungry?'

'What a lovely thing for the new owners to do, to open up the grounds of their home to the community for this event,' Abbey said, following the direction of Lizzie's gaze.

'Well, I suppose it's no good having a country pile like this if no one else gets to see it. It needs showing off. You can catch glimpses of the hall from Primrose Wood through the fence, especially at this time of the year with the trees bare, but you can't really appreciate its magnificence unless you're standing here, right in front of it.' Sam was in full agreement with the others.

'Hi, Abbey!' Abbey turned at the sound of her name to see a face from the past. Connor was standing there, hand in hand with his girlfriend Ruby.

'Hi!' She instinctively moved forward to hug him. She'd known Connor for years, he was like the big brother she'd never had, even if she hadn't seen him in a while. 'It's great to see you. I got the invitation, by the way. Thank you! And congratulations to you both! I will reply formally in the new year, but yes, we'd love to come. This is Sam, by the way, my plus one.'

'Great to meet you,' said Sam, holding out his hand to Connor and nodding, with a big smile, at Ruby.

'How's Pia? Is she here tonight?' Abbey glanced around her, hoping one of her very best friends might be here too. It had been far too long since they'd had a proper catch-up.

'No, she decided to give it a miss,' said Connor. 'She's fine, although she's obviously had a tough year, what with losing Mum, but she's slowly getting herself sorted. We've put the house on the market, so she's looking around to find herself a new place to live and a job too. Next year's going to be a big one for us all.'

'Yeah, I bet,' said Abbey, wondering how her friend was really doing. Pia had spent most of the years since leaving school acting as a carer, first to her dad and then to her mum. To start all over again in her late twenties must be daunting.

'Well, send her my love, won't you, and tell her I'll give her a call soon to arrange a catch-up.' Abbey felt a pang of guilt watching Connor and Ruby go, realising how long it had been since she'd seen Pia, but it had always been a feature of their friendship, going for months without seeing or talking to each other, and then picking up instantly when they did finally get together, the weeks and months falling away, as if they'd never been apart.

The group wandered on a little before huddling together to join in with a hearty rendition of 'Jingle Bells', which left them all smiling, their cheeks made rosy from the cold night air. As they moved on, they were interrupted again.

'Hey, Katy, is that you?'

The group turned as one to greet a man who'd approached their little huddle. He was tall, his physical presence imposing, with dark hair just visible beneath a grey beanie. Katy looked up to face him, her expression flitting from one of bemusement to one of recognition in a few moments.

'Jackson Moody! Blimey!'

A wide grin spread across his face.

'It's great to see you, Katy. It's been a while.'

'I should say so...' Her brow furrowed as she tried to remember how long it had been exactly. Memories flooded her brain as she tried to reconcile the teenage Jackson Moody, who had certainly lived up to his name back then, with the man standing in front of her now. There had been quite the transformation, even if she'd have recognised those prominent cheekbones and strongly defined jawline anywhere. In a vintage-style sheepskin jacket, Jackson looked cool and edgy, and certainly stood out from the crowd. 'It would have been when we were at school and that was a lifetime ago. I didn't realise you still lived around here.'

'Well, I was away for a good few years, but yeah, it's great to be back,' said Jackson. 'What about you?'

'The same. I've been living in Australia for the last couple of years with my family, but I've just got back with the children. I'm staying with Mum at the moment.' She gestured towards Lizzie, who smiled and nodded at Jackson. She knew a lot of Katy's friends from school, but couldn't remember meeting this one. Katy went on, 'I'm looking for a place with my husband but he won't be home until the new year. It'll definitely be somewhere round here, though, so I can stay close to Mum.'

'Great. That means we'll probably run into each other again.' At that moment, a tall, willowy woman appeared at Jackson's side, placing a proprietary arm on the sleeve of his jacket. Her ash-blonde hair was just visible from beneath a Cossack-style faux fur hat, a long plait hanging down her back. Her wide bright smile dazzled them all. 'This is my girlfriend, Tara. Katy and I went to school together,' he told her.

'Hey, it's great to meet you,' she said, with a natural and likeable confidence. 'What do you think to all of this?' Tara gestured to the activity around them. The crowd had grown now, people were milling around chatting and laughing, holding warming mugs of mulled wine or hot chocolate in their hands, the aromas of roasting chestnuts wafting in the air.

'Aw, it's brilliant, such a great atmosphere. It's lovely to see everyone out enjoying themselves,' said Katy.

'Yes, isn't it great what they've done here? For as long as I can remember, Primrose Hall has been left neglected and abandoned, so to see it restored to its former glory is absolutely wonderful. It benefits the whole community,' said Lizzie.

'That's great to hear.' Jackson's face lit up. 'That's exactly what I intended.'

'What?' Katy immediately turned on his comment, her eyes wide and her mouth open. 'What do you mean? Don't tell me this is your place?'

Jackson laughed, and Tara joined in, threading her arm around his waist. They made such a glamorous couple standing there together, obviously very much in love and, now Katy came to think of it, looking just like lord and lady of the manor.

'It is. I bought it a few years back, but I've only recently moved in. We've had extensive works carried out, so this is a bit of a celebration for us, finally getting to this point. It was something we wanted to share with the local community.'

Katy couldn't hide her surprise. The wayward rebellious boy she remembered from school had obviously done very well for himself in the intervening years. There were so many questions she wanted to ask him, but now wasn't the time. Instead, she simply said, 'You've done a great job, Jackson, that's for sure.'

'I don't know if you've had a chance to look around the stables yet, but we're planning on opening them up on a few weekends throughout the year to pop-up shops and food stores. We're particularly keen to offer local craftspeople the opportunity to sell their products, so if you know anyone who might be interested, then please spread the word. We'll put all the details up on the website after Christmas.'

Katy nodded her head keenly, still trying to assimilate what

Jackson was telling her. To think that this was Jackson's place was astonishing. She liked the sound of what he had planned for the stables, a kernel of an idea popping into her head. It was definitely something she would be interested in finding out more about.

'I work at Treetops Café at Primrose Woods and we'd be happy to put up any posters when the time comes,' offered Lizzie.

'Ah, great, so we're neighbours then?' said Jackson, with an engaging smile.

'Yes! And Sam's a ranger at the park too.' The two men acknowledged each other with a nod of their head. 'We're all local so we'll hopefully be getting to see you again.'

'Let me give you one of my cards.' Jackson dug inside his jacket pocket and pulled out a wad of business cards and handed one each to Katy, Lizzie and Sam. 'If there's anything at all, just give me a call.' Then he leaned over and addressed Rosie, who'd been kicking her feet on the ground, growing restless. 'If you go across to the stables, you'll be able to say hello to the newest members of our family – there's a donkey and a little pony.'

Rosie looked up at Jackson, her eyes growing wide with excitement.

'What are their names?' she asked seriously.

Jackson's brow furrowed. He might have overlooked that small detail. When he was offered the animals, he immediately said yes, knowing what a great addition they would be for tonight's event, and already they'd proved to be a huge hit with the visitors. Now, though, he had a sweet little girl looking at him expectantly, waiting for an answer. He glanced at Tara, whose eyes grew wide in the same way as Rosie's, before shrugging her shoulders.

'Well, they only arrived here yesterday so we haven't decided on their names yet.' He turned to Katy, lowering his voice. 'They came through a friend of a friend from a farm over the other side of the valley. Sadly, there was a bereavement and all the animals had to go. We don't know much more about them, but hopefully we can offer them a good home here.' He turned back to Rosie. 'Maybe you could go and see them and tell me what you think their names might be?'

'Mummy, Mummy! Can we go and see the donkey and pony?' she said, stomping her little yellow wellies on the ground.

'Yes,' said Katy, laughing, 'we'll do that next. Thanks for the heads up, Jackson. It's been lovely to see you and great meeting you too, Tara.'

As Katy was led away by little Rosie, she shook her head, smiling, still unable to believe what had just happened. Fancy that! Jackson Moody, the bad boy from her school days, had obviously made good, and had done it in considerable style too.

21

Rhi stood on the gravelled frontage of Primrose Hall amongst her friends, soaking up the beauty of the imposing manor house where a warm and welcoming glow radiated from behind the mullioned windows, Christmas carols rang out around her, and lights twinkled on the Christmas tree. She took a deep breath, the cold air tingling on her cheeks. She thought it was probably the most romantic setting she'd ever been in and when she felt Luke's arm around her shoulders, she could almost imagine she was playing the starring role in a seasonal romantic comedy film. Her leading man was looking particularly gorgeous tonight in a navy hooded parka that highlighted his natural good looks. His blond hair stuck out in random strands from beneath his hood and Rhi only had to look up into his deep blue eyes to feel the familiar lurch of her stomach. She wished she had a time machine so that she could travel into the future to see where she and Luke might be in a year's time or even three months' time. Would they find their own happy ending like they always did in the movies? She could only hope that Luke would think it worth a try, rather than forgetting all about Rhi as soon as he was out of sight.

'Hey, you were a million miles away there.' Luke's words shook her out of her reverie. She'd been gazing up at the night sky, lost in thought, transfixed by the lights of Primrose Hall and the stars sparkling in the heavens above.

'It's just so beautiful,' she said dreamily, not wanting any reminders of Luke's impending departure to spoil the moment. She had to push those feelings to one side and make the most of the time they did have together. Glancing sideways at Luke's profile, she suspected he wasn't troubled by the same sense of impending loss and regret. He was positive and excited for the next chapter in his life, talking about his new flat and job with enthusiasm, his bright blue eyes as sparkly as the stars above.

'Very beautiful indeed,' he said, his gaze locking onto hers for a lingering moment, a half-smile on his lips. The way he said it suggested he could be talking about her rather than the setting, or perhaps she was imagining that. Then he leaned forward and kissed her tenderly on the forehead, the sensation of his mouth upon her skin sending a shiver down her spine. 'Come on,' he said, taking her hand in his. 'Let's go and have a look around the stables.'

Together with their group of friends, they mooched slowly across to the beautifully restored stable blocks, the melodious tones of the carol singers accompanying them. Rhi looked on fondly at the parents with their children, their excitement palpable in the air, and felt thrilled to be part of such a lovely festive occasion. The sense of belonging wrapped her in a warm hug. Suddenly, in front of her, Rosie let out a squeal of delight.

'Nanna, Nanna, it's snowing.' The little girl lifted her face to the sky, catching light feathery snowflakes on her cheeks.

'My goodness, so it is. I never expected that. Isn't it lovely?' So lovely, in fact, that Lizzie had to wonder if Jackson hadn't arranged it specially, an expensive special effect designed to enthral his guests. Lizzie held up her palms to the air to make absolutely sure that what she was seeing was real, sharing Rosie's infectious enthusiasm at the sensation of the snow on her skin. It was a light, swirly, dancing snowfall that had no intention of settling on the ground, but it was enough to make her granddaughter's Christmas wish come true, and anything that made Rosie happy made Lizzie happy too.

As they walked through the opened double doors to the stables, they were greeted by the scent of seasonal spices wafting in the air: gingerbread, cinnamon, roast chestnuts and mulled wine.

'This looks amazing,' said Katy, peering along the central walkway where the overhead oak beams were festooned with garlands of holly and berries. There were several stable units, all similarly decorated with foliage, and abuzz with activity; one offering warm drinks with a selection of delicious sweet treats, another serving mugs of mulled wine, and others selling quirky gifts and decorations.

'Who fancies a hot chocolate?' Katy asked, spotting a fellow reveller carrying a mug overflowing with whipped cream and fluffy marshmallows.

'I want to see the donkey and the pony first, Mummy. Please!'

'Come on then,' said Katy, laughing, the rest of the group following behind. They made their way along the length of the stables, Katy taking a sneaky peek inside each one, thinking what a terrific way it was of utilising the space. Before she'd left for Australia, she'd occasionally taken a table at one of the local craft fayres, selling her floral illustrations in frames and her handmade greetings cards and bookmarks. She'd always enjoyed those occasions as there was a lovely atmosphere between the crafters and her items were always popular with the visitors. She'd been thinking about expanding her range of products when the job in

Australia came up for Brad, and all of Katy's personal plans had fallen by the wayside. Now, she felt excited at the idea of setting up her small business again. It might never bring her in a fortune, but it offered a welcome outlet for her creative skills. As much as she loved Brad and the children, they'd somehow become the whole focus of her life and she'd lost sight of herself and her own needs.

'Mummy, Mummy!' Rosie's cries interrupted her musings. 'It's here, the donkey and the horsey.' Rosie had run along to the end of the block and was peering through the wooden struts to the stable, jumping up and down excitedly at seeing the animals mooching around happily, seemingly unperturbed by the constant flow of visitors. At the back of the stable was a wooden nativity scene displayed on a wooden plinth.

'Can you see the baby Jesus?' Katy said, pointing to show her, but Rosie's attention was distracted by the two cute animals, a light grey donkey with white markings on its nose and legs, and a sturdy Shetland pony that was cream in colour with large wide eyes, a long straight mane and a lively expression.

'Aren't they adorable?' Katy said, lifting Rosie up into her arms and beckoning the animals over with a clicking of her tongue. Bill pushed the buggy right up to the side of the stable so that Pip could see too. Tentatively, Rosie reached out to pat the pony's head and giggled as the pony bobbed its head up and down in a friendly greeting. The others in the group peered into the stable, just as entranced as Rosie. Sam put an arm round Abbey's shoulder, pulling her into his side, and Luke squeezed Rhi's hand tight. Lizzie glanced at Bill, who gave her a friendly little wink.

'This one's name is Twinkle,' said Rosie, patting the donkey on the head, with all the gravitas of an official naming ceremony, 'and this one is called… Little Star,' she declared triumphantly.

'Twinkle and Little Star,' said Abbey, with a big grin. 'They sound like perfect names.'

'We have to tell the man,' insisted Rosie, wriggling in her mum's arms, 'because he doesn't know their names. And it's not very nice to not have a proper name.' Katy popped her daughter back down on the floor and took hold of her hand.

'Hopefully we'll find him on the way out and you can tell him what you think their names should be.'

'No, Mummy,' Rosie pleaded, a touch of impatience reaching her voice. 'We have to see him now and tell him.'

Thankfully, at that moment, Sam leaned forward and put his hand on Katy's shoulder, turning her in the direction of the opened doors where Jackson was making his entrance. As if greeting an old friend, she lifted her arm and beckoned him over. Immediately his face lit up in a smile and he wandered across.

'Ah, I see you've met the newest members of the Primrose Hall family. What do you think?'

'They're very cute, and Rosie's already decided on their names. I hope you meant what you said earlier,' Katy said half-jokingly.

'Of course I did. Rosie will be doing me a big favour.'

The little girl had been looking up eagerly at Jackson, waiting for her opportunity to speak. He bent down on his haunches so that he could hear Rosie properly amongst the excited hubbub all around them.

'Twinkle!' she called gleefully, pointing at the donkey. 'And Little Star!' She ran round the side of the stable to point at the pony, just in case Jackson was in any doubt as to who she might be talking about.

'What fab names,' he said genuinely. 'Thank you. You've saved me a job and I'm not sure I could have come up with two such perfect names.'

Rosie beamed proudly, and all the adults looked on with warm appreciation. If Jackson was on a mission to win the local community over, then he'd certainly succeeded with his charm offensive as far as they were all concerned and in particular with one delighted little girl.

22

Abbey had a big smile on her face as she cupped her hands around a warming mug of hot chocolate topped with whipped cream and marshmallows. It felt hugely decadent, but she didn't care as it was so delicious and, besides, if you couldn't indulge at Christmas, when could you? Already, with still a week to go to the big day, Abbey knew that this year, with Sam at her side, was going to be the best Christmas in years.

Looking at Sam's handsome profile beside her as they stood outside the stables, tucking into sausage rolls and mince pies, Abbey thought how lucky she was to have had Sam come into her life at a time when she'd most needed her faith in men restored.

'We're good, aren't we, Sam?' she said, surprising herself with the question.

'What kind of question is that?' he said, with that beaming smile that was reassurance enough. 'We're great, Abbey.' He kissed the hair on top of her head.

Okay, so they might have just experienced their first major falling out but that was because of misunderstandings and assumptions on both their parts. In the last few days, they'd spoken about it, argued about it and even laughed about it. They'd promised to communicate with each other better in the future to avoid anything similar happening again. In a way, Abbey was relieved that they'd got their first argument behind them. It was bound to have happened at some point. Now they could forget about it and move on.

Deep down, she knew that Sam was a really genuine guy. Kind, caring and thoughtful, characteristics that, she realised now, her ex Jason hadn't really possessed. Now, standing in the beautiful grounds of Primrose Hall with a light fluttering of snow falling on their faces, Sam looked down at her, a crooked smile on his lips, and gave a tiny wink, which lifted her heart. It felt wholly intimate, as though it was just the two of them, alone against the backdrop of the magnificent house. She leaned into his side, relishing the sensation of his arm around her shoulder as an image of that sparkly ring she'd discovered under the bed popped into her mind. Had she imagined that? No, she really hadn't, although she still found it hard to make sense of what it meant. Was Sam really intending to propose over the holidays?

'Isn't it romantic?' she sighed, taking in the view around them.

'It is... I guess. Although, as you know, I'm hardly the most romantic man in the world.'

Her gaze snagged on his. He was teasing her, downplaying his true romantic intent so that when the proposal came, it would be a complete and utter surprise to her. Only a true romantic would have a big surprise in store of the kind Sam was planning. Besides, however much Abbey was eagerly anticipating Sam's romantic gesture, she knew romance wasn't about those big declarations of love. It was more about the little things; a mug of tea delivered to the bedside table first thing, the car defrosted before she headed off to work on a wintery morning, an appreciative comment about her appearance when she least expected it. It was those small gestures that made her feel so loved and appreciated.

'I think you're much more romantic than you're letting on,' she said, looking up at him now. 'You're a big softie at heart, that's for sure.'

'Well, as long as you keep that fact to yourself,' he said, brushing a finger against her nose. 'I have my manly image to maintain,' he said, adopting an hysterically deep voice that made her giggle.

Abbey suspected Rhi was feeling the romance of the occasion too as she and Luke had spent the entire evening holding hands, sharing loving gazes and whispering into each other's ears, while giggling like a pair of lovestruck teenagers. It was heart-warming to see Rhi so happy. She and Luke made a great couple, and Abbey hoped they'd be able to keep seeing each other once Luke moved away. She definitely needed a girly catch-up with Rhi soon to find out all the latest news.

'I hope Jackson makes this an annual event,' Rhi commented.

'I can't see why he wouldn't,' Sam said, looking around him. 'Especially after the success of tonight. Word will spread and I'll bet they'll be back bigger and better next year.'

'I really hope so,' said Rhi. 'Sounds as though Jackson wants to place himself at the centre of the community. I'm looking forward to seeing what other events he will put on here.'

'Well, if this happens again next year, then we should make it a new tradition to come along as a group,' suggested Lizzie.

'I'd love that. It would be something for the children to look forward to and next year Brad will be with us too. Besides,' said Katy, giving Rosie's hand a little squeeze, 'we'll need to find out how Twinkle and Little Star are getting on, won't we?'

'Yay! Twinkle, twinkle, little star…' Rosie's impromptu rendition of the nursery rhyme had everyone smiling.

'I wonder if you'll be able to come along next year,' said Rhi quietly, looking up at Luke.

'Are you kidding? Just try and keep me away. I'm sure I'll be back to stay with my folks over Christmas, which will be a great opportunity to catch up with all my old friends.' He tipped up her chin with a finger, and she forced a smile in return. Is that all she was to him, a friend? With some obvious benefits now too. Would he be back next Christmas with someone else in tow, someone special, someone more than just a friend?

The cold air whipped around her skin and her eyes stung, although she knew she couldn't blame that entirely on the chill. She delved into her pocket for a tissue and blew her nose noisily as a distraction, gathering her feelings close. Did Luke really have no idea how much he'd come to mean to her?

There was no point in imagining where they might be in a year's time, because who knew what fate had in store for them all, although she could make a pretty good guess on behalf of her friends. Sam and Abbey would be as strong as ever and probably planning the next step in their relationship, maybe a wedding or a baby. Lizzie and Bill would still be as much in love, laughing and joking all the time, making the most of every moment they shared together. Katy would be settled in a new home with Brad and the children. That only left Rhi and Luke.

Hopefully her business would have taken off and she would have a string of satisfied customers. She would have her own place to live by then, somewhere cosy, a little sanctuary where she would surround herself with books and crocheted blankets and fairy lights. Whether or not Luke would still play a part in her life, she didn't know, but she really hoped that he might. Whatever he was doing, she knew he would be making a success of it because that was the type of person he was, forward-thinking, positive and determined to make the most of the opportunities that came his way. She sighed, as she looked up at him longingly, and he planted a kiss on her forehead, the look in his eyes telling her that he knew exactly what she was thinking. It would be more than she could hope for that Luke really could know her mind. Then he might actually be able to put her out of her misery.

'We should be making a move,' said Lizzie. 'We need to get these little ones to bed. What a lovely evening it's been. Next time we see you all will be next Saturday at mine. We're really looking forward to it, aren't we, Bill?' she said, squeezing his hand.

'So are we,' said Abbey, 'although I can hardly believe it's only a week until Christmas.' It had been a whirlwind of a year and Abbey was just pleased that she'd made it here with Sam, her dad and her friends.

'I can't wait,' piped up Rosie. 'Santa is coming to bring us all presents,' she said gleefully.

'That's right, and I can't wait either,' said Rhi, ruffling the bobble on Rosie's hat. A week closer to Christmas meant a week nearer to Luke moving away, but she would ignore that thought for now. There was still plenty of time for kisses under the mistletoe and making memories. Christmas was full of surprises and magic, whether you were three or coming up to twenty-three.

Back at Lizzie's place, with the children exhausted after visiting Primrose Hall and tucked up safely in bed, Bill poured himself and Lizzie a small Baileys on the rocks, while Katy pottered about upstairs, getting herself ready for bed.

'Thanks, Bill,' said Lizzie, tucking her legs up beneath her on the sofa and taking a sip.

'My pleasure,' he said, sitting down beside her and chinking his glass against hers. He placed his arm around her shoulder. 'Cheers.'

'Oh, I don't mean the drink, lovely though this is.' She took another sip, before turning her head and looking up into his eyes. 'I meant you, thank you,' she squeezed his arm affectionately, 'for everything.' Bill's eyes grew wide, his expression one of questioning bemusement. 'For all that you do for me and Katy, and the grandchildren,' she explained. 'It's funny, but it's as though you've always been in our lives. When I think back to the last couple of Christmases, when I spent most of the time on my own, I can remember how sad and miserable I felt. Katy was living abroad then, and I was left alone with my memories of David, thinking I would never be really happy again. Then, unexpectedly, you and Abbey turned up in my life, and I got to know Rhi and Luke too, and I can't tell you what a difference it's made to my life. It's as though I've discovered another part to my family. Most of all, though, I'm grateful that I found you, Bill. Everything is better with you at my side.'

'Well, let me tell you that the feeling is entirely mutual.' He chuckled, kissing her lightly on the forehead. 'You've welcomed me into your heart and your home and I feel as if I've been given a new lease of life. I thought the best years of my life were behind me, but you came along and lit up my entire world. It's so wonderful to be part of family life again. I think it's taken us both by surprise, hasn't it? We're lucky. We both had fantastic marriages and we both know the pain of losing that special person in our lives, so to have a second chance at happiness is more than I could ever have wished for.'

'Too true.' They sat snuggled together in companionable silence for a few moments, with Bill lightly stroking Lizzie's arm. 'It looks as though Abbey and Sam are back on track too. I'm glad they've sorted out that little misunderstanding. Young love, eh?'

she said with a chuckle. 'And what about Luke and Rhi? I think there was definitely some Christmas magic at work tonight because those two looked very much in love.'

'I noticed that. They're great kids. I hope it works out for them.'

'Me too,' said Lizzie. 'Honestly, Bill, Christmas this year, with Katy and the children home, has already turned out to be the best one in years.'

'It really has.' Bill smiled, giving her another squeeze. It just goes to show that Christmas dreams can come true, thought Lizzie. All you have to do is believe.

23

Abbey poured herself a cup of tea and went and sat down beside Stella Darling. She'd thoroughly enjoyed watching the last twenty minutes of *The Polar Express* with some of the residents in the main lounge. A well-deserved opportunity to have a breather. Each afternoon this week, a different Christmas film had been showing and it had proved very popular with the residents, even if a great deal of them ended up nodding off during the film. In fairness, had Abbey been at home, curled up on the sofa, she too would have succumbed to a nap.

'How are you, my lovely?' Stella asked, taking hold of Abbey's hand and giving it a friendly pat. Out of all of Rushmere Lodge's residents, Stella had to be the most outgoing and chatty. Her grey-green eyes sparkled with curiosity and intelligence, and she was always eager and interested to know what was going on in everyone's lives.

'Good. It's nice to sit down and share a cuppa with you, Stella. I love all the Christmas films, even if I've seen them plenty of times before. Shall we have one of these chocolate biscuits?' Abbey picked up the plate and offered it to Stella, who duly took one. 'I was just thinking about what I still need to do for Christmas, but I've just realised I'm pretty much ready for the celebrations. I've delivered all of my cards and done all of the wrapping. I've bought the choccies and the booze too, so we're all sorted.'

'It's such a busy time, I remember all too well. I expect you'll be spending it with your young man, the one with the reindeer jumper?'

'No, that was Matt,' Abbey quickly corrected her. 'He's the general manager of the care homes? He came and introduced himself the other week. Sam is my boyfriend, he's been here a couple of times with his dog. Do you remember, he showed us around Primrose Woods in the summer?'

'Oh, of course, Lady, she's such a sweetheart. And Sam, I'm very fond of that young man. You must admit the pair of them are quite similar, him and the other one, no surprise I get them muddled up. Mind you, it never hurts to have more than one man in tow.'

She twisted her lips together, suppressing a smile, and Abbey suspected Stella had known all along who she was talking about. She was just being mischievous, but then again, you could be forgiven for getting Sam and Matt confused.

'You're a very bad woman, Stella Darling!'

'I'm only teasing,' she giggled. 'Sam is lovely, and I've noticed that twinkle in your eye, ever since you've been together. Your happiness radiates about this place these days, we've all noticed it. You've got a good one there. Nothing less than you deserve, though.'

'I know. I feel very lucky to have found him, especially after what happened earlier in the year.' Abbey rolled her eyes, and Stella shook her head, tutting in sympathy. 'We're really looking forward to spending our first Christmas together.'

'The first of many together, I hope,' said Stella kindly.

'I hope so too.' Abbey squeezed Stella's hand. How she wished she could confide in her, tell her what she'd found underneath the bed that day and how she was eagerly anticipating Sam's proposal. Stella would have squealed with delight, wanting to know all the details. But however much she loved Stella, she knew she had to keep on the right side of professionalism. Besides, Stella was such an outrageous gossip that any secrets Abbey might divulge wouldn't stay secret for long.

'Anyway,' she said, eager to move the conversation on to safer territory. 'I meant to tell you we went to Primrose Hall on Saturday night. They had carollers and a small band in the grounds and served mince pies and mulled wine too. We got to see the renovated house up close. Gosh, they have done an amazing job, it looked beautiful, especially with all the Christmas lights on it.'

'I know they've been talking about doing the old place up for years. It's good they've finally got round to it.'

'We met the new owners too, Jackson and his partner Tara, they make quite the glamorous couple. He's from around here, went to one of the local schools, but left to make a career in London. Apparently, he made an awful lot of money in the City. I did a bit of Googling about him when we got home. Anyway, he's always had a soft spot for Primrose Hall, he used to play in the grounds when he was a kid and has spent the last couple of years overseeing the rebuild. He's intending to open up the grounds a few times in the year to the local community. They have a lovely stable block and each of the renovated stables can be used as little sales units for different craftspeople or food outlets. I think it's very exciting what they have planned.'

'It does sound good. See if you can arrange a visit for us sometime,' said Stella, who was never one to miss out on any opportunity going. 'I'd love to see it too.'

'Funnily enough, Stella, I had the very same idea. It would make an ideal outing as it's not very far, but it's in such a beautiful setting. I took Jackson's card, so I'll give him a call in the new year to see if we can get something in the diary.'

After catching up with some of the other residents as they enjoyed their afternoon tea and sticky gingerbread, Abbey returned to her office and just caught Lydia as she was pulling on her coat before leaving for home.

'Oh, just to let you know, Christine rang this afternoon. Matt's had a bereavement in his family so he's taking some time off work. He won't be back until after Christmas so if there's anything important, she said to contact her.'

'Of course.' Abbey knew how efficient Matt's assistant was, so there were no concerns on that front, but she felt a wave of sympathy for Matt. She'd barely given him a second thought since he called into the office last week. 'Do we know who it was?'

'His mum, apparently.'

'Oh!' Abbey's stomach twisted involuntarily at the thought of Matt's pain. He'd mentioned over dinner how he was intending to spend Christmas with his parents, so this must have come as a huge and unexpected shock. It brought sharp reminders of when she'd lost her own mum, the numbness of those first few days, not knowing how life could ever be the same again. She sighed, before gathering herself.

'There's never a good time to lose a loved one, but it always seems that it's so much worse when it happens at Christmas. I'll pick up a card and we can send it to Christine to pass on to Matt.'

The news of Matt's loss played on Abbey's mind as she drove home, her own feelings of sadness bubbling beneath the surface. She still thought about her mum all the time, but these days, the memories usually made her smile, like hearing one of her mum's favourite songs on the radio, and picturing her dancing around the kitchen, a silly grin on her face. Or when one of her mum's trusty and reassuring sayings tripped off her own tongue as though it was her own. At home, she was surrounded by reminders of her mum; she particularly loved her well-thumbed cookery books and the exquisite millefiori paperweight that had always been on the old dresser when Abbey was growing up. Now it took pride of place on the front windowsill of her cottage where the light filtered through the window, picking out the coloured jewel-like glass flowers. There were plenty of framed photos of her mum too, so she felt her presence all around her, which was a huge source of comfort, but hearing Matt's news and knowing what he must be going through right at this moment brought back all the emotions she'd felt so strongly at the time of her mum's passing.

She was relieved to get home, back to the sanctuary of the cottage, closing the door on the dark and dank December evening, finding reassurance in Sam's arms. The cottage, with the Christmas tree lit up in the window, the festive cards dotted on the mantlepiece and the fire crackling in the hearth, wrapped her in a warm welcoming embrace.

'Bad day?' Sam asked, knowing instinctively something was wrong. He greeted her with a hug before peeling his chest away to look into her eyes.

'Kind of. Nothing a cuddle won't make better.' She returned to the safety of Sam's arms, squeezing him tight, not wanting to ever let him go. Her emotions were so close to the surface she had to fight back the tears. Matt's news today had reminded her how fragile life was, how easily her newfound happiness could be snatched away. She couldn't take anything for granted and needed to make the most of every moment with Sam, and with her dad, and all of those people she loved most in the world.

'Let's have a drink,' she suggested, as his gaze appraised her thoughtfully.

While Sam made gin and tonics for them both, she kicked off her shoes and gave in to Lady's insistent demands for attention. She smiled, exhaling a sigh of relief. You couldn't stay sad for long with a faithful and loving dog around.

'Do you want to tell me about it?' Sam asked, handing her a glass tinkling with ice and lemon. She took a sip, running her tongue around her lips, instantly appreciating its restorative effect. She remembered how she'd vowed never to utter Matt's name in Sam's presence again, but of course she hadn't reckoned on learning something quite so personal about Matt. She took a deep breath.

'Lydia heard from Christine today, Matt's secretary, to tell us that his mum has died, so he's going to be out of office until after Christmas. It's funny, I don't know Matt that well and certainly not his mum, but the suddenness of the news took my breath away. It took me back to that time when we lost Mum, and those feelings of grief and shock took hold of me again. You think you've come so far, that you're over the worst of it and that you're coming out the other side, when something like this can throw you totally off-balance again.' She lifted her lashes to look up at him, wondering if the mention of Matt's name had reignited the anger he'd shown before, but all she saw in those deep brown eyes now was kindness and understanding.

'Oh, Abbs, come here.' He wrapped her in his embrace and she was able to let go, the emotion she'd been holding on to for the last couple of hours escaping in a river of soft tears rolling down her cheeks.

'Look at me,' she said, mopping up her tears with the heel of her hand. 'I'm just being silly.'

Sam reached for a tissue from the box on the worktop, taking over the job, gently wiping away her tears.

'Not silly at all. Totally understandable. Grief has a habit of doing that to you, catching you unawares.' He stroked his hand over her hair, kissing the top of her head. 'Matt, though? I'm sorry to hear that. I only met his mum a couple of times, but I remember her as being a lovely lady. She made the effort to come to my mum's funeral, actually, but I never spoke to her. I wish I had, but it was a difficult time, as you can imagine.'

She nodded, knowing he wasn't talking solely about his mum's passing, but also the recent break-up with Sophie when he'd lost Matt as his best friend at the same time.

'Oh, sorry, Sam, this must bring up bad memories for you as well, but I thought I should tell you.'

'I'm glad you did. The other night, that was a moment of madness. It won't happen again, but you must never think you can't talk to me.' He sighed, brushing away the dampness from her cheeks. 'Puts things into perspective, I guess. You and I both know the pain of losing our mums. It creates a gap that can never be filled. Your heart can only go out to anybody going through the same.'

Abbey relaxed into his arms again, her head resting on his chest.

'It's a reminder of just how fragile life is,' she whispered, 'how things can change in a heartbeat.'

'It is, and I understand that,' agreed Sam, 'but you can't live with that fear.' He tipped up her chin with a finger, his gaze roaming her features. 'You just have to acknowledge those feelings and then put them to one side. We owe it to our mums to live our best lives and to be happy, it's what they would want for us.'

'You're right.' She breathed a huge sigh of relief. Sam had a way of knowing exactly the right thing to say which always made her feel better. Her tears had dried now, just talking through her feelings with Sam had lifted her mood and given her a different perspective on the situation.

'Besides, you and I have so much to look forward to together,' said Sam. 'Dinner tonight... Christmas, the rest of our lives together.' Lady thumped her tail on the floor beside them, as if in total agreement.

That sounded pretty good. The casual way he said it, as though it was a given and that nothing could possibly get in the way of their future. If anything, the misunderstandings of the last few days had given them a deeper understanding of each other and only brought them closer together.

'When you're next in contact with Matt, pass on my condolences to him, won't you?' He squeezed her hand and smiled.

'Of course I will,' she said, feeling relieved, glad that Sam's compassion for an old friend was greater than his antagonism towards him.

24

'Hello, lovely!'

Abbey's face lit up to see Rhi, who was wrapped up in her fur-lined parka, her face glowing beneath all her layers, her arms held wide, inviting a big hug. Before Rhi's trip to Australia, the pair of them had met regularly at Primrose Woods to walk one of the several trails around the park, where they would gossip and laugh, offer advice if it was sought or just listen if a sympathetic ear was required. Abbey had missed those times, so it was good to be back in the familiar routine. The habit had stemmed from the very first time they'd met, when Rhi had tracked Abbey down, following her into the park with the sole intention of apologising to Abbey for inadvertently having fallen for Abbey's fiancé, Jason. Rhi had felt awful and humiliated when she discovered that Jason was due to be married in a few weeks' time, and was compelled to find Abbey to tell her that she would never have got involved with him in the first place if she'd known the full story.

That day was full of hurt, anger and recriminations, and Abbey had just wanted this young, beautiful and wilful girl to say what she'd come to say and then leave. She'd believed she'd caused enough damage as it was, but Abbey hadn't banked on Rhi's persistence and determination, and her refusal to fade into the background. Not long afterwards, they found themselves on the same quiz team and slowly an unlikely friendship formed. Now, when they got together, they barely ever mentioned Jason and if they did it was only ever in passing, peppered with a good dose of ridicule and scorn. They believed they'd had a lucky escape from the man who had lied to them both and they were much happier now at not having him in their lives any more.

'Come on, let's walk before we freeze to death,' said Abbey, linking her arm through Rhi's. 'How are you? Wasn't Saturday night fun at Primrose Hall?'

'It really was. I loved it! It was such a beautiful and magical setting and really set the mood for Christmas. It was great to see everyone too, especially little Rosie. Didn't she have the best time, especially when she got to name the donkey and the pony? It was so sweet seeing her little face light up. Such a lovely thing for Jackson to do.'

'Hmmm, yes, I thought Jackson played the part of country squire to perfection.'

'Didn't he just?' Rhi's eyes lit up mischievously. 'He's very easy on the eye, isn't he?'

'I should say so,' said Abbey, tapping her chest theatrically to slow her heartbeat. 'Good-looking, rich and charming, I think he's a very welcome addition to the area. It's great what he has planned for the stables, it'll be a great facility for the local community.'

'And any excuse to see Jackson again has to be a good thing, right?' Rhi's laughter rippled through the trees around them, and Abbey joined in. It was bracingly cold, and even though the sun was low in the sky, filtering through the trees, it had little effect upon the temperature.

'Anyway, I thought you only had eyes for one man at the moment. It was great to see you and Luke getting on so well the other night... so touchy-feely.'

'Yes,' Rhi sighed. 'After all these months, we finally get together just as he's about to move to away. Our timing's not great, is it? I really like him, Abbey. I just wish we could have more time together before he leaves.'

'But it doesn't have to be the end for you and him, does it? Couldn't you make it work at a distance if that's what you both want?'

'That's the thing, I'm not sure it is what Luke wants. Don't get me wrong, he's been great, and I know he really likes me too, but we've not really talked about what happens after he moves. He's just said let's see how it goes. Once he moves away, settles into his new job and makes new friends, I think he'll probably move on emotionally too.'

'Can't you talk to him about it?'

'What, and risk spoiling the time that we do have left together? I think I'd probably get too upset, and I don't want to put that kind of pressure on Luke. I think both of us know in our heart of hearts that it can only ever be a fling. There were times when we might have got together in the past, but it didn't happen for one reason or another, and now, well, we're just enjoying the moment.'

'But you two are so good together, made for each other, I'd say,' said Abbey. 'It would be a shame to throw away what you have together for the sake of a few miles. Besides, for purely selfish reasons, I want you two to stay together. I love how things are between us in our little friendship group and don't want anything to change.'

Rhi gave a resigned shrug, grateful that Abbey saw the situation in the same light and shared her frustration too. If only Luke would see it in the same way too.

'Anyway,' Rhi said, turning to her friend. 'We've not had a chance to catch up properly after what happened in the pub last week. Is everything okay now? You and Sam seemed pretty good together on Saturday.'

'Yeah.' Abbey exhaled a big breath through pursed lips and shook her head dramatically. 'I think we're back on track now, but it was pretty awful at the time. It came out of the blue. I'd never seen Sam like that before, he was furious, and the worst part about it was that I had no idea what it was all about. I thought it was something I'd done or that I'd suddenly discovered that Sam had this awful jealous streak. It turns out that Matt, the guy I went out to dinner with that night, the general manager of the care homes, my boss, no less, is in fact Sam's ex-best friend. Ex-friend because he went off with Sam's girlfriend. They'd all been at university together. I suppose it was a huge shock for Sam, running into Matt again like that.'

'Blimey. I guess it explains why he reacted so strongly.'

'Yeah, I couldn't understand it at first and wondered if it was because he'd never really got over losing his girlfriend, but I think it just brought up a whole raft of bad memories for him. It was just a little while later that his mum died too, so it was an especially bleak time for him.'

Thinking about how upset and hurt Sam must have been pulled at her insides now. Sam rarely displayed his innermost feelings, he gave off an aura of being strong, capable and unsentimental, so to see that vulnerable side of him had only increased her love and protectiveness of him.

'Fingers crossed, we've worked it through and it's all sorted now. I'm not sure I'll be inviting the boss round to dinner anytime soon, but we can live with that.'

Rhi laughed. They walked on, arm in arm, stopping on the little rickety bridge that crossed the stream as they always did. How Abbey would love to tell Rhi her suspicions that Sam was planning to propose, but she felt guilty enough at her own underhandedness in discovering that fact, so keeping the news to herself was her penance.

'I love this place, don't you?' Rhi exhaled, spreading her arms wide and looking up at the bare trees. 'Every time I come here, I find something new to look at, something I haven't noticed before. Being in the woods is very therapeutic. It always lifts my mood.'

'Me too,' said Abbey. 'It's definitely my happy place. If ever I have a bad day at work or there's something else troubling me, then the first thing I will want to do is come over here. Being amongst the trees, seeing the squirrels, and hearing the birds helps me forget, even if just for an hour or so, any problems going on outside of the park. I don't want to sound like a tree hugger, but sometimes when I've been really low, it's felt as though the trees have wrapped their branches around me in a reassuring embrace and whispered that everything will work out for me in the end. Ha, do you think I'm mad?'

'Not at all. I totally get that.' Rhi laid a hand on Abbey's arm. 'Let's not forget it's where we first met too, so that's another good reason for it being a special place to us both.'

As they walked around the lake, passing Primrose Hall on the other side of the fence, looking magnificent in the winter sun, they spotted a Dalmatian up ahead, just emerging from the water. He was all frisky from his dip and acting goofy, running around in circles, spraying water everywhere.

'Bertie, come here!' called its owner to no avail, as it looked intent on causing as much trouble as it possibly could. As they got closer, Abbey realised with a sense of dread that she might

soon have a very close encounter with a very sopping wet dog.
'Bertie!' cried the owner again. 'Oh, crap, I am so sorry. Look what he's... Abbey...?'

Abbey looked up from where she'd been examining the muddy footprints left on her coat by the dog, who was greeting her like she was a long-lost friend.

'Pia! How are you? I didn't realise you had a dog,' she said, laughing.

'I don't,' she said wryly. 'He belongs to my neighbour who's not too mobile at the moment, so I'm helping her out. Sorry about Bertie. Sometimes he forgets his manners.'

Didn't that sound just like Pia? She was always helping out or caring for someone, running errands, popping in on her neighbours or tending to their animals. It really had been far too long since they'd last had a proper catch-up. After Pia managed to grab Bertie and put him on the lead, the two old friends hugged.

'Don't worry, I'm used to over-friendly dogs. Sam has a springer spaniel who takes liberties all the time.'

'Oh, yes, your new man! How's it going?'

'Good, we're very happy together. It's still early days, but I'm in a much better place than I was this time last year.'

'That's good to hear. I never did like Jason,' said Pia, with a curl of her lip.

'And you only decide to tell me that now!' Abbey said, in mock despair.

'Well, I could hardly say anything while you were with him. I was just very relieved when you called the wedding off.' Pia had been a great support at the time. She'd sent messages and kept in touch on an almost daily basis, even though she was nursing her mum through the last stages of her illness at the time.

'If it makes you feel any better,' Rhi said to Pia with a wide grin, 'I thought he was a dickhead too.' Abbey laughed, taking the opportunity to introduce her friends to one another.

'I bumped into Connor and Ruby the other night. They said you'll be selling the house soon.'

'Yep, we'll have to,' said Pia, with a flicker of sadness. 'Connor and Ruby want to move out of their rented flat and buy a place, hopefully before the wedding, and I'll need to find somewhere of my own too. Next year will be my year, Abbey. I'm going to find a job, a place to live and who knows, maybe even meet a man, preferably a rich one. Well, a bit of positive thinking never hurt anyone.'

'Well, it's about time,' Abbey said, with a fond smile, as she stroked Pia's arm. 'Let's get a date in the diary for a coffee in the first week of January or even a walk with our two mad hounds.'

'I'd like that,' said Pia, as she waved goodbye, hanging on for dear life to Bertie's lead, as he dragged her in the opposite direction.

Later Abbey and Rhi caught up with Lizzie at the Treetops Café. She joined them at their table with their order of cinnamon lattes and hot buttered teacakes.

'We've had a lovely walk, even though it was pretty nippy out there. I met one of my old friends, got far too close to a wet and smelly Dalmatian and then Rhi and I have been reminiscing over everything that's happened this last year.'

'It feels as though we've all known each other for years,' said Lizzie, biting her teacake with gusto. 'The boys too.'

Abbey smiled, glancing across at Rhi, delighting in the way Lizzie always referred to Bill, Sam and Luke as the boys.

'I had a couple of miserable years after David died, being on my own for the first time in thirty-plus years. Then, with Katy moving to the other side of the world, I felt so lonely. It was only this place, and Sam and my customers, that kept me going. But this year, meeting you both and the others, has really opened up my world. I would never have believed it could happen. Being with Bill too, well, it's such a lovely surprise. Just goes to show that you're never too old to fall in love.' She leaned across and tapped them both fondly on their hands.

Abbey pulled her hand out from beneath Lizzie's and laid it on top, and Rhi did the same, the three women's hands locked in sisterly support. They might be of different ages, different generations even, but their differences, their individual strengths and weaknesses, only enhanced their newfound friendship.

'I started the year with great plans to marry my fiancé and am ending it madly in love with another man,' said Abbey. 'When I say it like that, it sounds terrible, but I'm just relieved I didn't make the biggest mistake of my life.'

'Sometimes what seems like the worst thing that could happen to us turns out to be the best thing for us in the long run. The universe works in peculiar ways,' said Lizzie. 'And who knows, maybe there will be another wedding in the offing very soon!'

'Lizzie! Now you're getting carried away.' Thank goodness Lizzie couldn't hear the thump of Abbey's heartbeat or see the way her palms had grown clammy. Lizzie was exchanging mischievous looks with Rhi. Lizzie and Sam were very close, did Lizzie know something she wasn't letting on about?

'I remember you telling us when we had lunch that day, the day that you were due to be married, that if there should ever be another wedding for you, then you would invite us all along. I was just wondering if I should get myself a new hat, ready for the occasion, that's all?'

Abbey laughed. She could remember saying that, but only flippantly, never believing for one moment that there would be another wedding and certainly not with the extremely attractive man she'd only just met who was funny, charming and entertaining, totally distracting her from any reminders of what she should have been doing that day, marrying another man. It was enough to send anyone's head into a spin. So maybe she'd got carried away by the occasion, drunk too much wine, laughed far too loudly, but surely on such an auspicious occasion those were all the things she was supposed to do, and it had given her wonderful memories of her very nearly wedding day.

Now, back in the moment with her good friends, she glanced across at Rhi for some more moral support, but her younger friend only raised her eyebrows. 'Well, it's not the worst idea I've ever heard,' Rhi said, with a shrug, and although Abbey secretly agreed, she shook her head, tutting, as though it was a ridiculous thought. She knew that Lizzie might soon be choosing a hat for that special occasion, after all, and however much she wanted to spill the beans, Abbey knew she would have to keep her thoughts to herself, for the time being, at least. Just until Sam had proposed – which wouldn't be very long now, she thought, anticipating the best Christmas present ever – then she would be shouting her news to the whole world.

25

Rhi peered out of the window of the taxi as the car pulled up outside Lizzie's house, thinking how pretty the street looked with all the houses aglow, shimmering with Christmas lights and decorations, a sense of expectation tangible in the December night sky. She might be in her twenties, but she still felt the same sense of awe and wonder as a small girl on Christmas Eve, awaiting Santa's arrival.

'That looks to be Abbey and Sam in front,' she said to Luke, as they climbed out of the car. Lady jumped out of the taxi first, her nose immediately to the ground, before she noticed Rhi and Luke approaching, and wagged her tail furiously in greeting.

'Hello, you.' Rhi bent down to greet the excitable dog, tickling her under her chin.

The couples hugged each other, their mood already giddy at their anticipation of a good evening ahead. Both Sam and Luke were clutching bottles of booze, Rhi held a beautiful blowsy poinsettia plant in her arms and Abbey carried a tin of her home-made mince pies.

'Brrr, it's freezing.' Rhi shivered. 'Quick, let's get inside.'

'You know, I think we might get a snowfall tonight.' Sam stopped halfway down the front path, looking up at the sky. 'I've been saying it all day. You can feel it building in the air.'

'That's just wishful thinking on your part,' Abbey teased Sam. 'Next you'll be saying that you can see Father Christmas up there flying past on his sleigh.'

Inside, Lizzy and Bill greeted them warmly and poured glasses of sparkling wine for the girls and beers for the guys. Rosie squealed on seeing Lady and hung her arms around the dog's neck, following Lady around the room, as she sniffed her way around every nook and cranny, making herself very much at home. Knowing it would be a late night, Lizzie had insisted Sam brought her along this evening.

Once Rosie had finished petting Lady and the dog was sitting patiently in front of Bill, obviously believing he was her best bet for receiving a treat, Rosie grabbed hold of Sam's hand and led him in the direction of the fireplace.

'Look! These are for Santa. Mince pie and beer. You mustn't eat them. And the carrot and water is for Rudolph.' She showed him proudly, her little face beaming, as she stood there in her cute reindeer pyjamas, looking adorable. 'They're not for you,' she reiterated, addressing the whole group this time.

'Don't worry, we won't touch them,' said Luke kindly.

'I have a *big* stocking.' Rosie held out her arms wide. 'And Pip does too, in the bedroom.' She gave a little dance on tiptoes, her face a picture of excitement. 'Santa is coming!'

'He is, but remember what I told you,' said Katy. 'Santa won't come until you're fast asleep so you can stay up for a little while, have a drink and a biscuit with us, but then you must get upstairs to sleep.'

'Okaaaaaay.' Rosie couldn't keep still, she danced all around the living room, skipped around the tree, and giggled joyously, her laughter infectious. She ran across to the front windows, peeking through the curtains, and peering up at the night sky.

'I think I can see him,' she squealed. 'Brrr.' She wriggled on the spot. 'I think the snow is coming too.'

Lizzie exchanged a smile with Katy. Rosie hadn't wavered in her belief that she would wake up to snow on Christmas morning. Her mum and grandma had done their best to convince her that it probably wouldn't be the case, but even they couldn't persuade little Rosie otherwise. They only hoped that with all the excitement of Santa Claus's visit, Rosie might forget about the wished-for snowfall.

'Do you know, Rosie, I think you could be right,' said Sam unhelpfully. 'You can always tell when it's about to snow. You can feel it in the atmosphere. I bet when you wake up in the morning, there'll be plenty of crisp white snow outside.'

'Yay!' cried Rosie, spinning around on the spot.

Katy gave a little internal groan. With these levels of excitement, she wondered if Rosie would ever get to sleep tonight.

'Aw, well, I don't think snow is forecast for tonight, but you never know!' Bill piped up, trying to manage expectations.

Lizzie quickly distracted Rosie with a drink and a biscuit, and a promise of presents, but only if she got to bed very soon.

Much later, with Rosie and Pip upstairs and both of them finally asleep, after several visits from Katy, Lizzie, Bill, and even Sam, Katy reappeared and breathed a huge sigh of relief.

'Fingers crossed, they'll both sleep all the way through now. They should do, they were both shattered.'

'Here, have this,' said Lizzie, handing her daughter a flute of Prosecco. 'You deserve it. Just relax now and enjoy the evening before all the madness tomorrow.'

Katy took the proffered glass and collapsed down on the sofa. Rosie wasn't the only one who was shattered. The last few days had been hectic, wrapping all the last-minute presents, helping her mum with the food shopping and preparing the vegetables for dinner tomorrow, as well as trying to keep Rosie entertained, but she'd done it, they'd made it to Christmas Eve and Katy could finally relax. All she needed to do now was fill the children's stockings hanging at the bottom of their beds, which she'd do last thing tonight just before she went to sleep. *And breathe*. A few sips of the fizzy bubbles dancing in her flute would help to give her a second wind, ready for the night's celebrations.

She loved her children with all her heart, but some days, like today, were tough. Back in Australia, Brad had usually taken care of the bed and bath routine, and he also made breakfast for everyone to give Katy a chance to get herself showered and ready for the day. She missed him so much. A pang of sadness filled her chest, but she pushed the negative thoughts away. It wasn't for much longer now.

Thank goodness her mum was around to help out. She wasn't sure how she would have managed without her these last few weeks. They'd miss having her on hand hugely when they moved out, which was looking to be in a couple of weeks' time, as Katy had heard today that her offer on a lovely three-bedroom house in the next village on a short-term let had been accepted. She'd sent the details over to Brad and he'd given them the thumbs up, but she couldn't wait to talk to him about it in more detail and make some proper plans. She'd tried calling him earlier, but his phone had gone straight to voicemail. No doubt making the most of the Christmas festivities. Never mind, they'd arranged a call for early in the morning so that he could see the children open their presents, she would just have to wait until then for their catch-up.

'There's some cheese straws straight out of the oven or some sticky chipolatas, if you fancy them.' Lizzie came out from the kitchen holding a large platter, offering a napkin to each of the guests. She chatted to each person on the way, her laughter ringing out around the room as she sashayed along to the music playing in the background. This was just one of many plates of small, delicious canapés that she produced effortlessly, the aromas emanating from the kitchen divine. If there was anything that could bring Katy round, it was her mum's cooking. She jumped up from her chair and helped herself to a honey and mustard cocktail sausage on a stick.

'I love this point on Christmas Eve.' Lizzie grinned, putting a couple more plates down on the buffet table. 'All the presents are wrapped, the vegetables are prepared for tomorrow, the shops are shut and the children are tucked up safely in bed. What could be better? Now I get to enjoy myself with all my favourite people in the world.' She wrapped an arm around her daughter's shoulder.

'Hey, guys, I hate to say I told you so, but have you seen it out here?' Sam was peering out through the front curtains, a big grin on his face as he looked over his shoulder at them.

'It's not snowing, is it?' Katy asked.

'Come and have a look.'

They all went to join him and huddled round the window, peering outside, where big fat snowflakes were dancing in the sky before tumbling to the ground in a steady onslaught.

Katy gasped.

'Wow, it looks like a Christmas card. Do you think it will last until morning?'

'Looks like it,' said Sam. 'It's settling out there and showing no sign of letting up anytime soon.'

They all stood gathered at the window, craning their heads to see the snow as though they were witnessing it for the first time, the ground covered in a smooth white crisp blanket as far as the eye could see.

'I can't remember seeing snow at Christmas before,' Rhi said, her voice full of wonderment. Luke put an arm around her shoulder and pulled her into his side and she dropped her head onto his chest, savouring the moment.

'Well, you know who we have to thank for this, don't you?' said Lizzie, laughing. 'Must have something to do with Rosie putting her wish out to the universe. The universe has clearly been listening.'

'We've all been listening to Rosie going on about it snowing at Christmas,' said Katy. 'Bless her. Wait until I tell Brad, he'll never believe it.'

'Do you think we'll be able to get home okay?' Abbey asked Sam. 'Do we need to get the taxis to come a bit earlier, they might have trouble getting through on the roads. I think this snowfall will have taken everyone by surprise.'

'Oh, you don't want to worry about that at the moment,' said Lizzie, shepherding everyone away from the curtains. 'Let me top up your drinks. We'll keep an eye on it and see if it gets any worse.' Lizzie really didn't want the evening to end before it had even started.

Bill closed the curtains on the winter wonderland outside and everyone settled on the sofas and chairs, the mood fun and convivial. Someone suggested a game of 'guess who' written on Post-it notes and stuck on people's foreheads, but Sam groaned, complaining that he wasn't nearly drunk enough for playing games. Abbey and Lizzie were doing their utmost to persuade him otherwise when they were interrupted by a knock on the door, which called a temporary halt to all their celebrations.

'I'm not sure who that could be,' said Lizzie, glancing at her watch. 'Probably one of the neighbours.' She jumped up from her seat and hurried across to the window. She pressed her head against the glass, unable to see round the porch to see who was there, but her focus was distracted by the scene outside.

'Oh, goodness, look at the snow now!' she gasped. 'It's coming down even heavier. The cars and the roofs are covered, and it's still falling.' She'd been so distracted by the sight that momentarily she'd forgotten about the knock on the door, until another one came, more insistent this time. 'I'm coming!'

She rushed to the door, the act of opening it bringing a cold blast of air rushing into the hallway, before reaching the living room with its ferocity too.

'Good grief!' Lizzie's high exclamation was heard by the others and Bill dashed out to the hall to see what it might be. Or rather who it might be.

'Good heavens,' Bill's voice called out moments later.

'Maybe it's the abominable snowman,' said Luke to the others, as they all giggled, straining to hear what was going on.

'Katy! Come here,' called her mum.

Katy shrugged and climbed out of her seat, the curiosity of the others roused now, so they all followed her out towards the front door.

'Oh, my god!' Her squeal resounded through the whole house and it was a wonder the noise didn't wake Rosie and Pip sleeping upstairs, let alone all the other sleeping children in the neighbourhood.

It was the abominable snowman. Or rather Brad doing a very good impression of one, as his broad frame filled the doorway, and snow clung onto his hair and lightweight hoodie, his face wet, shiny and smiling as snowflakes fell into a puddle around him.

'Merry Christmas, guys!'

26

'What...?' Katy had to strain her eyes to make sure it really was her husband standing in front of her and that it wasn't an elaborate prank. 'What are you doing here? Why didn't you say anything?' The questions came thick and fast as Brad simply laughed and shrugged off his wet top and slipped off his pumps, wholly unsuitable footwear for a snowstorm, leaving them beneath the radiator.

'No wonder I couldn't get hold of you! I thought you were out enjoying yourself.' Katy didn't know whether to pummel his chest in frustration or hug him so tightly she might never let him go. Her bemusement was quickly replaced by a surge of relief and happiness. 'Did you know about this?' Katy turned to her mum accusingly.

'I didn't. Although I suppose I should be used to people turning up unexpectedly from the other side of world by now.' Lizzie laughed. 'Let me go and fix you a nice warm cuppa.'

'Hello, mate,' said Sam, slapping Brad on the shoulder. 'I'll get you a beer too.'

That suggestion elicited a warm smile from Brad and a thumbs up.

'Well, this really is going to be the best Christmas ever! I still can't believe you're really here, standing in front of me. The kids are going to be made up. Oooh...' Katy threw her arms around his body, making sure he was real and not an apparition. 'You've given me the absolute shock of my life.'

'Hopefully a good shock, though,' said Brad, pulling her into his chest and kissing her head. She looked up into his handsome face, and beamed with happiness. There was so much she wanted to tell him and so many questions to ask, she barely knew where to start.

'How long are you staying for?' she plumped for.

'That's it. I'm home for good now. I've still got a few weeks' more work to do on the project, but I can just as well do that from here. The Department Head said I needed to be back home for Christmas, and I wasn't going to argue with that.'

Lizzie's heart swelled with warmth and pride at seeing Katy and Brad back together again. She knew how much Katy had been struggling these last few weeks, counting down the days until her husband was home again. His unexpected early arrival would do Katy the power of good and make Christmas more special for them all.

'Can I go and wake the kids up?' Brad said eagerly.

'Noooo!' The resounding response came from Lizzie, Katy and Bill, plus some laughter from Abbey, Sam, Rhi and Luke.

'We'll never get Rosie back to sleep again if you do. Make the most of the peace and quiet while you can. She was excited enough as it was, without knowing her dad's home, and there's now a foot of snow outside. Go and peek round the bedroom door at them. Although I'm not sure Rosie would dare to open her eyes even if she sensed you were there. I've told her Santa will only bring their presents if they're fast asleep.'

Brad grinned and collapsed into the armchair instead, grateful for the beer in his hand.

'I'll go up and see them in a while. I can't wait to give them a cuddle. I've missed you all so much.' He held out his hand to Katy and pulled her down so that she fell onto his lap, laughing, her joy evident to see as he planted a big kiss on her cheek.

'How was your journey?' Bill asked. 'You must be shattered, travelling all that way.'

'In fairness, it was absolutely fine. Everything went pretty smoothly until we hit the village. I've never seen anything like it. The snow came down so heavily that in the space of about ten minutes, we could barely see where we were going. The driver apologised, but said he'd have to turn round, so that's why I had to walk the last part of the journey. Mind you, another fifteen minutes or so and I might have had to turn back with the driver.'

'Crikey, it's mad,' said Rhi, excited and terrified in equal measure. 'I'd better call the taxi company and get them to come sooner,' she said to Luke, noticing how he glanced across at Brad and Sam, and the way their faces crumpled into the same doubtful expression.

'I'm not sure any cars will be getting up here now,' said Brad gently.

'No,' said Sam. 'The roads won't have been gritted.' His phone vibrated in his pocket at that very moment and he pulled it out to look at it. 'In fact, that's the taxi company now. They've said that because of the weather conditions, they're not going to be able do the pick-up, they've pulled all their cars off the road for safety reasons.'

'We'll have to walk,' said Rhi, gulping. It was a lovely walk on a summer's day, and would normally take thirty-five or forty minutes, but in these conditions, it might take them hours, especially when Rhi was wearing a pair of suede high-heeled boots and had only brought her little grey faux fur jacket with her, which was designed for style and not for warmth.

'Not sure that's the best idea,' said Bill. 'It's still snowing and though it might look like a Christmas card out there, it will be pretty treacherous underfoot.'

'I fell over twice on the way up the hill,' said Brad.

'Of course you can't go out in these conditions. You'll catch your death of cold. And I would never forgive myself if anything were to happen to you. There's only one thing for it. You'll have to stay here,' said Lizzie. 'You'll have to sleep on the sofas, I'm afraid, but I have plenty of spare duvets and pillows.'

'What a pain!' shrieked Rhi.

'Well, hopefully it won't be as bad as all that,' said Lizzie, in mock horror. 'I know it's a shame, Rhi, and it'll mean your plans will be spoiled, but it's just one of those things.' Lizzie came across and put an arm around Rhi's shoulder. 'All we can do is make the most of the situation.'

'I didn't mean it like that, Lizzie,' said Rhi, giggling, looking up at her friend. 'Mum won't mind, she's got Robb with her. I just feel bad that we're intruding on your Christmas when you have all your family here...' Rhi's voice trailed away, overwhelmed by the events, but really not sure why. It was Christmas Eve, there was a picture-perfect scene outside, she had all her friends around her, and at her side was the man who she'd fallen in love with.

'Well, you're part of my family too now. And we'll have the best time together. I have enough food and drink to feed the whole neighbourhood, so you'll be doing me a massive favour, actually. The more the merrier, as far as I'm concerned. You need to contact your mum, though, and let her know what's happening.'

There was a flurry of activity while Rhi went off to phone her mum, Luke called his dad and Brad tiptoed upstairs, followed by Katy, and peered around the bedroom door, his heart swelling at the sight of his sleeping children. What little angels! Lizzie removed the latest batch of sausage rolls from the oven while Bill topped up everyone's drinks and Sam and Abbey collected all the empties and tidied them away into the dishwasher. Later, when they all reconvened in the living room, they opened another bottle of fizz and the silly games started. By this stage, Sam was more than happy to get involved, throwing himself into the party spirit wholeheartedly. Brad was excused because he was clearly exhausted. He settled himself in the comfy armchair next to the fireplace as his eyes fluttered closed, a benign smile on his face as he listened to the babble around him. Katy sat on the floor in front of him, resting her head on his long legs, a solid reminder that he was actually here and she hadn't imagined his return, after all.

Katy's earlier exhaustion had miraculously lifted, and she was filled with excitement for the following morning, imagining the children's faces and their excited squeals. It was more than she could ever have hoped for, having her entire family under the same roof, along with Lizzie's friends too, who in such a short space of time had become her friends as well.

After a couple of hours of games, funny voices and tuneless singing, Lizzie went off in search of the duvets and pillows.

'I've found some pyjamas and some big T-shirts for you, girls, if you want them. I wish I had beds to offer you, but hopefully you'll be comfortable enough sleeping down here. I will warn you, though, that Rosie will be up at the crack of dawn so you won't have much of a lie-in, I'm afraid.'

'Well, hopefully if the snow has thawed we'll be up and out of your way early in the morning, we won't get in the way of your plans,' said Rhi.

'No chance,' piped up Brad, who everyone thought had nodded off, but who had actually been listening to all the merriment.

'You're very much part of our plans now, Rhi, whether you like it or not. And don't tell your mum, but I'm very happy that you'll be here for Christmas Day,' said Lizzie, chuckling. 'I've just had a look at the forecast and the thaw won't be coming until tomorrow evening, so you're stuck with us for a while at least.'

Katy gently nudged Brad out of his sleepy state and sent him upstairs to the comfort of their bed. She was looking forward to feeling his solid reassuring form beneath the covers, wrapping her arms around his chest, relishing the sound of his deep and heavy breathing that she'd so missed these last few weeks. First, she needed to see to some last-minute preparations for the morning, taking the mince pie from the plate in the fireplace and removing it from its wrapping, leaving a few crumbs in the empty case. She offered it to Sam, who was only too happy to oblige, finishing it off in a couple of bites, while Luke gallantly volunteered to drink the beer.

'It's a tough job,' he joked, 'but someone has to do it!'

Katy snapped off most of the carrot and left the knobbly top in the fireplace as evidence of Rudolph's visit, and got rid of most of the water in the saucer too. She stood back and admired her handiwork. She wasn't sure who would be more excited, her or Rosie. This year was the first one where Rosie could really take part and enjoy all the festivities, and Katy felt grateful that her mum and Brad were here to see it too. She'd already received the best Christmas present she could ever have hoped for.

'Right, well, I'm going to head up to bed, I've still got to fill the children's stockings, but I'll see you all in just a few hours, I reckon,' she said, yawning.

Lizzie glanced at her watch and grimaced. 'Come on, we need to get some sleep too,' she said, taking Bill by the hand. 'It's going to be a very busy day ahead.'

'Goodnight!' everyone called together.

Once Rhi had accepted that she wouldn't be going anywhere tonight, she quickly realised there could be much worse places to be stuck on Christmas Eve. Fortunately there were two sofas, both with deep cushions, which meant two people could fit on quite easily, as long as they were friendly and didn't mind snuggling up together, which was no hardship as far as Rhi was concerned. Sam and Abbey bagsied one sofa while Rhi and Luke settled down on the other.

'No giggling or snogging, you two,' teased Sam, when the others had gone up to bed. 'I don't want to be kept up all night by you two canoodling over there.'

Rhi giggled and snuggled up against Luke on the sofa, wrapping her arms around his chest. It was very intimate, she could feel his breath on her skin and see deeply into his eyes, but their makeshift bed for the night was surprisingly comfortable, even if it felt weirdly illicit, as though she was a teenager on a sleepover again.

'What an amazing evening it's been,' sighed Abbey. 'This will certainly be a Christmas to remember. Something to tell the grandchildren, eh?'

'Mmmm,' grunted Sam, who sounded as though he was already well on his way to sleep.

'That Christmas when we all got stuck at Lizzie's house,' Luke chuckled.

'Yeah, definitely something we'll dine out on, that's for sure,' sighed Rhi. She and Luke were making a habit of collecting memorable stories to tell their grandchildren; first their near miss with a deer in the dead of the night and now being snowed in at Christmas. She didn't really want to think of a time, though, when Luke would be only a fond memory.

'Night night, you guys,' said Abbey sleepily. 'Night night, Lady.' Abbey dropped her arm down the front of sofa to pet Lady on the head where she was curled up on the floor beside them, before Abbey turned round to face Sam, resting her head in the crook of his arm.

'Night night,' Rhi whispered across to Abbey.

Luke pulled Rhi closer into his side, the limited room on the sofa making it necessary for their limbs to naturally intertwine, his gorgeous scent reaching her nostrils, the sensation sending waves of desire through her body. Their faces were so close that when he pulled back to look at her, their lips immediately found each other, their eyes alight with desire. They kissed tentatively, quietly, or at least trying to keep the noise down, which was almost impossible. She giggled, pulling away, knowing that however lovely the temptation, they would need to be on their best behaviour tonight.

'Are you tired?' Luke asked, mouthing the words.

'Not really,' she laughed. 'I'm too excited to sleep!'

'Me too. Come on, let's go outside. The snow is too enticing to ignore and when will we ever get the opportunity again?'

What opportunity was he talking about, exactly? The one to see the snow or the two of them being able to go outside together at midnight again? Momentarily, Rhi was transfixed by Luke's eyes, which were shining a bright blue even in the darkened room, his enthusiasm highly contagious, but it was only a moment before she came to her senses.

'Are you mad? Besides, I've hardly got the right gear on for going out in the snow.'

'Don't worry, there's some wellies by the back door, I think they're Bill's, you can use those and there'll be a coat in the hall. Come on, it'll be fun.'

She didn't have chance to protest further because Luke was already on his feet and held out his hand to lead her outside. As soon as they were standing, Lady's ears pricked up and she looked up expectantly. If something was going on, she wanted to be a part of it.

'Okay, you can come, but you need to be quiet. No barking. All right?' Luke spoke solemnly as he held a finger to his lips, before beckoning Lady to his side. He couldn't risk leaving her behind in case she did bark and wake up the whole house. Rhi giggled like a teenager sneaking out to meet a forbidden boyfriend.

'Come on,' Luke urged, desperate now to get outside. In the kitchen they found the wellies, which Rhi slipped on her feet. They were two sizes too big, but much better than her own boots and they found Bill's waxed coat, which swamped her, but would keep her warm out in the December night.

Luke quietly turned the key in the lock of the back door and they slipped outside, the bitter freshness momentarily taking their breath away. Lady was keen to explore, tentatively lifting and dropping her paws in the snow.

'Wow!' They stood at the top of the garden, looking down its length, in awe at the sight in front of them. Thick snow covered the ground as far as the eye could see, the crisp whiteness glowing under a night sky filled with stars. 'It's so beautiful,' gasped Rhi.

Romantic, too, she thought, as Luke led her further into the garden. They jumped into the untouched snow, which had to be over three inches deep, while still the flakes tumbled down around them. Luke broke into a trot and Lady joined in the game, lolloping along, seemingly oblivious to the cold. Rhi laughed as

Luke pulled her along, her feet feeling as though they didn't belong to her, in the immovable baggy wellies.

'Hey, wait, I'm stuck, my feet won't...' It was too late, Luke wasn't waiting for anyone as he lifted his knees high to gallop through the snow and with Rhi's feet refusing to budge, there was no way she could keep up with him. She toppled over, letting out a shriek, falling sideways into the thick white cushion of snow.

'Luke!' she cried, giggling. The snow covered her face, buried her bare hands and seeped down the sides of her wellies. Lady came over to investigate what was going on with her wet nose, licking the snow off Rhi's face.

'Eugh! No. Stop it.'

'What on earth are you doing, Rhi?' Luke asked with a huge grin on his face as he stood over her, holding out a hand to help her up.

'What do you think I'm doing? This is all your fault, Luke!' She couldn't resist the temptation to reach out and grab a handful of the powdery snow, throwing it up in his direction, the white flakes wetting his head and face. She laughed, doing it again, before holding her hand out for him to pull her to her feet.

'Huh! No way, not after that,' he said, drying off his face on the sleeve of his coat, snow falling around him. He let go of her hand. 'You are in big trouble now, you do realise that?'

'No, Luke, please don't! I didn't mean it,' she said, laughing so much so she could barely get her words out. She turned over onto her front, on all fours, trying to prise herself off the ground, her hands going numb through the cold, the damn wellies proving much more of a hindrance than a help.

'You didn't, huh? Are you sure about that?' He grabbed some snow with his hand and she yelped.

'No, please, Luke, don't!' But it was far too late for Luke's forgiveness and he nudged her with his leg just as she was finding her feet so that she toppled over again, landing on her back. 'Stop it, I can't,' she said, looking up at Luke, who was standing astride her body, two handfuls of snow above her. She was squirming, trying to move away from his direct aim, but she was captive beneath his hold and slowly he allowed the snow to slip through his fingers so that it fell in a shower over her face and hair.

She grinned, actually quite enjoying the sensation of the snow melting on her face but not letting on to Luke. Instead, she protested noisily.

'Eugh, it's horrible!' She was laughing so much it made her stomach ache.

'Hey, let's call a truce.' He stepped to one side of her body and then bent down on his haunches to help her up with the benefit of both of his hands, but not before he'd leaned down to kiss her, mopping up the snow on her face with his mouth. She took the opportunity and grabbed hold of him and pulled him over so that he fell onto the ground next to her, rolling over onto his back dramatically.

'We're quits now, Luke. Really, enough is enough. You don't want me getting hypothermia.'

'Hmmm, I suppose not,' he said, taking hold of her hand and squeezing it tight. 'How would I explain that to your mum? You're freezing,' he said, genuinely concerned now.

'I know I am! That comes from having snow sprayed all over me, thank you, Luke.'

'Come here.' He pulled her up against him and they lay there for a moment gazing up at the stars, embracing the stillness and wonder of the night, while Lady mooched about around them. 'Isn't this great?' His face was a picture of awe as he turned to look at her.

'It is. Like Abbey said, a Christmas to remember.' Although whether it would be something they would be reminded of together in years to come, laughing at the memories, she really didn't know. More likely, she would look back fondly on it alone and think, *That was the year I lay in a heap of snow in the early hours of Christmas morning, gazing up at stars with that funny guy, Luke. I wonder whatever happened to him.*

'Crikey, did you see that?' Luke's urgent words brought her out of her daydreaming and back to the moment. He was sitting up now, looking ahead into the distance. He had Lady's full attention too.

'What? What was it?'

'I'm not sure, but I think it might have been... Come on, let's go and look.' He scrambled to his feet and this time he took hold of Rhi's hand with some strength, pulling her up too. Was it an animal? A fox perhaps, or a badger. Maybe even a muntjac deer, you sometimes spotted them around here, emerging from the darkness to reclaim their landscape. She didn't have time to ask all those questions, though, because she was concentrating on staying upright, taking high steps through the snow hanging onto Luke's arm for dear life, determined not to fall over this time. They reached the fence at the bottom of the garden and looked out into the distance to the fields beyond, seeing nothing but a wide stretch of white snow disappearing off into the distance. 'Look, there it is again, over there?' Luke put an arm around her shoulder, pulling her into his side, and she followed his outstretched arm, trying to see what it was he was pointing at.

'I can't see, what is it, Luke? Tell me,' she asked, impatient now.

'Aw, don't tell me you missed it, Rhi. It was over there. Look, if you're quick, you can just see the lights tailing away in the sky.'

Still she couldn't see a thing. She looked up at him, her brow furrowing as she caught the spark of devilment in his eyes.

'It was some sort of vehicle, I couldn't quite work it out, but it looked like a... I dunno, like a sleigh, pulled by about nine reindeer and there was this big fat guy driving it. Honestly, Rhi, I'm surprised you didn't see him, he gave us a cheery wave as he went past.'

'Aargh, you!' she said, pummelling him playfully in the side, exasperated that Luke had managed to trick her into believing there was actually something out there.

'Really, Rhi, I'm telling you, it was the most magical sight ever!'

Coming from Luke, as she stood hand in hand with him in the midst of the winter wonderland scene around them, she could actually believe that it might be true.

27

Christmas Day dawned in a riot of squeals, laughter and unbridled joy. Lizzie was pottering in the kitchen, peeling a few extra sprouts for the additional guests she'd have around her Christmas table today when she heard Rosie's heartfelt cry from upstairs.

'Mummy, Mummy! He's been,' she shrieked excitedly, discovering her stocking overflowing with presents.

Upstairs, Rosie ran into Katy's bedroom, dragging her stocking with her, and stopped suddenly in the doorway when she spotted something, or someone, she hadn't been expecting to see in her mum's bed. Brad quickly wriggled his way up the bed and opened his arms wide.

'Merry Christmas, sweetheart,' he said sleepily.

'Daddy, Daddy!' Little Rosie could barely believe her eyes and she promptly burst into tears, her stocking immediately forgotten as she scrambled up on to the bed and threw herself at Brad's chest, hugging him tight. Katy wandered in with Pip in her arms and her own eyes filled with tears from the relief and happiness she felt at having her family back together. She handed Pip to Brad so that he had both children in his arms.

'Hello, little man, I've missed you.'

'Did you come with Father Christmas?' Rosie asked, tears running down her cheeks, overwhelmed by the occasion. Katy stroked her daughter's hair from behind. They hadn't even had their breakfast yet and already there'd been plenty of tears.

'No, but I think I might have spotted him on my way here.'

'Did you?' she asked, her eyes wide.

'I really did. He was on his sledge gliding through the sky and he saw me and turned and waved. I bet he was on his way here because it looks as though he's left you, and Pip, with lots of presents. Aren't you lucky?'

'I am, I am, I am,' sang Rosie, with the biggest smile ever on her face.

'Come on, then,' Brad said, tapping the space next to him on the bed. 'You ought to make a start on opening them. Quick, go and grab them.'

Rosie slid off the bed, grabbed her discarded stocking and returned moments later, nestling in her dad's embrace on the bed as she pulled out the presents, looking in awe at each one before she started unwrapping them. Katy sat down alongside them, taking hold of Brad's hand, while Pip's gaze was transfixed by the bright shiny paper that crinkled beneath his fingers.

* * *

Downstairs, Bill was making mugs of tea for Sam, Abbey, Luke and Rhi, as they slowly stirred after their night spent on the sofas.

'Good morning,' Sam whispered in Abbey's ear, gently shaking her awake and kissing her on the forehead. 'Merry Christmas, my darling!'

'Aw, Merry Christmas to you too, Sam!' She stretched out her body as she looked up at Sam lovingly. 'Our first Christmas together, eh, that's pretty cool.'

'There's no one else in the world I'd rather be sharing it with, that's for sure,' he said, squeezing her shoulder.

It wasn't how she'd planned Christmas morning, but it didn't matter because she was with Sam and her dad, and her friends, and that was most important of all.

It was a shame about her new dress, bought especially to wear today, left behind at the cottage, but it would save for another day. And the presents, wrapped up, waiting beneath the Christmas tree. They could exchange their gifts later when they got home. She looked up at Sam now with a smile, knowing that his plans will have been thwarted too by the unexpected snowstorm. When had he intended to propose? she wondered. Probably this morning as they'd shared a glass of champagne and opened their presents together, just the two of them, before leaving to spend the day with Lizzie and her dad. They might have announced their exciting news over Christmas lunch when she could have shown off her sparkly ring to everyone around the table. Never mind, it would only make it all the more special when Sam finally had the opportunity to ask her the big question.

'What about you two?' Abbey asked, as Rhi and Luke eased themselves up to a sitting position on the sofa. 'Did you sleep okay?'

'Best night's sleep ever,' said Rhi, a smile spreading across her lips at the memory of her and Luke's midnight adventure. It had all felt terribly illicit and wonderful. When they'd got indoors, they'd climbed out of their wet clothes and Rhi had found some towels to dry off with, before wiping Lady down too. Luke had popped on the kettle and made warming drinks for them both. Lizzie had offered them one earlier in the evening, so it had been easy to find the mugs, the hot chocolate and the milk, and they'd sat in the kitchen, closing the door on the others who were sleeping, along with Lady, who had reclaimed her position near to Abbey and Sam. Luke and Rhi had whispered and giggled into the early hours of the morning, talking about everything and nothing. When they finally settled on the sofa to sleep, Rhi rested her head on Luke's chest and relished the comfort of his arm around her shoulder. It was no surprise that she was asleep within moments. Now, Luke wriggled above her and edged his way up the sofa, still holding Rhi in his embrace.

'Hey, you! Merry Christmas,' he said, bending down to leave a gentle kiss on her forehead.

'Merry Christmas to you,' she replied, smiling up at him. The only thing she'd wanted for Christmas was to find Luke underneath her Christmas tree and here he was, in all his gorgeousness, all her wishes had come true! Today, she wouldn't think about the new year when Luke would be moving away, she would simply make the most of this precious time they had together.

'It's Christmas!' Rosie bowled into the living room, dragging Brad with her, their hands intertwined as though she might never let him go. Katy followed with a bright-eyed Pip in her arms.

'Merry Christmas, everyone!'

'Look,' Rosie squealed. 'Santa did eat the mince pie and Rudolph has eaten the carrot. He made a mess,' she said, spotting the perfectly placed puddle around the saucer. 'Silly Rudolph.'

'Have you looked outside yet?' Luke asked Rosie.

'No! What is it? Daddy, Daddy, let's look!' She dragged him over to the back window and her little face widened in awe as her gaze settled on the beautiful snowy scene outside. 'It's snowing, I told you it would snow, Nanna!' Rosie said accusingly. Lizzie and Katy exchanged a smile, and Lizzie could only wonder why she ever had cause to doubt Rosie in the first place. 'Can we go outside, Daddy? And build a snowman.'

Brad laughed. Talk about being thrown right back into the thick of it. Not that he minded. Being home only reminded him how much he'd missed the noise, the chaos and the joy of family life. Now, it was as if he'd never been away.

'Yes, we can do that later if you'd like to, but you need to have some breakfast first, and what about all those presents under the Christmas tree?'

'Presents!' Rosie spun round, spotting the colourful wrapped parcels nestling beneath the tree, her eyes growing ever wider. 'Oh, no!' she exclaimed, lifting her palm onto her face in a gesture that made everyone laugh. 'Are they all for me?'

'Not all of them,' said Lizzie, 'but I suspect a great deal of them are for you and Pip.'

The morning passed in a flurry of Christmas paper, carols playing on the radio, squeals of delight from Rosie, big smiles from Pip, and lots of laughter and chatter from the adults. They cracked open the Buck's Fizz early, sharing a toast to friends and family, and enjoyed a breakfast of orange and cinnamon-scented muffins, warm from the oven.

'Right, we're going to head outside to make a snowman,' Katy said later, when they were all wrapped up in their winter coats, hats and gloves. 'I've had a peek out the window and it seems that the rest of the street have had the same idea.'

'Come on, Mummy!' Rosie tugged at her mum's hand, impatient now to get outside. 'Let's go!'

'We'll be out there with you in a while,' said Sam. 'Luke and I are going to get the driveway cleared.'

The snow had stopped falling in the early hours of the morning, but the thaw wasn't expected until at least the evening, and even then the forecasters were warning against travelling as the roads were treacherous. The unexpected downfall had come at exactly the right time, though, with people at home for the holidays with fridges full of food, and nothing else to do but enjoy the snowy conditions and the festivities.

Outside, there was an air of palpable excitement, with children shrieking as they delighted in discovering the snow, jumping up and down, making impressions in the untouched landscape. Lady was having the best time joining in with the fun. For Brad, it was surreal. A few days ago, he was wearing shorts, T-shirt and flip-flops in the intense heat of a Sydney summer, and now he was here in the midst of a British winter, making snowballs and lobbing them at Katy.

'Hey,' she cried, as a well-aimed shot landed on her head, dispersing snow all over her head and shoulders. 'Come on, Rosie, let's get Daddy.' Rosie and Katy giggled, scrabbling around on the ground forming snowballs and throwing them towards Brad, although their aim wasn't particularly good and Brad simply blocked their attempts by turning his back on them both, laughing at their feeble attempts. Pip was on his dad's chest in a front carrier and kicked his little legs excitedly, enjoying all the activity going on around him.

While they got down to the business of building the best snowman on the street, Luke and Sam started clearing the driveway and path outside Lizzie's house. The neighbours had had the same idea, so there was a lovely community spirit in the air and Brenda at number twenty-four brought out trays of warming mulled wine for the adults, and orange squash for the children.

'Look at our snowman.' Rosie pestered Luke and Sam to come and admire their handiwork once they were finished. Lizzie had provided them with a hat and a scarf, a carrot for the nose, and some black olives for the eyes and buttons.

'Doesn't that look fantastic!' Luke said, leaning on his shovel, grateful for the rest. 'Well done, Team Rosie, you've done a great job there.'

Later, with the cold seeping through to their bones, Pip becoming scratchy and Rosie needing a drink, they all decided they'd had enough winter air for one Christmas Day and they headed back indoors where the smells emanating from the kitchen greeted them in a warm and enticing fog.

'Lunch will be in half an hour,' called Lizzie.

'Let me sort out the drinks for everyone,' said Bill.

Rhi had been watching Luke through the window, hardly able to drag her eyes away from him. He and Sam had worked hard to clear the snow, the pair of them larking around together, their friendship and respect for each other evident to see. They'd struck up quite a bromance since they'd got to know each other and however much she would miss Luke when he moved away, she knew that Sam would miss him hugely too.

'Here, let me help you with that.' Now, Rhi helped to pull off Luke's coat from his shoulders, hanging it over the radiator in the hall, reminders of their romantic night-time flit springing to her mind. As she turned, her gaze snagged on his, his potent blue eyes shining brightly, and she had to wonder if the same memories were uppermost in his mind too.

'Sorry that I can't give you your present today,' she said, as they snatched a moment together, holding hands as they faced each other.

'You bought me a present?'

'I did.'

'What is it?'

'Well, I'm not going to tell you or else it won't be a surprise,' she laughed.

'Can't wait,' he said, kissing her on the lips. 'Come on,' he said, taking her by the hand and leading her towards the kitchen. 'Bill said something about drinks.'

A little while later, they all converged to find a seat at the table. Bill and Sam had brought in the small-leafed table from the kitchen and positioned it at the end of the dining room table so they could all sit together, even if it was a tight squeeze. Rosie, who hadn't stopped since she she'd woken up this morning, clambered up on her seat and looked around her, a big smile on her face, delighted to be at the centre of this family gathering.

Lizzie and Bill were a great team, delivering the plates overflowing with food to the table, and everyone took a moment to survey the feast in front of them.

'Everything looks and smells delicious,' said Sam.

'I must take a photo, to show Mum,' said Rhi. 'It looks absolutely amazing.'

'Compliments to the chef,' said Luke.

There was every conceivable Christmas treat on the table; roast turkey, gammon, sausage meat stuffing, pigs in blankets, roast potatoes and parsnips, Brussels sprouts with chestnuts, honey-roasted carrots, cauliflower cheese, red cabbage, Yorkshire puddings, cranberry sauce and bread sauce. Bill was working his way around the table pouring water, and either red wine or white wine.

They paused only for a few moments to check everything was in place and to take some photos of everyone sitting around the table, but they couldn't hesitate for too long because everyone was impatient to get stuck into the delicious feast in front of them.

'This looks yummy,' said Rosie, summing up everyone's sentiments.

'Happy Christmas!' Lizzie said, and they all responded in

kind, holding their glasses up to pass on their compliments to the chef and her very affable assistant, Bill.

Abbey looked across at her dad, who gave her a discreet wink, and she felt a huge swell of love for him. This really had turned out to be one of the best Christmases ever, what with the snowstorm and being with her dad, Sam, and all their friends, and she knew there would be even more Christmas surprises in store when she and Sam finally made it home to the cottage, whenever that would be.

28

'I'm shattered. I didn't realise eating and drinking everything in sight for two whole days could be so utterly exhausting. It's been lovely, though, I wouldn't change a thing.'

Well, maybe just one small thing, the matter of the engagement ring and the missed proposal, although she could never admit that to Sam. In the end, they'd stayed at Lizzie's until Boxing Day, as she'd insisted they had to help in eating all the leftovers, which as far as Abbey, Sam, Rhi and Luke were concerned was no hardship at all. Still, it was good to be finally back at the cottage, with the fire blazing and all the fairy lights and decorations alight. Abbey felt only the slightest sense of deflation after all the excitement of the last few days. What had she been expecting? That she would walk through the front door and Sam would immediately drop to one knee? But there had been no hint from Sam, no mention at all that there could be something in the offing. They'd opened their presents together, but Abbey had known looking at the wrapped parcels that the small ring box wasn't among them. Her mum's voice resounded in her ear. '*Patience is a virtue, young lady!*' Although Abbey had never quite got the hang of that idea.

Now, she stretched her arms high above her head. 'I'm just going to change into my brand-new pyjamas and I'll be back down.'

'When you'll be ready for a glass of red wine and some cheese and biscuits, no doubt?' Sam suggested.

'Of course,' said Abbey mock-seriously, rubbing her tummy, as though she might actually be hungry when nothing could be further from the truth.

Upstairs, she quickly undressed, removed her make-up and brushed out her hair, and pulled on her new cotton squirrel print pyjamas, a present from Lizzie and her dad, facing her reflection in the mirror. She sighed. It was true she was exhausted, definitely too much food and drink, but she knew her tiredness wasn't down solely to her over-indulgence. Her emotions had been heightened over the whole holiday, anticipation filling every cell in her body, and the excitement and joy from spending time with her dad and friends had bubbled through her veins like a vintage champagne. She'd chatted and laughed so much it had made her tummy ache, but it had been spending time with Sam that had made this Christmas quite so special.

Now, back at the cottage, the fizz had turned flat. Of course, if she had never been snooping in the first place, then she wouldn't be trying to second-guess when Sam might make his move. Unless she'd got it all entirely wrong. It wouldn't be the first time. She should go straight back downstairs and join Sam in the kitchen, but she was desperate to satisfy her own curiosity.

It would only take a moment, and she wouldn't find any peace until she did. Carefully making sure the door was properly closed, she tiptoed across the bedroom floor and bent down to peer beneath the bed, her heart thumping in her chest, her cheeks burning with heat. Her gaze swept the patch of carpet underneath the bed, but the space was now entirely empty. There was no sign of the carrier bags she'd stumbled upon previously, but then what was she expecting? She'd opened all her lovely presents from Sam earlier today, just after they'd arrived home, sitting in front of the fire with a cup of tea and a slice of Lizzie's Christmas cake. She hadn't needed to feign any surprise as they were all such delightful, thoughtful gifts which hit the spot perfectly. She loved each and every one of them. She wasn't ungrateful, it was just that there was one small present missing.

She'd been full of anticipation for how Sam might present the small black box, so where exactly was the beautiful ring? She hadn't imagined it. She'd held it in her hands, marvelled at its sparkliness and had imprinted on her brain the words engraved on the interior lid of the box: 'Christmas 2022'. Which, if you were being pedantic, had passed. So if not now, then when? Maybe Sam was waiting downstairs, ready to spring his surprise upon her. Should she really be in her cosy pyjamas for such an auspicious event? Or maybe, and this was what was beginning to niggle at the back of Abbey's brain, Sam had changed his mind.

Sadly, over the next couple of days, Abbey had to accept that it might actually seem that way. Sam didn't propose that evening, or the next one. They'd even watched her favourite Christmas film together, *Love Actually*, and her heart had twisted at the part where poor Emma Thompson's character is gifted a CD for Christmas when she'd earlier found a beautiful necklace in her husband's jacket. She'd tried to catch Sam's eye then, but his attention had been distracted by the new photography book that Lizzie and Bill had bought him, and she suspected he hadn't been enjoying the film as much as she might have wanted him to. It brought home to Abbey that no good ever came from snooping about in other people's business.

'Come on, then... What's the matter?'

It was a couple of days later over breakfast that Sam quizzed her. She'd been lost in thought over the missing ring, stirring her spoon around aimlessly in her bowl of porridge, his question jolting her out of her musings.

'What? Nothing, I'm fine,' she said brightly, trying to bring herself back to the moment as she looked up into his dark, appraising eyes.

'Are you absolutely sure, because I've noticed that you've been distracted these last few days? As though something might be troubling you.'

'No... I don't think...' Her words trailed away. Damn Sam for being quite so perceptive.

'Ever since we came home from Lizzie's, actually. I wondered if it was the Christmas presents, if you didn't like them?' There was a wry smile on his lips, but his comment hit a nerve. She obviously hadn't hidden her true feelings as well as she thought she had. Now he was looking at her with those deep, penetrating eyes that seemed to pierce her soul and reveal her innermost secrets.

'What? I loved all my presents. You thoroughly spoilt me. I guess it's just Christmas... it is a time for relaxation and reflection, isn't it?' she said with a smile, collecting the used plates from the table and heading towards the kitchen to place them in the dishwasher. She hoped she might have got away with it, but she hadn't reckoned on Sam's persistence.

'Not sure I believe you, Abbey.' He followed her out to the kitchen and spun her around to face him, his hands resting on her waist. His gaze ran across her features, making her feel exposed beneath his gaze. 'Come on, I know you well enough by now to know when something's wrong. And didn't we always promise each other there would no secrets?'

'Yes...' she said, half-heartedly. Sam made a good point. They'd both been cheated on in previous relationships, so it was important to both of them that any relationship was based on honesty and trust. They'd had that conversation early on, so it wasn't fair of her now to be economical with the truth. Especially after their big misunderstanding just before Christmas and their subsequent promise that they would always talk things through in the future.

Abbey busied herself with wiping down the worktops with a cloth, but Sam was a patient man and simply waited until every surface was sparkling clean. When she could no longer put off facing him, she turned towards his expectant gaze. He raised an eyebrow at her and she knew she couldn't put it off a moment longer.

She sighed, guiltily, a heat flaring at her cheeks.

'Well, there is something... I suppose.'

'I thought as much. Is it about Matt? Sophie? I told you, that's all in the past.'

'What? No!' She was quick to reassure him, before pausing to consider his question for a moment. 'Well, indirectly, I suppose it does have something to do with Matt.'

'Do you want to tell me about it?' He kept his voice neutral, but she could detect an icy undertone to his words.

'You'll be cross. I should never have done it. It was that night when you didn't come home, you were late, and we'd had that falling out the previous night, so all sorts of thoughts were running through my head. I thought you might have left for good and I needed to know for sure. I was just checking if your bags were still there, underneath the bed.'

Sam's brow furrowed. He had no idea what she was talking about. 'Abbey.' He leaned across and grabbed her wrist, pulling her towards him, looking at her imploringly. 'Just tell me what's going on.'

She took a deep breath. She knew she wouldn't come out of this very well, but she couldn't put it off any longer. She started again at the beginning.

'It was the night after I went out to dinner with Matt. I was waiting for you to come home. I knew how angry you were and when you didn't turn up at the expected time, well, I didn't know what to think. I was up in the bedroom, looking out of the window, hoping to see your Jeep come down the road, and with each passing moment I was becoming more and more panicky. I thought you might have had an accident or something. Then I had this awful idea that you might have left and gone back to your cottage, taking Lady with you. I was only checking under the bed for your holdall and that's when I found the carrier bags.'

Sam's expression creased, his eyes narrowing to observe her more closely, her skin prickling under his scrutiny.

'The carrier bags?'

'Yes, I just stumbled upon them. I didn't realise until it was too late that it was actually your Christmas shopping. I wouldn't have looked inside had I known, but I wasn't thinking straight at the time. I'm not sure what I was expecting to find, but…'

'Right, I get it.' He turned away, holding his hands on the edge of the worktop, the power and strength in his broad shoulders clearly visible. 'You were snooping around in my private things, was that it, Abbey?' She saw his shoulders rise and fall, his strong frame remaining resolutely turned away from her. She could tell even from this angle that he was angry with her, disappointed even, which was so much worse. 'So I guess there were no surprises for you when we came back here on Boxing Day and you opened your presents?'

'I'm sorry, I should never have done it.' She wished he would turn round to look at her so that she could see into his dark eyes, find some understanding there. Now it was her turn to grab him from behind, placing her hands on his waist, pulling him round to face her. 'Please, Sam. It didn't spoil a thing for me. I loved all of my presents. Really, it's been the best Christmas ever, the best presents ever.'

His expression was fierce, but his lips had been pursed together this whole time, twisting to contain the laughter that now spluttered to the surface, his eyes brimming with amusement.

'Honestly, Abbey, what are you like?'

'I'm glad you find it so funny,' she said morosely.

'Did your dad never tell you that no good ever comes from poking your nose into other people's business? So what happened then, you ended up discovering something you wish you hadn't?'

'No!' Her cheeks stung with shame. That's exactly what had happened. Sam knew it too and was teasing her, enjoying her discomfort at being found out. He must know what else she'd discovered beneath that bed, the present that hadn't materialised, the one she simply couldn't get out of her mind. 'Well, yes... I guess I did,' she admitted begrudgingly. 'I'm sorry about that. What else can I say?'

Sam laughed, pulling her head into his chest, his hands stroking her hair so that his fingers massaged her scalp.

'Hmmm, I can see I'm going to have to find a much better hiding place for your presents next year. Under lock and key, maybe?'

She breathed a sigh of relief at having owned up to her small transgression, resting her head against Sam's firm body, hearing the solid beat of his heart through his shirt. Why had she been worried about Sam's reaction? He seemed more amused than anything else, even if the mystery of the missing engagement ring had yet to be solved. When would he put her out of her misery, though?

She ran a hand down the front of his shirt, looking up into those dark enticing eyes that shone back at her, now alive with amusement.

'What?' His brow furrowed. 'Unless there's something else you need to tell me?' She noticed that imperceptible quirk of his eyebrow.

Her stomach tumbled. He wasn't going to make this easy for her. He was going to make her ask, but it was too late to go back, they couldn't finish the conversation, leaving the matter unresolved. She needed to get it out in the open, even if her cheeks were already stinging with shame.

'The ring, Sam?' There was an extended pause between them. 'In amongst the bags I found a beautiful ring, an engagement ring. I rather foolishly thought it was for me. Or perhaps I got the wrong end of the stick entirely?'

Sam gave a resigned smile and shook his head.

'No, you didn't get it wrong, how could you? It was... it is a ring, but...' He ran a hand through his hair. For the first time since this conversation had begun, Sam appeared uncomfortable. He dropped his gaze for a moment, before lifting his eyes to meet hers. They stood a hair's breadth away from each other, his lips within kissing distance, but they both knew this moment was too important to be interrupted by the instant and fleeting gratification of a kiss.

'But what, Sam?' she asked, her heart in her mouth, not entirely sure she was ready for his answer.

'I guess... well, I thought... The thing is... I decided...' His head dropped to one side, his mouth twisting, as he attempted to find the right words. 'I... well...' He took a deep breath, and

Abbey knew instinctively that she wouldn't like what she was about to hear. 'I decided not to.'

'You changed your mind?' she pressed, her stomach twisting in pain.

Sam grimaced and shrugged his shoulders. When she put it like that, he really couldn't deny it.

29

'There you go, sweetheart.' Bill placed Lizzie's favourite mug filled with a milky coffee on the side table next to the armchair, where she'd been doing a word search puzzle in a magazine.

'Thank you, darling, that's lovely.' She put her magazine down, stretching her legs out on the pouffe in front of her and focusing her full attention on Bill.

'Isn't it quiet?'

It was the first day they'd had together, just the two of them, in several weeks. Brad, Katy and the children had gone out for the day. First they were taking another look at their new house, with a view to measuring up for a few pieces of furniture, then they were off to lunch at the pizzeria in town, and in the afternoon they were going to see the pantomime, *Snow White and the Seven Dwarfs*.

'Are you missing them already?'

'No!' Lizzie chuckled. 'I love them all dearly, but I'd forgotten how lovely it is to have this place to ourselves, just the two of us. It is a bit full-on when they're all here, as much as I love them. Mind you, we did have a lovely Christmas, didn't we?'

'You surpassed yourself, Lizzie. You wouldn't have got that quality of food in a Michelin-starred restaurant. You were the perfect host, and everyone said what a lovely time they'd had.'

'I couldn't have done it without you, Bill. Honestly, I think I must have been running on adrenaline these last few days because I've been absolutely fine, and then today, it's hit me, a wave of tiredness. It's probably because I know I can relax, with Katy and children out for the day.'

'They'll be moving into their own place in a couple of weeks' time and then you'll miss all the noise and the mayhem.'

'You're right, I will. But at least then I'll have the best of both worlds with them being round the corner. I'm just pleased that Katy seems a lot happier these days, almost back to her old self. She's going to look for some part-time work in the new year, which I think will do her the power of good. And she wants to get back to her drawing. She's done some lovely pictures in the past and sold some of her work too as framed prints and greetings cards. I think speaking to Jackson the other week gave her the idea of taking up one of the pop-up stores at the stables. At least it's given her something to focus on, something she can apply her creative energies to that's just for her, and not for Brad or the children. That's definitely what she needs.'

'My place will soon be ready for me to move back into as well, so you'll be able to get back to some sort of normality in the new year.'

'Oh, but Bill. I don't want you to go. I've loved having you here. However will I manage without you now? Do you really have to go? Couldn't you stay for a little while longer?'

Bill laughed, flattered by Lizzie's reaction.

'Well, to be honest with you, I wasn't much looking forward to going back to my lonely little flat anyway, so maybe I could stay for another week or two. Shall we see how it goes and then decide?'

'That makes much more sense,' said Lizzie, laughing with relief. Perhaps they would need to have a proper conversation about their living arrangements, some other time, but it seemed daft to have two properties when they spent so much time together.

'Well, the day is our own,' said Bill, sitting on the arm of the chair next to Lizzie. 'What would you like to do? We could do battle at the shopping centre and see if we can pick up some bargains in the sale, or we could drive out to a pub and have a spot of lunch, or we could go for a walk down by the canal, and then find somewhere to have a nice cream tea later.'

'Ooh, I'd love to do all of those things, but can we organise them for some other time? Do you know what I fancy doing today? Absolutely nothing! Just staying here, making the most of the peace and quiet, having a nice lunch and maybe watching a film this afternoon. What do you think? You're not disappointed, are you?'

'Never. I'm just happy being with you.' It was one of his common sayings and it always made Lizzie feel so very special. His eyes twinkled as he observed her closely now. 'This is your day, so your wish is my command. I'll make you your favourite for lunch, how about that, a prawn and mayonnaise sandwich. Make sure you have a proper rest today, love, while you can.'

Lizzie lifted her arm across her chest and reached up to take hold of Bill's hand, which was resting on her shoulder. She threaded her fingers through his.

'You spoil me, Bill, do you know that?'

'It's only what you deserve. You do so much for everyone else, sometimes you forget to take care of yourself. I've realised it should be my job, looking after you.' He held up his hands. 'Only if you want to be looked after, that is?'

'Well, I think it's rather lovely having someone to care for you. You take it for granted when you have it and then when it's gone, you miss it terribly. You'll know as well as I do that it's the simple pleasures you miss the most; having a cup of tea made for you, sharing a meal, watching something together on telly. Having someone to put the bins out.' She laughed aloud. 'Oh, how I hate that job!'

'I'll be your bin man for as long as you want me to be,' said Bill, deadly serious.

Lizzie sighed contentedly. She wouldn't describe herself as romantic, but she wondered if those were possibly the loveliest words she'd heard in a long time. She couldn't imagine a time when she wouldn't want Bill in her life.

'I love this song,' said Lizzie, the bars of 'Dancing Queen' just reaching her ears from the radio playing in the kitchen.

'Come on then, my very own dancing queen, up on your feet.' She didn't need asking twice, the music stirring her senses and re-igniting her energy. Bill turned the music up and held her hand, twirling her about the living room floor in a series of moves that had them laughing out loud and gasping for breath, so much so that when the music finished, Lizzie fell onto the sofa, pulling Bill on top of her. Their lips met and they kissed passionately, and Lizzie had to marvel at how the sensations swirling around her body, the thumping of her heartbeat, the butterflies dancing in her tummy and the goosebumps running all over her skin could have her believing that she was a teenager all over again. They were so lost in the music, too swept up in the heat of the moment, that they didn't hear the front door open. The first they knew of someone being there was when they sensed a movement in the doorway to the living room, shortly followed by Katy's strangled cry.

'Oh, God, I am so sorry.' She clasped her hand over her eyes in horror. 'I didn't realise. I just came back to collect the tickets, I left them in my other handbag. Please pretend this never happened, that I never saw... I'm not stopping. Oh, my god...' She shuddered, running past the doorway and snatching up her other handbag, burrowing around for the tickets, before grabbing them and dashing back towards the front door again.

'Katy!' Lizzie called, laughing. 'There's no need for you to rush off like that. Have you got everything you need?'

'Yep, everything, it's fine, Mum. Absolutely fine. I'll leave you both to it. Sorry! And see you later.'

Lizzie and Bill dissolved into giggles as Katy left, seemingly unable to get out of that front door fast enough. Another reminder of being a teenager, thought Lizzie, smiling to herself, remembering how she went to great lengths to hide her sexuality from her parents back in the day. Now, it was the exact same feelings, only she was hiding her sexuality from her dear daughter.

'Oh, Bill,' she said, snuggling into his warm embrace on the sofa, still laughing. 'I love my family dearly, but it's definitely time for them to move into their own place. We can't have them cramping our style for much longer. And I don't know who was more embarrassed, me or Katy.'

'Ha, I do,' said Bill, chuckling, planting a kiss on Lizzie's neck, making her sigh, 'and it was very definitely Katy.'

30

'What do you mean you've changed your mind?' Abbey could barely voice the words as a feeling of nausea gathered in her throat.

'Hey, come here. Don't look so horrified.' Sam cupped Abbey's face in his hands, gently brushing some stray strands of hair away from her face. 'I haven't changed my mind about you. Or about us. It's just... well, we're really happy as we are, aren't we?'

'Yes, but...' Anything she might say would sound churlish and ungrateful. Sam was right, they were happy as they were, but he'd clearly wanted to propose at one time and now he'd changed his mind, so saying that was clearly just an excuse. Was it really such a bad idea, them getting married? Why exactly had Sam had a change of heart?

She suppressed a sigh. It was her own fault. Before she knew about the ring, she'd had no expectation of any proposal, but the idea was in her head now and it had been tumbling through her thoughts ever since she'd found the ring. She had worked herself up into such a huge ball of excitement and anticipation that now she was left deflated and disappointed.

'Don't worry, I get it,' she said, pulling away from his proximity, waving her hand around. 'I had a change of heart about a marriage earlier in the year too.' She'd meant to sound light-hearted and funny, but instead her words tumbled out tinged with bitterness.

'Hey, don't be like that,' said Sam. 'This is completely different.'

'Is it?' She turned on him.

'Yes, entirely.' Sam pulled her down so they were sitting together on the sofa. He turned to face her, his dark brown eyes imploring as they roamed her face. 'I love you. I've never been happier than I am now with you, and I love being here with you, it's almost as though we were always meant to be together. I didn't want to do anything that might change what we have between us. Do you understand?'

She nodded morosely, although she wasn't sure she did understand. Surely getting married would only make their connection so much stronger.

She turned away. She had no reason to be cross with Sam, he'd done nothing wrong, and she only had herself to blame at finding herself in this position. If she hadn't gone poking around in his business, or rather his shopping bags, then her hopes for a wedding would never have been raised in the first place. Perhaps she was an idiot to even want to entertain the idea of another wedding after what had happened last time, or more pertinently, didn't happen last time. But this was different, she knew that what she had with Sam could in no way be compared with what she had with Jason.

Sam pulled her back into his embrace again, the temptation to drop her head on his chest too strong to ignore. She sighed. She'd be lying to herself if she pretended that she wouldn't love a glorious wedding with all her family and friends around her, but she knew deep down it wasn't the most important thing in the world. What was most important of all was the love they shared for each other. If Sam had entertained the idea of getting married briefly, then changed his mind, that didn't mean that his feelings for her had changed. Besides, if she really wanted to marry him, if it was that important to her, then she could always ask him to marry her instead. Which she was never going to do. She'd had enough humiliation and rejection to last her a lifetime.

'I understand, it's fine,' she said breezily, her tone not quite matching her words. She would put it out of her mind and try to forget that she'd ever seen that gorgeous sparkling ring nestling under the bed. What on earth would he do with it now, she wondered. Could you even return an unwanted ring for a full refund? She didn't know. Perhaps he'd already taken it back to the shop, or maybe he was keeping it in a safe place for a future moment. *If only*. She'd put that thought straight out of her head, or else she'd drive herself mad trying to anticipate if and when that moment might ever come.

'Hey!' Sam gently shook her beneath his arm to gain her attention. 'You're upset, I can tell. Look, full disclosure time. Yes, I was going to propose. On Christmas Day. It was meant to be a big surprise, only, well, I decided against it. Besides, I realise now, if I had gone ahead with it, it wouldn't have been much of a surprise, would it?' His brow furrowed, chastising her lightly, but there was warmth in his eyes and a smile on his lips.

'It doesn't matter now.'

'And of course my plans would have been dashed anyway because of being snowed in at Lizzie's, so maybe it wasn't meant to be.'

She glanced at him through narrowed eyes.

'You could have done it on Boxing Day,' she countered, unable to stop herself, sounding sulky to her own ears.

'I know, but...'

'But what? Is it such a terrible idea?'

'No, not at all.' He paused, taking a deep breath. 'After what happened with Matt, I decided it wasn't the right time to ask you. I didn't want you thinking my big gesture was a knee-jerk reaction. That I was only proposing to you to make up for acting like an idiot in front of Matt.' He screwed up his face with frustration, as if struggling to make his point clear. 'Does that make sense?'

'That would never have occurred to me.'

'I thought it might come across that way, even though I'd picked up the ring weeks before that night in the pub. Seeing Matt again after all those years was weird. It brought back all sorts of feelings from way back when, but it had absolutely nothing to do with Sophie. I promise you that. I hadn't thought about her in years. It was seeing you with Matt that scared me, the realisation that I had so much to lose. I couldn't bear the thought, Abbey, and I just didn't know what to do with myself. I suppose it was jealousy, a gut reaction which, I know now, was totally unreasonable. My only defence was that I wasn't thinking that night, I was only feeling.'

'I do get it, you know,' she said, squeezing his hand.

'Once I'd got a bit of perspective on it, I realised I didn't want those bad feelings impacting on what we had together. I put the idea of proposing to one side. If I was going to do it, then I wanted to make it really special, a reason for celebration, with nothing getting in the way or tainting the occasion. Not that my feelings changed in the slightest. I still feel exactly the same way about you. Believe that, if nothing else.'

How could she not believe him when it came so utterly from his heart?

'I do believe you. I just feel bad that my actions messed up things quite so spectacularly. If I hadn't found that ring, then I would have been none the wiser and we wouldn't be having this awkward conversation now. I'm kind of embarrassed.'

Sam gave a wry smile.

'There's no need to be embarrassed. It's just one of those things. Although it is quite funny when you stop to think about it.'

Abbey didn't consider it funny. She thought it sad, disappointing and frustrating. What were they supposed to do now? Simply not mention it ever again and pretend that Sam hadn't once intended to propose to her.

'What did you do with the ring?' she asked, her desperation to know getting the better of her. She wanted to see it again, to check that it really was as large and sparkly as she remembered it to be. To see it with her own eyes one more time.

'It's upstairs, in my sock drawer. Safe and sound.'

'Good.' Well, at least he hadn't returned it, or worse, sold it. The special black box she'd stumbled upon with the beautiful ring inside was tucked away for a future moment in time. Okay, so the box, with its inscription, might be a little dated by the time Sam felt inclined to propose to her again, but that wasn't important. She was relieved to have had this conversation with him, to have it finally out in the open, even if it hadn't yet delivered the happy ending she would have hoped for.

'You know what I wish? That we could just forget that any of this ever happened, and we can get back to normal.' She was fed up of second-guessing Sam's intentions and having awkward conversations about engagement rings and wedding proposals. If it was that difficult to sort out between them, then surely it wasn't meant to be.

As Sam had told her, they were happy as they were, so was there any reason to change things?

31

Rhi peered through the passenger door window of the car as Luke pulled off the motorway onto the country roads and she spotted the first signs to Dashford-upon-Avon. She glanced at her watch. Already they'd been in the car for over an hour and still they had some way to go yet. She didn't know the area at all, but noticing the passing fields, country pubs and traditional villages, it seemed like a beautiful part of the country. Only it was a long way from home. Which meant a long way from Luke. Not a journey you'd be wanting to do on a weekday night after work for the sole purpose of going to a quiz night at the Three Feathers.

When Luke had invited her to come along to pick up the keys to his new flat, she jumped at the opportunity. The days between Christmas and new year stretched out interminably and it was good to have the opportunity to get away for the day, to get a fresh focus on the week. Besides, it gave her an excuse to spend more time with Luke, which she was never going to say no to. Arriving in Dashford-upon-Avon, it was clear that it was a very picturesque spot. The traffic slowed as they crossed a stone bridge into the town and Rhi was able to look each way at the pretty river meandering beneath them, noticing the waterside bars and cafés.

Even in the post-Christmas lull, there were lots of people around, families taking advantage of the clement weather, couples arm in arm enjoying together time and lots of dogs walking their owners. It was a happy and vibrant scene and even though she'd only just arrived, she could tell it would be a lovely place to live. As they drove on through the town, Rhi spotted some of the usual shops you find on every other High Street in the country, but alongside these were specialist bakeries, independent bookshops, and enticing boutiques. It was the sort of place you would visit on a daytrip, mooching around the vast array of shops, visiting one of the many inviting eateries before taking a walk through the park and along the riverbank. The perfect place to visit, as if she needed any excuse. She'd definitely have to arrange a weekend to come and visit soon, get a date in the diary before Luke even made the move.

After picking up the keys from the estate agent, they drove back through the town and turned into a side road just before the bridge that ran alongside the river.

'My flat is in this block here,' he said, bringing the car to a halt in the car park.

'Really? What a great spot. Just beside the river. And you have the town centre right on your doorstep too.' Rhi was thrilled for Luke and the adventure he had ahead of him, although she had to squash the unwelcome feeling of jealousy spreading through her veins. How she would love to live in a spot like this, in her own flat. Still, this was Luke's moment, and it only made her more determined to find her own place in the new year, even if she knew her funds wouldn't stretch to anywhere as lovely as this. The most she could hope for on her budget was a room in someone else's house, and didn't she already have that at home?

Even if it meant sharing a house with a pair of second-time-around lovebirds.

Inside, the flat was just as impressive as it had been from the exterior. It was newly renovated with a contemporary black shiny kitchen, an open-plan living area, two bedrooms and even a small balcony, with a wrought-iron table and chairs, that overlooked the river. The perfect spot for that post-work glass of wine, Rhi thought. The flat was furnished with a small brown leather sofa and a glass-topped round dining table with two chairs. On one wall there was an electric fire with a stone surround. Minimalist in style, it was definitely a bachelor pad and Rhi could imagine Luke settling in here quickly, making the most of his newfound freedom.

She sighed, wondering if it would be a case of 'out of sight, out of mind' for Luke, as far as she was concerned. He'd told her she would always be welcome at his new flat and how Dashford-upon-Avon was a great place to visit for a weekend away. She'd seen that for herself now, but would those casual invitations really come to anything?

'What do you think, then?' Luke turned to look at her as they stood on the balcony, taking in the view around them.

'It's perfect. You've really landed on your feet here.'

'It's great, isn't it? I'm thinking I'll start running in the mornings before work, get to see a bit more of the local area. There seem to be a couple of good routes alongside the river.' The slight breeze lifted his spiky blond hair and she saw the enthusiasm shining in his bright blue eyes. 'It's only a ten-minute drive to work as well.'

'Brilliant.' She nodded her head keenly. She was making all the right noises, not wanting to quash Luke's excitement, but already she could feel him pulling away from her, his head and heart now firmly ensconced in Dashford-upon-Avon.

'Come on, let's go and collect the bits from the car,' he suggested, 'then we can go and find somewhere nice for lunch.'

They did a couple of trips up and down the stairs, mainly with Luke's bed linen, clothes and personal belongings. He'd be moving in the rest of his gear next week just before he started his new job. On their final trip up to the first-floor apartment, they'd just reached the landing when the door on the opposite side of the corridor opened. A woman appeared, early twenties, sporting a short swingy bob and a wide smile.

'Ah, hello! I thought I heard some activity out here. You must be the new tenants. I'm Louise, lovely to meet you.'

'Hi!' Luke stepped forward and held out his hand to her, by way of greeting, matching her big grin. Rhi's arms were full of clothes, but she managed to give a small wave from beneath her bundle as she edged her way into the flat, leaving Luke to meet his new neighbour. Her ears strained to hear their conversation. 'I'm Luke, and yes, just dropping a few bits and pieces off today. I'll be moving in properly next week.'

'Great, well, if there's anything you need to know, just give me a knock. I think you're going to love living here. It's so handy for town and there's a really lovely community in this block. We get together for supper evenings, weekend walks, quiz nights, all sorts of things, really.' She gave a small laugh. 'Only if you'd want to, of course. There's absolutely no pressure.'

'Sounds great,' said Luke. 'I'm new to this area, so it's nice to see a friendly face and to know there's some stuff I can get involved in.'

'Yes! As much or as little as you like. Well, I thought I'd just come and introduce myself. Good luck with the move. I'll come and give you a knock when you're properly settled in. You're always welcome round at mine. The kettle's normally just boiled.'

'She seems lovely,' said Rhi brightly, through gritted teeth, when Luke came through to the bedroom. She was trying hard to ignore the negative feelings of jealousy and regret worming their way beneath her skin, but the constant reminders of the new opportunities opening up to Luke were wearing her down.

'Yeah, good to know that there's plenty of stuff going on around here too.' He dumped the suitcases he'd been carrying onto the floor, then fell dramatically back onto the bed, flinging his arms and legs wide as he bounced his body against the mattress, which still had its brand-new wrapping around it. 'Seems pretty comfy, what do you think?' He shuffled over on the bed, making room for her, and patted the empty space, inviting her to come and join him.

She lay down beside him, adopting a similar position, their gazes settling on the ceiling, before he reached across and turned her face to look at him.

'Thanks for coming with me today, Rhi. You are okay, aren't you?' His fingertip trailed along her jawbone.

'Fine,' she said, forcing a smile. *Damn*. She'd always found it hard to hide her true feelings, but she didn't want Luke to pick up on the low mood which had slowly taken a grip on her, ever since she'd arrived at the flat, seeing what a wonderful place Luke was coming to. Wonderful neighbours too, by the sound of things. 'Thanks for inviting me along. It's been really fun, and of course I had to come and see where you'll be living. Don't worry, I'll be booking my stay very soon.'

'Well, you know you'll always be very welcome, don't you?' He leaned across and gently kissed her on the forehead. She wanted to grab hold of him, tell him not to come here, that he should stay with her and their friends. It was beautiful here, but Primrose Woods and its surrounds were just as beautiful, perhaps even more so.

'Are you ready for some lunch?' Luke asked, that big wide

smile back on his face again. He jumped off the bed and held out a hand to Rhi, pulling her to her feet.

'Oh, hang on a minute. Something important to do.' Luke searched through his bags for his rucksack, unzipped the pocket and pulled out the cute plush deer that Rhi had given him for Christmas. He'd been genuinely touched when he'd accepted the gift, or else he'd been putting on a very good act, admiring, with a smile on his face, the toy's soft brown fur, long legs and large eyes and ears. It had long, thick dark eyelashes too that gave the deer a coquettish appeal. 'There, pride of place,' he said, gently placing the deer on the centre of the headboard.

'Well, at least you won't forget about me now,' said Rhi.

'There was never any chance of that,' he said, turning to face her with a genuine smile.

They walked the short distance into town, where they were spoilt for choice for places to eat. In the end, after wandering around and peering into several windows, they decided on an inviting tapas bar that had patterned tiled walls, dark wooden furniture and verdant plants spilling over from high shelves. Settled at a table at the back of the restaurant, they ordered several dishes to share and a jug of Sangria, although it was only after they'd ordered that Luke told Rhi he'd only be having the smallest of glasses.

'Well, cheers then,' she said, raising her glass to his, 'and here's wishing you every success in your new job and much happiness in your new flat too.'

'Thanks. To think that this time next week I'll actually be living here, it's mad. It's come round so quickly since Christmas has been and gone.'

Far too quickly, as far as Rhi was concerned.

'Of course, I'll miss my family and friends,' he gave an almost imperceptible nod in her direction, 'but I certainly won't miss my old job. It was the best thing I did, leaving there. It's time for a new start.' He paused, pondering on that thought for a moment. 'Anyway, how about you? Are you excited to get stuck into your new business?'

'I am!' It wasn't a lie, but in truth, all that had occupied her headspace these last few weeks had been Luke. If she'd been hoping that by spending every available moment with Luke over Christmas, immersing herself in his company, enjoying the quick-witted banter they shared, the laughter and affection, somehow she might be able to get him out of her system, then she'd been very much mistaken. All it had caused her to do was fall deeper and deeper under Luke's spell and she hadn't thought that even possible.

'Did I tell you I found another client? One of the customers at the pub runs a small management consultancy and I was talking to him about my new business and he said how they really needed someone to manage their admin facilities, so I'm going to be handling their email accounts and diary management.'

'That's great, Rhi. I'm really proud of you. See, you're going great guns already. Those companies will be really fortunate to have you on board.'

She hoped so. It would also give her something to focus on in those first days following Luke's departure. She was determined to make a success of the business, it was a long-held ambition to work for herself and she was full of ideas and enthusiasm about how to take the company forward. She'd probably be so busy she would barely have time to think about Luke.

Just then, the waiter delivered some sweet peppers in olive oil, a tortilla and some patatas bravas, along with a basket of bread for the aubergine pâté. They eagerly filled their plates and when Rhi looked up, Luke was observing her closely.

'So are you going to miss me then?' This was the Luke she

knew and loved. Cheeky, irrepressible and utterly charming. He had that all-too-familiar lopsided smile on his face too, making light of their impending separation, but what else would she expect from him?

'Maybe,' she said airily, her stomach churning. If only he knew just how much she was already feeling his absence. 'Perhaps, a little bit, but you know...' She gave a nonchalant shrug. 'I'm sure in a few months' time, I'll be saying "Luke who?"'

Their relationship had always been marked by gentle ribbing, light-hearted banter and teasing. Whenever they were together it was never very long before the pair of them would be giggling, usually about something silly, laughter that would end up making their ribs aches. She couldn't imagine laughing in the same way with anyone else.

'Will you, though?' He pursed his lips, and creased his nose and brow at her, narrowing his eyes too. He looked gorgeous, even when he was pretending to be cross. She smiled, expecting to see her smile returned, but Luke's gaze was unwavering and deadly serious now, an electricity sizzling across the table. 'You don't really mean that, do you, Rhi?' His tone was altered too. Perhaps he wasn't pretending to be cross after all.

'Okay, so maybe I'll miss you more than just a bit, but hey, we'll keep in touch and you know I'll be down to visit just as soon as you'll have me.' She was keeping her tone light, flirty, but there'd been a shift in mood from the other side of the table.

'I've been thinking.'

'Well, that's always a dangerous thing,' said Rhi flippantly.

'No, really...' His hand reached out across the table and took hold of hers, and she looked at it, surprised, her heartbeat suddenly sounding in her ear, not knowing where this conversation was heading, but knowing instinctively it was important. What was he about to tell her? That while their Christmas romance had been fun, it had only ever been destined as a fling. Was this the big brush-off? He would let her down gently, say that while they would always remain friends, there could be no future for them romantically and he was letting her know, as it was only fair, as he didn't want her holding out any hope of anything more serious or permanent. She braced herself.

'Okaaay...'

'Well... I was thinking... Ha, well, I hope this doesn't seem completely random, because it's not. I've been thinking about this for a while now, but...' She really wished he would just come out and say it. 'Well... I wondered if perhaps you would want to come with me?'

'What?' She suspected that even the waiter, who happened to be delivering some chicken and ham croquettes, and a dish of meatballs, to their table at that moment caught her surprise. She lowered her voice. 'Come with you?'

'Yes. You could come with me here, to Dashford-upon-Avon. You've seen how lovely it is. I mean, why not?'

She gave an imperceptible shake of her head. Was she really understanding him correctly? He answered her puzzled expression.

'You could move up here with me.' He leaned across the table. 'You're looking to move out from home and the great thing about being a virtual assistant is that you can do it from *virtually* anywhere. You told me that yourself. There's two bedrooms at the flat. You could have the second bedroom as your office.'

An unexpected wave of emotion swept through her body as she gazed at Luke, still uncertain whether he was about to burst into laughter and tell her he was only kidding. It honestly wouldn't surprise her, knowing Luke, but for once he was being deadly serious.

'You must know how much you've come to mean to me, Rhi.'

She didn't, she really didn't. They'd been having a great time together over the holidays, and Luke was very attentive, but he'd given her no indication that what they had together would be anything more than a Christmas romance.

'Hell, it took us long enough to get together,' said Luke. 'It was almost as though fate was conspiring to keep us apart. First you were with Jason and would barely even register my existence.'

'That's not true,' she protested, blushing, but knowing that it was absolutely the truth.

'Then, when you left Jansens, it made me realise just how much I'd looked forward to seeing you each day. The office wasn't the same without you and I couldn't bear the thought of not seeing you again. That's why I came and tracked you down. I wanted us to stay in touch as friends and maybe see if anything developed. I couldn't make a move too soon, though, you'd just broken up with Jason and I didn't want to put any pressure on you.'

She smiled, hardly believing what she was hearing, every nerve end in her body tingling. To think that back then she'd been desperate for Luke to make a move, and for the same reason as him, she hadn't wanted to take the initiative in case she scared him away.

'Then you announced you were heading off to Australia, and it looked as though you and me weren't meant to be.'

Relief rushed through her, she understood exactly what he was saying. That same sense of frustration had been bubbling inside of her for the last six months as her feelings for Luke had been growing all the time. There were so many occasions when she wanted to tell him just how much he'd come to mean to her, but her fear of rejection had always stopped her from taking that next step.

'I kept in touch from Aus, sent you loads of messages and videos.'

'I know you did, and I've kept every one of them. I loved hearing from you, but I had to pull back and keep some distance between us. I didn't want you feeling that you had to keep in touch. I didn't know, you might have met someone on your travels, and well...' He shrugged, taking a sip from his water glass. 'I didn't want to stand in your way.'

'You're too saintly for your own good, do you know that, Luke Barnfield?' she said, with only the faintest hint of sarcasm. She copied his gesture, taking a sip of the fruity wine, the flavours exploding in her mouth, her head bursting with thoughts as she tried to make sense of what Luke was telling her.

'I know I am. Just call me Saint Luke, but honestly, Rhi, I'm deadly serious now. Spending Christmas with you, having all this time together has made me realise just how much you've come to mean to me. That night in the car, where a few moments later and we might not have had such a lucky escape, was such a wake-up call. It made me wonder why I was holding back when I knew I'd already fallen in love with you.'

'Sorry... I didn't quite hear...' Rhi definitely needed some clarification on that point, in case her ears had been deceiving her. Luke was only too happy to oblige.

'Yes, Rhi, I love you. For a long time, I fought those feelings, not wanting to admit it to myself, unsure whether you felt the same or if I might be a stepping-stone for you, from Jason to the next guy.'

'No, it was never like that. I really liked you, but I got the distinct impression that you only wanted to be friends, and nothing more.'

He shook his head, smiling wryly.

'We got our timing wrong, spectacularly wrong, didn't we?' He leaned across and took hold of her hand. 'Now we have finally got together, I don't want to lose you again. We can make this work, can't we, Rhi?'

It was everything she'd wanted to hear and so much more. She adored Luke with all her heart, and she'd discovered only this morning that she really rather loved the beautiful town of Dashford-upon-Avon too. She'd even imagined, in a flight of fancy, living here, popping into the bakeries and the bookstores, walking through the streets hand in hand with Luke. Perhaps it wasn't as fanciful as she first thought.

'Just tell me you'll think about it?' Luke pressed, clasping her hand and squeezing it tight.

'Of course I'll think about it,' she said with a big grin on her face, knowing her mind was already made up. What was there to think about? *Breathe*, she cautioned herself, taking another sip from her Sangria. She needed to make sure she wasn't being swept away by the romance of Luke's suggestion. There were practicalities to consider. It would mean giving up her job at the pub and being away from her mum and her friends, but as she'd been trying to convince herself these last few weeks, it really wasn't *that* far away from home. Her emotions had spun in a 360-degree turn. Earlier she'd been battling feelings of loss, disappointment and regret. Now excitement and anticipation stirred inside her. Her gaze drifted out the front window of the tapas bar, into the charming streets of Dashford-upon-Avon. Could she really up sticks and follow her heart to be with Luke?

32

It was a couple of hours later, after a moreish supper of cheese and biscuits, a bottle of decent red wine shared between the pair of them and a game of Scrabble, which Abbey won, as she usually did. Now she felt nicely mellow, and only the tiniest bit smug. They were about to watch a Bruce Willis action film on the telly, when Sam suddenly jumped up from the sofa and brandished the remote control at her.

'This is stupid.'

'What is?' she asked, alarmed.

'This whole thing. That conversation we had earlier. What are we doing, Abbey?' he said, throwing his hands in the air and pacing up and down the living room

'Oh, don't, Sam.' She was weary, she really didn't want to go over it again, tying them both up in knots. 'I thought we'd sorted all that.' An uneasy sensation of dread lodged in her chest.

'But we haven't, have we? And it's all my fault. I told you that I didn't want to jeopardise what we have together.'

'Yeah, and I understand that. We're fine as we are, aren't we?'

She held out a hand to him from her position on the sofa. 'Why fix it if it ain't broke, eh?' She was trying to lighten the mood, but Sam was unreachable, ignoring her gesture, lost in his own thoughts. He turned to look at her.

'I do love you, you know,' he said gravely. Her stomach slid, as she waited for what was to come next. He loved her, but... what? Was he going to let her down gently? Tell her *he couldn't do this any more, they worked better as friends, they should consider having a break from each other*?

Instead, his gaze swept over her, his dark brown eyes shining with fondness and love.

'Do you want to get married?' His sudden question took her aback. As far as proposals went, it wasn't what she'd imagined or hoped for. Her expression must have given that away because Sam quickly held up a hand to her. 'No, I'm not proposing, don't think that, I was just asking if that's what you want to do?'

She gave an imperceptible shrug, wondering what the right answer should be.

'Uhh! I've been overthinking it, haven't I? Allowing what happened with Matt to get in the way of my plans. Making it much more complicated than it needs to be when really what's most important is you and me, our commitment to each other, our future together.'

Now he took hold of her hand and their eyes locked, and she allowed that kernel of excitement to swirl and grow deeper inside her.

'Shall we do it, Abbey? Get married? It's what I want, more than anything. No, wait, don't say anything!'

Abbey wasn't sure that she could, her emotions had been on a white-knuckle ride tonight.

Sam jumped up from his spot on the sofa and dashed upstairs. Abbey gave a small squee of delight, hunching her shoulders, and exchanged a conspiratorial grin with Lady, who thumped her tail on the floor as if knowing exactly what Sam was doing up there. Abbey heard his footsteps across the bedroom floor, the opening and closing of a drawer and then his return back down the stairs, her anticipation building with his every movement until he suddenly reappeared.

'Right, you need to close your eyes. Have you got your eyes closed?'

'Yes, yes!' Abbey sat on her hands, barely able to contain her excitement. She could hear Sam moving around in front of her and the sound of Lady getting up from her basket, then padding about in circles, following Sam around, no doubt, always interested to see what he was up to.

'Right. No, wait a minute. I just need to grab something else. Keep your eyes closed.' She could hear him rush over to the other side of the room and Abbey couldn't think what he might be doing. Whatever it was it didn't take long because within moments he was back again.

'Can I open my eyes now?' she asked, impatient.

'Let's do it on three. Okay? Are you ready?' She'd never been more ready for anything in her life. 'So, one... two... three! You can open them now.'

She pinged her eyes open and there he was, as she suspected, or rather hoped he would be, on one knee in front of her, holding that beautiful black box in his hand. She couldn't help but gasp, before breaking into laughter. She hadn't expected to see the red rose clutched between his teeth, which he'd clearly filched from the vase of flowers on the windowsill. Lady, who obviously had grasped the importance of the occasion, sat keenly and obediently beside Sam.

'Abbey Carter,' he spluttered, before pulling out the rose from his mouth and tossing it to one side. 'I love you with all my heart. Will you marry me?'

'Oh, Sam, what a surprise,' she said airily, placing the palms on her hands on her chest, feigning shock.

She looked down at the ring and tears filled her eyes as he gently slid it onto her finger. It was every bit as beautiful as she'd remembered it to be, perhaps even more so, but what touched her most was what the lovely sparkly ring represented, their future together.

The ridiculousness and the frivolity of the situation, the mock surprise and the rose prop, was lost when Sam cupped Abbey's face in his hands, and his eyes roamed her features imploringly.

'Honestly, Abbey, in all seriousness, I really, really want this, it's surprised me how much I want to marry you. I mean, I was certain that I wanted to spend the rest of my life with you, but more than that, I really want us to be husband and wife. It sounds pretty cool, doesn't it?'

She'd had to agree with him, nodding keenly, feeling intensely joyful, unable to wipe the wide grin from her face.

'I'm sorry that we're not on top of a mountain, or overlooking the ocean, or in a Michelin-starred restaurant, we can do all those things on our honeymoon, but I realised there's no point in waiting for the ideal moment to present itself. As far as I'm concerned, this is the ideal moment.'

Sitting in her jim-jams in front of the crackling fire, with Lady at her side, and Sam in front of her, pouring his heart out, Abbey agreed it probably was the right moment.

'Definitely,' she sighed dreamily, quickly distracted by his lips, which were within touching distance, too enticing to ignore. When she felt his mouth upon hers, she delighted at the sizzling sensations which darted around her body, reaching the very tips of her fingers and the end of her toes. They were soon kissing urgently and fervently, sealing their love for one other, until Sam suddenly pulled away, his eyes heavy with desire, his lips full.

'Wait, you haven't answered my question yet, Abbey.' He stroked her face with his fingers. 'Will you marry me?'

'Oh, Sam, of course I will,' she said, quickly succumbing to his kisses all over again.

33

It was the last day of the year and Abbey was looking forward to the new year celebrations at the Three Feathers. It seemed a fitting place to see out the old year, being the venue for so many happy times during the past six months with her friends Rhi, Luke, Lizzie, her dad, and not forgetting Sam, of course. Brad and Katy would be there as well, having secured the services of a babysitter, and no doubt there would be more of her friends and neighbours there too, seeing in the new year.

First, though, after a scrumptious breakfast of poached eggs and bacon served up on granary toast, lovingly prepared by Sam, she was going to pop into work and Sam had volunteered to go along with her. It was actually her day off, she'd taken the extra days between Christmas and new year as holiday, knowing the Lodge was in safe hands under the care of Lydia and her team of carers, but she wanted to drop in to wish the residents and friends there a very happy new year.

'Oh, look who's here,' said Reg Catling, with a big grin on his face, when they arrived at Rushgrove Lodge and went into the main guest lounge. Making sure all the residents were sitting safely in their comfy armchairs, Sam undid the lead on Lady and she scampered off, roaming around each of the residents in turn, and greeting them warmly, as though a member of the royal family on an official visit. Once she'd been round the room once, she did a second sweep, making sure there weren't any stray crumbs that needed seeing to. Abbey's heart lit up to see the smiles and cries of delight from the residents; Lady brought with her an energy and joy that was infectious and rippled around the entire room.

'How are you doing, Reg?' Abbey sat down beside him and squeezed his hand. 'Are you feeling better?'

'Much better now,' he said, hugging Lady, who had somehow managed to jump up on Reg's lap and was taking full advantage of the fuss Reg was providing. Abbey was certain they would be breaking some kind of regulation, but for the joy it was giving to this particular animal lover, then it had to be worth it. 'Those pills obviously did the trick.'

'Good, I'm glad to hear it. You're looking much better too. I just wanted to pop by to wish you a very happy new year,' said Abbey, planting a kiss on his cheek.

'Of course. I'd almost forgotten. Back in the day, we used to make a big thing of new year. Always had a party round at ours with all the neighbours. We'd be dancing out on the street at midnight. Happy times.' Reg's eyes misted over at the memory as Lady looked intently into his face as though she was listening to his every word. 'I shall look forward to a couple of small drinks later then,' he laughed.

Tonight at Rushgrove Lodge there would be a celebratory tea, some party games, music and definitely a tipple or two, although the celebrations would be over well before midnight and most of the residents would be fast asleep as the old year turned into the new.

Abbey took her time to speak to each of the residents in turn. She thought of them all as her friends, and made a point of discovering as much as she could about each of them, the names of their family members, and their personal likes and dislikes so that she could always find something pertinent to chat with them about. She liked to catch up with them one-on-one at least once a week to make sure they were happy and well, and there weren't any problems brewing.

After she and Sam had had a mug of tea and a couple of biscuits as they chatted with the residents in the lounge, they did a quick visit to those who had opted to stay in their rooms. Some had taken the opportunity for a mid-morning doze and others were busy reading the papers or entertaining visitors. When they reached Stella Darling's room, her voice rang out brightly to greet them.

'Hello, you two, or three, should I say? How lovely to see you.' Her face lit up to see them as she folded up her newspaper, where she'd been attempting to do the cryptic crossword, and put it down on the side table, laying down her pen on top. 'Did you have a lovely Christmas?'

'We did!' Abbey explained how the snowstorm had impacted their plans and how they'd all had to camp out round at Lizzie's. 'It was a lot of fun and felt extra Christmassy with all that snow outside. There was quite a crowd of us, so we all mucked in and helped out. It was a lovely Christmas, definitely one to remember, that's for sure.'

'It sounds lovely. I loved seeing the snow through the window. It reminded me of when I was a small girl and all the fun we had on our sledges. We missed you here, though.' Stella laid a hand on Abbey's.

'Aw, I missed you all too, but it sounds as though you had a good Christmas lunch, from what the others were telling us.'

'Oh, yes, it was a very good day. You always look after us so well here. I had a couple of those Zoom calls too from my nieces and nephews. They were meant to be coming on Christmas Day, but of course they weren't able to with all that snow. Anyway, they're coming over this weekend instead, so that will be something to look forward to.'

'Well, I'll be back to work on Monday, Stella, so I'll make a point of coming down and you can tell me all the news.'

'Hmm, before you two lovebirds sneak off, I think you might have some news for me, and I can't possibly wait to hear about that until next week. Now, is that what I think it is?' she asked, gleefully picking up Abbey's left hand.

Abbey laughed, and Sam smiled fondly while Lady, who was sitting at Stella's feet, thumped her tail. Abbey might have known she wouldn't get anything past Stella. She was the first one to notice the diamond ring sparkling on Abbey's finger, even Lydia hadn't spotted it when they spoke to her briefly in reception, although Abbey had to wonder how anyone could miss the huge sparkly rock. Abbey and Sam were intending to announce their news tonight in the pub with all their friends and family around them, but obviously Stella had beaten them to it.

'Yes,' said Abbey, feeling inordinately proud, waggling her fingers to show off the ring in all its glory. 'It's true, Sam asked me to marry him, and I said yes.'

'Well, isn't that the best news to start off the new year. Congratulations to you both. I shall keep my fingers crossed that this wedding will actually come off, then,' she said, with a quirk of her eyebrow.

Coming from anyone else, Abbey might have been offended at this, but she knew from the mischievous glint in Stella's eye and the smile twitching at her lips that she was teasing in her usual inimitable manner.

'There's no worry on that front.' Sam was quick to reassure Stella. 'Nothing's going to stand in the way of us getting married, I promise.' He took hold of Abbey's hand and squeezed it tight.

'Well, in that case, do you think we should have a little something to celebrate? Over there on the shelf, Sam, is a bottle of sherry. I keep it for these very occasions. There's some glasses in the cupboard below.'

Sam did the honours and poured small measures of sherry, an especially small one for himself, as he wasn't a great fan of this particular tipple, but some moments were worth celebrating and this was definitely one of them.

'So tell me, Abbey, how did Sam propose?'

Now, recounting the story to Stella, Abbey smiled at the memory, deciding to omit the finer details. It was touch and go for a while as to whether the longed-for proposal would ever materialise, but it had happened in the end, and they were both utterly delighted about that. She'd been hugging the secret to herself these last few days, excited at the prospect of announcing their news at the pub tonight, and she wasn't bothered in the slightest, only amused, that eagle-eyed Stella had got there before them.

'Well, it sounds very romantic,' Stella said now, her face beaming. 'Congratulations,' she said, raising her glass to the air. 'I'm thrilled for the pair of you.'

'It will only be a small wedding, just close family and friends, and hopefully quite soon too. In the next couple of months or so.'

There was no point in waiting. Abbey didn't want this engagement to be protracted, like her previous one. Those preparations for the wedding that never was had made her ill with stress and anxiety, although now she saw that it was probably down to instinctively knowing that something was wrong, but not being brave enough to admit it. This time, she had no such concerns.

'Well, it's marvellous news. I always said you two make the perfect couple.'

Abbey hugged Stella tight, and wished her a happy new year. She realised that her news would have spread around the entire care home by lunchtime, but it didn't matter. Her friends and loved ones would hear the news tonight at the pub, and then she wouldn't care if the whole world knew.

After saying their goodbyes to Stella, they walked down the corridor and into the main reception area, where Abbey spotted an unwelcome visitor entering through the double doors. In that moment, her whole body tensed as she gave a sidewards glance at Sam, who was so far oblivious to who they were about to run into. If she could have, she would have grabbed Sam's arm and bundled him into one of the side rooms, but it was too late for that. Matt had spotted them both and judging by his stony expression, he was just as horrified at running into them as Abbey had been.

Matt gave a tight smile, but kept his head low, avoiding eye contact with Sam, clearly intending to walk straight past them towards the main office, but Sam stepped forward into Matt's path, and Abbey stiffened, hoping that there wasn't going to be a repeat of the scene in the pub. Thankfully, her fears were immediately allayed.

'Hey, Matt, do you have a moment? Look, I'm sorry about the other week, in the pub.' Sam clenched his hands together in front of him, looking pained. It was never going to be easy. 'It was a shock, that was all, coming face to face with you again after all those years, but it in no way excuses my behaviour. I was out of order.' He held out his hand and Matt hesitated only for the briefest moment before stepping forward and accepting his handshake, slapping his other hand on Sam's upper arm, in a friendly greeting.

'Hey, it's all forgotten about, honestly.'

Abbey was hugely grateful to Matt for his easy forgiveness, and she breathed a huge sigh of relief, knowing that the two old friends had cleared the air, and called an unlikely truce.

'We were so sorry to hear about your mum,' said Abbey.

'Thank you.' A flicker of pain spread across his features as he ran a hand through his hair. 'It's been tough. I still can't really believe that I won't get to see her again. I keep thinking of different things and find myself saying, "I'll text Mum about that," which is always a sharp reminder.' He gave a nonchalant shrug of his shoulders. 'I guess you'd know all about that.' He gestured to Sam with a smile of understanding. 'Anyway, I thought I'd have a drive out today for a change of scene. I've got a box full of brochures here.'

'Thanks, Matt,' said Abbey. 'Lydia's in the office. Pop in and have a chat, she'll be only too happy to make you a cuppa.'

'Great, I will do. Good seeing you again, Sam. Maybe we can get together for a beer one of these days?'

Last time Matt had made that suggestion, Sam had thrown him up against a wall, but Abbey hoped the bad feeling might have evaporated now. She couldn't imagine that these two guys would ever be best buddies again, but life was too short to hold onto resentments from years ago.

'I'd like that,' Sam said with a genuine smile. Hearing the emotion in his voice and the warmth of his expression, Abbey knew that Sam absolutely meant it too.

34

Fortunately, Rhi had taken the precaution of booking a table for the New Year's Eve celebrations at the Three Feathers, one of the perks of working at the pub. She'd been so grateful that Jan hadn't asked her to work tonight, which meant she could enjoy the celebrations along with her friends. With a band booked, a disco and one of Jan's legendary buffets, it had all the makings of a great evening.

There was a lively atmosphere in the pub from the outset, with most people taking the opportunity to dress up in the black and white theme Jan and Malc had chosen for the event. Bill looked dapper in his dinner suit, with a ruffled white shirt and red bow tie, while Lizzie wore a black flapper dress with fringing that shimmered every time she moved. Luke and Sam had opted for the same outfit of black smart trousers and open-necked white shirt, which was effortlessly stylish, even if Bill said they looked like a couple of waiters from the local pizzeria. Abbey wore a floating black dress with a layered skirt and a sequinned bodice. Her gorgeous auburn hair was worn loose on her shoulders and Sam felt inordinately proud every time he looked over at her. He still had to pinch himself to believe that this amazing woman would soon be his wife. Rhi turned everyone's head in a short black skirt with thick black tights and a sequinned top, which showed off her natural good looks to perfection.

Already by eight o'clock the place was filled with partygoers, and chatter and laughter rang out around the eaves. In the back bar, the food was laid out on a long table, the selection offering delicious small tasters of food from around the globe, with everyone desperate to get stuck in. The band had set up in the front bar and their repertoire of popular classics already had people toe-tapping and jigging along to the music.

Bill had just got a round of drinks in when they became aware of a young couple standing at their table.

'Hey, guys, great to see you again.' It was Jackson Moody, the new owner of Primrose Hall and his girlfriend Tara, who were looking as sophisticated and glamorous as the last time they'd run into them.

'Hi, Jackson. Hi, Tara. This is Brad, my husband,' said Katy, with a broad smile. 'I think I might have told you he wasn't due home until the new year and then he only went and turned up unexpectedly on Christmas Eve, the best present ever.'

Brad stood up and held out his hand to Jackson.

'I've heard a lot about you, especially from Rosie, who's told me all about your animals and how you let her choose their names. That was such a lovely gesture. You made one little girl very happy. Thank you.'

'No, honestly, she did me a great favour.'

'Actually, she's not stopped chatting about Twinkle and Little Star since that night, wondering how they're getting on and asking lots of question about what they eat and where they sleep.' It was probably the several glasses of fizz that made Katy uncharacteristically bold. 'She'd love to come along and see them again sometime if that would be possible?'

'Absolutely,' said Jackson effusively. 'I gave you my card, didn't I? Just give me a call in the new year and we'll get something sorted.'

Just then, Jan appeared with an ice bucket filled with two bottles of champagne, and a tray of glass flutes.

'With the compliments of this lovely gentleman here,' said Jan, gesturing towards Jackson as she placed the tray and bucket on their table.

'What on earth is this for?' said Lizzie, her face bright with surprise and gratitude.

'My way of saying thanks for coming along to my do the other week and for being part of the great naming ceremony. And to wish you a happy new year too, of course.'

'How lovely,' said Katy, glancing around the table. 'Why don't you find a couple of chairs and come and join us?'

'We're not stopping, thanks. We've somewhere else we need to be, but hopefully we'll get to see you again in the new year. I think I mentioned we have lots of plans for the stables, so look out for those and we hope to welcome you back to Primrose Hall very soon.'

With a wave, Jackson and Tara departed, and the group were left slightly bemused and very grateful for Jackson's generosity.

'He's a flash so-and-so, isn't he?' Brad said, with a sardonic smile.

'Not flash,' said Katy, elbowing him in the ribs. 'Charming. It was very lovely and generous of him to buy us these drinks.'

'Hmm, I guess,' said Brad, clearly not as enamoured by Jackson as his wife, but smiling at her indulgently all the same.

'He is quite good-looking,' said Rhi absentmindedly.

'Really?' said Luke, his brow furrowing in disbelief, as he turned to look at her.

'Very,' said Abbey, swooning. Luke and Sam exchanged a glance that showed exactly what they thought of Jackson Moody.

'And rich too, by all accounts,' said Lizzie, laughing. 'Quite the catch, when you come to think about it.'

'What is this?' said Sam, looking affronted. 'The Jackson whatshisname appreciation society?'

'No,' said Abbey, laughing, 'but credit where it's due. Jackson has made a real effort at befriending us all. He seems lovely to me, and I think it's very commendable that he's putting the money he's made back into the community.' She picked up one of the champagne flutes that Luke had filled. 'Cheers to Jackson Moody, that's what I say,' she said, raising her glass to the air.

'I think he seems a bit too good to be true, if you ask me,' said Brad, which elicited much head nodding from the other guys around the table.

'Oh, but we're not asking you,' said Katy, laughing. 'Come on, let's go and get something to eat.'

After they'd had some food, the atmosphere in the pub grew even more electrified as the new year drew ever closer. The noise rose to such levels that Lizzie could hardly hear what was being said across the other side of the table. Not that it mattered. She was just pleased to be amongst her family and friends. As her gaze swept around the table, she knew with an inner certainty that these people were her friends for life.

Abbey glanced at her watch.

'There's only fifteen minutes to go,' she said excitedly. 'Back in a while.' She got up from the table and headed to the loos. In the toilets, she checked her reflection in the mirror, running her hands through her auburn locks, applying a light covering of gloss to her lips. She saw the natural colour in her cheeks and the sparkle in her eyes. A shiver of excitement ran along her spine for what she was about to do. She looked back on the person she was a year ago and felt a pang for sympathy for that girl, knowing how unhappy she was then. Now, she gave her reflection a huge smile. She liked the person looking back at her now. How much could change in the course of a year!

She unzipped her black handbag that she'd worn close across her body all night long, and then further unzipped the pocket inside. She pulled out her engagement ring that had been nestling inside a black velvet pouch and slipped it on her finger. There! She would never need to remove it again now. It looked beautiful, she couldn't have picked better herself, and she wondered if she would ever get used to the sight of it glinting on her hand, as though it had always belonged there.

Back at the table, she squeezed in on the old oak bench next to Sam and laid her hand on the table. At the very same moment, she locked eyes with Rhi who put her own hand on the table, and as if they'd rehearsed it, they said together, 'We've got something to tell you.'

Abbey threw back her head and laughed, momentarily put off her stride. 'Well, you go first then.'

'Are you sure?' Rhi asked.

Abbey nodded and Rhi looked up at Luke, suddenly feeling self-conscious as she became aware of everyone's gaze upon her. Luke gave an encouraging squeeze of her lower thigh beneath the table.

'Well, the thing is, I've decided to move to Dashford-upon-Avon with Luke. We went up together the other day and it feels like the right thing for us.' Luke lifted his hand to take hold of Rhi's on the table. 'I can run my new business from the flat just as well as I can from here and we're really excited for this new start together.'

Lizzie clapped her hands together in delight.

'Well, that's wonderful news,' she said brightly, leaning over to give Rhi a big hug. Everyone else joined in with the congratulations and good wishes too. 'I'm really happy for you both. We've been wondering when you might properly get together.'

Rhi beamed, looking at Luke. Her mum had said exactly the same thing. Lisa had always had a soft spot for Luke and while she was sad that her daughter would be moving away, she was thrilled that she would be making a new start with that lovely boy, Luke.

'It is the best news,' said Abbey, genuinely pleased for her friend, knowing how much she'd longed for a future with Luke. 'But we're going to miss you both so much,' she said, feeling strangely emotional at the thought.

'Aw, and we'll miss you all too, but don't worry, we'll be coming back regularly for long weekends. I promise you, you won't be able to get rid of us that easily.'

'What about The Primrose Fancies?' Lizzie exclaimed, as if suddenly remembering, her face dropping with disappointment.

Luke gave a wry smile.

'Yes, I'm afraid we're going to have to relinquish our spot on the quiz team, which is a shame, but probably too far to travel for a weeknight.'

'Is that all you're worried about, Mum?' Katy said, laughing. 'I think you're overlooking the fact that you have the perfect replacements here.' She gestured to herself and Brad. 'Do you know how clever Brad is?'

Brad curled his lip doubtfully.

'Thanks for the vote of confidence, Katy. I'm not sure the stuff I know will be of any use in a pub quiz, but from what I've heard, it sounds like a lot of fun, and there's beer involved, so yes, definitely, count us in.'

'Oh, well, there you go then,' said Bill. 'We're sorted, but it won't be the same without you two.'

'Stop it,' Rhi said, waving a hand in front of her face to ward off the tears that were gathering in her eyes, 'or you'll set me off.' She would miss all her friends hugely, as well as her mum, but she knew that this was the right move for her, and being with Luke, building a future together, was the most important thing of all. 'Enough of me,' she said, wanting to change the subject. 'What was it you wanted to tell us, Abbey?'

Abbey's face lit up with excitement and she paused for a moment, taking in the rapt faces all looking in her direction, and with a dramatic flourish, she laid her hand on the table again, this time showing off the beautiful ring to maximum effect.

'Sam has asked me to marry him, and I've said yes!' There was a collective squeal of delight from everyone around the table and they all jumped up to hug each other.

'That's just wonderful,' said Lizzie, her face beaming. 'Isn't it, Bill?' But Bill was in no mood for words, he just held out his arms wide and welcomed his daughter into his embrace, his eyes welling up with tears.

'I couldn't be happier for you both,' he said, leaning back to look into his daughter's eyes, so reminiscent of her mum's tonight. 'I had a good feeling about you and Sam from the very first time you got together. Sam's a properly decent chap, you've definitely picked a good one there. Mind you, so has he,' he said, with a wry smile.

'Don't you worry, Bill,' said Sam. 'I know just how lucky I am to be marrying your daughter. I promise you I will look after her. I won't let her down.'

The two men embraced, and Abbey's heart swelled with pride.

'It's great to have you in the family,' said Bill, giving Sam a friendly slap on the back.

'Are you ready, folks?' called Malc, over the PA system. 'We're nearly there. Make sure your glasses are topped up. A minute to go and it'll be the big countdown to the new year.'

A wave of noisy excitement rippled around the pub as people stood up to get ready for the big event.

'Here we go then. Ten, nine, eight, seven...' Everyone joined in, chanting in unison, the tension increasing with each step closer to the clock striking twelve. 'Six, five, four, three, two, one!' The refrain of 'happy new year' rang out around the pub, people hugged and kissed and cheered, before everyone broke into a rousing rendition of 'Auld Lang Syne' that left them all with big smiles on their faces.

'I can't believe you made it home for Christmas,' said Katy, nestling into Brad's side, dropping her head onto his chest. 'It was the best surprise ever.' She hugged him tight. 'I'm sorry if I've been a pain this year. I sometime feel that I've let you down. That I should have tried harder to make things work in Australia.'

'Hey, we gave it a go and that's the main thing.' He turned her round to face him, tipping up her chin with a finger. 'And you're not a pain, well, only sometimes,' he said, with a cheeky grin that earned him a dig in the ribs from Katy. 'It wasn't the right thing for us, but this is a new start for us and if you and the kids are happy, then I'm happy too.'

'I love you, Brad,' she whispered in his ear, forever grateful for his kindness and patience.

Close by them, Sam grabbed Abbey's wrist and pulled her to one side, kissing her on the cheek.

'Hey, Abbey, you do realise you've made me the happiest man in the world by agreeing to marry me? I didn't even want to get married until I met you. And now look what's happened! You've completely turned my whole world around.'

'And you mine.' The noise and hubbub around them faded into the background as she looked up into his eyes. It could have been just the two of them in the busy pub for the intimacy of the moment. 'I love you, Sam.'

'I love you too, Abbey. Happy new year,' he said, kissing her gently on the forehead. 'This one will be the best one ever for us both.'

She couldn't disagree with that. She glanced over at Rhi, who had her arms thrown around Luke's neck, her lips pressed against his, their happiness radiating through the air around them. She would miss that girl so much when she moved away, their walks around Primrose Woods, their visits to Treetops Café to see Lizzie, her sunny presence and her unswerving support. Still, she was thrilled that Luke and Rhi had finally got together, and she knew that her friendship with Rhi and Luke would remain as strong as ever, in spite of the physical distance between them.

'Aw, I'm going to miss this place, the quiz nights, and this lovely bunch of people, our friends,' Rhi said to Luke.

'Me too, but you're not having any regrets, are you?'

'No! Never! I'm so excited about our move. About the new business. About living with you and starting a new life together. I still can't believe that we're actually doing it.'

'Well, you better start believing it, Rhi, because we're moving in a couple of days.'

'Aw, it will be a brand-new adventure together, and I just can't wait.'

'We can make some new memories as well, stories that we'll be able to tell the grandchildren.'

'Definitely. As long as they don't involve any near-death experiences, though,' she said, laughing. 'I've had enough of those to last me a lifetime. Oh, I do love you, Luke.'

'I love you too, Rhi,' he said, sealing his words with a kiss on her lips.

Bill led Lizzie up onto the floor so they could dance to the music being belted out by the band, a succession of up-tempo popular songs that had everyone moving to the beat. Bill held Lizzie's hand at arm's length and spun her around him in an action they'd perfected in their regular dance sessions, either at the tea dances they frequented or more likely in the kitchen when they were messing around. Bill pulled her in close and rested his hands on her waist.

'Are you having a good time, Lizzie?'

'I'm having the best time ever, Bill. What a year it's been, and it sounds as though next year might be even better. I'm so pleased Luke and Rhi have got together, and what about Abbey and Sam? Did you have any idea?'

'No, although I can't say I'm surprised. Those two were always meant to be together. Her mum would be so pleased to know she's found real happiness at last.'

'I bet, and she'd be proud of you, Bill, for getting Abbey to this point in her life and knowing that you're living your best life now too.'

'That's true,' said Bill, with a big smile. 'When she knew she would be leaving me behind, she told me she didn't want me to stay sad for long. That I had to try and find happiness again. I told her I would, just to make her happy, but I never really believed it would happen. She'd be so grateful to you, Lizzie, for making that change in me.'

'Well, you've done exactly the same for me,' she said, tapping him fondly on the nose. 'It's a good job we found each other when we did. We have so much living, laughing and loving still to do!' Her distinctive, affectionate chuckle washed over Bill in a warm embrace. He would never grow tired of hearing her laugh.

They were still swaying in time to the music, revelling in each other's company, when they realised they'd been joined by the others.

'Come on, you two, it's about time we had a group hug, don't you think?' Rhi said, laughing, putting an arm around Lizzie's shoulder. They all gathered in a circle; Lizzie and Bill, Abbey and Sam, Luke and Rhi, and Katy and Brad too, their arms wrapped around the shoulder of the next person in the circle.

'Happy new year to us!' said Sam, which was met with a cheer from the others. 'My future wife and I...' he said, poking his tongue in his cheek. 'We'd like to say how much we've appreciated your friendship this year and all the good times we've shared. It's meant the world to us. And here's to many more good times in the year ahead.'

Abbey felt a huge swell of pride as she looked around at the faces of her friends, beaming at one another. They were so much more than friends, their bond was much tighter than that, she looked upon them as her own family. She knew that whatever lay in store for them individually over the coming year, they could rely on the support and friendship of this lovely group of people.

There was so much to look forward to; more visits to Primrose Woods, her happy place, long walks with Sam and Lady in the glorious countryside, opportunities to pop into the Treetops Café for a chatter with Lizzie, and she was curious to discover much more about Primrose Hall too and its glamorous occupants. The quiz nights here at the pub would remain a regular feature on their social calendar and, who knew, perhaps they'd even get round to winning the quiz one of these days now they had brainbox Brad on their team. Despite Luke and Rhi moving away, she knew that they would still play a part in at least some of those occasions. Abbey was already planning when she and Sam might be able to make their first visit to Dashford-upon-Avon to see their friends.

Then there was the small matter of a wedding to plan. A small, intimate gathering with her close family and friends to share in the happy occasion. It would be her first job in the new year, and she couldn't wait to get started.

'Ooh, I love this one,' said Rhi, breaking up the circle as she heard the opening bars to 'Celebration' play on the PA system while the band took a well-earned rest. 'Celebrate, good times, come on,' she sang, urging the others to join in, which they didn't need any persuasion to do.

Abbey took hold of Rhi and Lizzie's hands and they danced joyfully around the floor, the guys joining in as well. Abbey spun round on the spot, her arms held wide. She wasn't in any doubt. There would be plenty of good times ahead for them all.

ACKNOWLEDGMENTS

Thank you for reading *Snowflakes Over Primrose Woods.* I really hope you enjoyed catching up with Abbey and Sam, Lizzie and Bill, and Luke and Rhi, and celebrating the Christmas holidays with them all. I know I did!

Getting a book out into the world is very much a team effort and I'm hugely grateful to the whole Boldwood crew for all their hard work and sterling efforts behind the scenes in making this happen. In particular, thanks to Claire Fenby, Jenna Houston, Nia Beynon, and of course, Amanda Ridout for everything that you do to help make the publishing process so seamless.

Special thanks must go to my lovely editor Sarah Ritherdon who is a joy to work with and who always brings such valuable insight and support during the editing process. I couldn't do it without you!

I'm indebted to all the book bloggers who waved the flag for Primrose Woods and helped to spread the word, and in particular to Rachel Gilbey for organising the blog tour.

Thank you to everyone who entered the competition to name the Shetland pony. I had a big smile on my face as I read through the entries, and any one of the names put forward would have been a good fit, but in the end I plumped for 'Little Star' as I think it's just the perfect name for the naughty pony. Thank you so much Andrea Davis for the fabulous suggestion! (We haven't seen the last of Little Star!)

As always, a big thanks to my husband Nick, and my grown-up children, Tom and Ellie, for always being there and cheering me on from the sidelines. I love you all so much.

Finally, a big thank you to you, my reader, for selecting this book to read. It really does mean the world and I'm so grateful for your support. I really hope you enjoyed the story.

Love Jill

X

MORE FROM JILL STEEPLES

We hope you enjoyed reading *Snowflakes Over Primrose Woods.* If you did, please leave a review.

If you'd like to gift a copy, this book is also available as an ebook, digital audio download and audiobook CD.

Sign up to Jill Steeples' mailing list for news, competitions and updates on future books.

https://bit.ly/JillSteeplesNews

ABOUT THE AUTHOR

Jill Steeples is the author of many successful women's fiction titles – most recently the Dog and Duck series - all set in the close communities of picturesque English villages. She lives in Bedfordshire.

Visit Jill Steeples's website: https://www.jillsteeples.co.uk

Follow Jill on social media:

Printed in Great Britain
by Amazon